Crosscurrents / Modern Critiques / Third Series

Edited by Jerome Klinkowitz

Michael Stephens

The Dramaturgy
of Style
Voice in Short Fiction

Southern Illinois University Press
CARBONDALE AND EDWARDSVILLE

Printed in the United States of America

Edited by Teresa White
Designed by Design for Publishing
Production supervised by Kathleen Giencke

Library of Congress Cataloging in Publication Data

Stephens, Michael Gregory.
    The dramaturgy of style.

    (Crosscurrents/modern critiques. Third series)
    Includes index.
    1. Fiction—Technique.   2. Style, Literary.
I. Title.   II. Title: Voice in short fiction.
III. Series.
PN3355.S77   1986   809.3'936   85-14327
ISBN 0-8093-1231-X

For J. R. Humphreys, a seeing voice

There comes the moment, and I saw it then, when the moon goes from flat to round. For the first time it met my eyes as a globe. The word "moon" came into my mouth as though fed to me out of a silver spoon. Held in my mouth the moon became a word. It had the roundness of a Concord grape Grandpa took off his vine and gave me to suck out of its skin and swallow whole, in Ohio.
                                        —Eudora Welty, *One Writer's Beginnings*

Contents

Crosscurrents/
Modern Critiques/
Third Series

IN THE EARLY 1960s, when the Crosscurrents/Modern Critiques series was developed by Harry T. Moore, the contemporary period was still a controversial one for scholarship. Even today the elusive sense of the present dares critics to rise above mere impressionism and to approach their subject with the same rigors of discipline expected in more traditional areas of study. As the first two series of Crosscurrents books demonstrated, critiquing contemporary culture often means that the writer must be historian, philosopher, sociologist, and bibliographer as well as literary critic, for in many cases these essential preliminary tasks are yet undone.

To the challenges that faced the initial Crosscurrents project have been added those unique to the past two decades: the disruption of conventional techniques by the great surge in innovative writing in the American 1960s just when social and political conditions were being radically transformed, the new worldwide interest in the Magic Realism of South American novelists, the startling experiments of textual and aural poetry from Europe, the emergence of Third World authors, the rising cause of feminism in life and literature, and, most dramatically, the introduction of Continental theory into the previously staid world of Anglo-American literary scholarship. These transformations demand that many traditional treatments be rethought, and part of the new responsibility for Crosscurrents will be to provide such studies.

Contributions to Crosscurrents/Modern Critiques/Third Series will be distinguished by their fresh approaches to established topics and by their opening up of new territories for discourse. When a single author is studied, we hope to present the first book on his or her work, or to explore a previously untreated aspect based on new research. Writers who have been critiqued well elsewhere will be studied in comparison with lesser-known figures, sometimes from other cultures, in an effort to broaden our base of understanding. Critical and theoretical works by leading novelists, poets, and dramatists will have a home in Crosscurrents/Modern Critiques/ Third Series, as will sampler-introductions to the best in new Americanist criticism written abroad.

The excitement of contemporary studies is that all of its critical practitioners and most of their subjects are alive and working at the same time. One work influences another, bringing to the field a spirit of competition and cooperation that reaches an intensity rarely found in other disciplines. Above all, this third series of Crosscurrents/Modern Critiques will be collegial—a mutual interest in the present moment that can be shared by writer, subject, and reader alike.

Jerome Klinkowitz

Preface

AT THE SUGGESTION of Professor Jerome Klinkowitz, the editor of the Crosscurrents series, I have attempted to write something about short fiction. It is a mark of his generosity and encouragement to suggest such a thing. For my part I have gone about this eccentrically, since I am a fiction writer, not a critic, and I have not disallowed my creative instincts to be varied simply because I am working the prose in a different genre. Because I still am involved in writing fiction—even as I write this Preface—I have not allowed myself to carve any theory or inclination in granite. At best I've written an intellectual sketch. What any kind of fiction is remains in flux for me; I have no exact point of view about how to write it or how to comprehend it. As a fiction writer who teaches said to me recently at the end of a semester: "Now I can forget all those rules I've given them and do some of my own writing." The best impulses for fiction usually come from a writer without preconceptions about what fiction is or about what a particular book is going to be until it is written. I recall a remark which the poet Robert Duncan made after a reading at the Guggenheim Museum in the late 1960s. Asked how his poems were conceived, he replied, "I take dictation from angels."

This is a work about short fiction, but it is bracketed by ideas I have about drama and poetry. That is because I came into fiction through poetry and because I have attempted to enrich my ideas about fiction by learning more about (and practicing) the drama. My background in poetry comes from a time in grade school; basically I grew up thinking I was going to be a poet, and I wrote poetry voluminously in high school and when I first went to college. In my late teens, after dropping out of college, I attended workshops at St. Mark's in the Bowery Poetry Project. I took classes with people like Joel Oppenheimer and Sam Abrams, and sat in on lectures by people like Ted Berrigan. I used to hear Paul Blackburn's poems every Monday night at the Open Reading run by St. Mark's. When a bunch of us from the neighborhood went out for beers on Avenue B, we talked about poetry, and the conversations were peppered with names like Spicer, Sorrentino, Oppen, Oppenheimer, O'Hara, Bremser, Olson, Creeley, Ashbery—anyone contemporary and not yet academic.

As for my dramatic influence, it is a peculiarity of our country that we need credentials in order to get anywhere in this life. I mainly am self-taught as a fiction writer, although I did attend workshops given by Seymour Krim at St. Mark's which ultimately made me decide to write prose instead of poetry—or rather to concentrate on prose, since I still do write poetry. In an academic, though probably not in a mature artistic, sense, I am most credentialed as a playwright, having received an advanced degree from the Yale School of Drama. My first experience at the Drama School was in the early 1970s, when I attended as a special student because I

had no previous degrees. Christopher Durang and Albert In-
naurato were classmates. But upon the publication of my
novel *Season at Coole* I left New Haven and spent a few hermetic
years in Wellfleet and Provincetown, and I did not go back to
Yale until the late seventies, more at the urging of my wife,
Okhee, a singer and actress. The Drama School is a professional conservatory, so that its emphasis is not merely academic excellence but instead combines academics and
professionalism. Its greatest advantage for a writer is that
you work with actors and directors and other theater people
constantly, around the clock, for three years. You eat, sleep,
poop, talk, and do theater. My dramatic sense comes from
these experiences in New Haven, and thereafter working in
New York with what is affectionately referred to in the theater world as the Yale mafia.

Poetry is an emotional instinct for me; drama is an acquired taste like learning to smoke and drink. Fiction, I
think, is what I was born to do. How I write poetry or plays is
quick and emotional, a word, a sound, a rhythm, and I am
off. Rewriting may take some time, but the first draft is always fast and from the heart. Fiction, though, is a labor of
love, a constant battle, a process of slow and meticulous accretions, small victories and major defeats. The fiction writer
gives to the prose most of his life, many hours in isolation,
many months in accumulations, many years—day after day,
year after year. One page of clear, readable copy from one
day's work is a major triumph. Ultimately writing fiction,
even short fiction—or maybe I should say *especially* short fiction—is backbreaking work, like sewing rice plants in a paddy
or digging ditches. (Nearly every fiction writer I know has
constant lower back problems, myself included, a kind of oc-
cupational affliction of the craft.) I often wish that writing fiction could be as spontaneous as a poem, but usually it is not.

The above explains my personal reasons for putting fiction within a parenthesis which includes drama and poetry. What follows, I hope, goes beyond my subjective preferences to explain that there are clear links between these forms. My purpose is not to be definitive but representative. I write of writers whose work I am taken by. None of the writers I have chosen as examples are obscure, and some of them are quite well known. Perhaps more could be written about some of these writers, both by myself and others. Every one of the writers covered here has multitudes of other qualities besides voice which could be enumerated. I have chosen really only one aspect of their craft, and that is the dramatic qualities of their voices. For me, this is a narrow, though important, consideration.

I also wish to thank my colleagues in the Writing Program at Columbia University's School of General Studies, where many of these ideas were developed over seven years in a course called Structure and Style, especially Dick Humphreys, Peter Rand, Glenda Adams, Austin Flint, and Phyllis Raphael.

Over the years I have had ongoing correspondences on writing with Andrei Codrescu, Guy Davenport, Jerzy Kutnik, and Tomek Mirkowicz, all of whom I would like to thank for general literary wisdom.

There are also ongoing conversations I have with local writers, this talk usually mixed with that of sports, drinking, sex, and food, and these writers include Mark Rudman, Mark Leib, Russell Banks, Bill Woods, Chuck Wachtel—as well as other talks with my wife and daughter, Okhee and Mora. Thank you.

Lastly, I must thank the writers from whose work this volume draws.

Part I

Introduction

1

The Dramaturgy of Style

My own words, when I am at work on a story, I hear too as they go, in the same voice that I hear when I read in books. When I write and the sound of it comes back to my ears, then I act to make my changes. I have always trusted this voice. — *Eudora Welty*

How Voice Influences Fiction

Fiction's imaginary landscape is evoked by virtue of a voice which sees. That a voice *sees* is not a facile synesthesia. The mind sees what the ear hears. Sight is called the privileged sense (Robbe-Grillet), but a voice which sees is a gift beyond measure. "The fictional eye," Eudora Welty writes, "sees in, through, and around what is really there." How a voice sees is by showing objects through the perspective of images. Word pictures, they are called. Broken down into the range of voice these word pictures create a vision for the auditory.

The poetics of fiction is not flying diacritical wings and struts, flapping, gliding, over the scanned page, left to right through a line length. But word pictures in fiction are similar to those in poetry, and as Charles Olson wrote they consist of "breath" and "syllable." Through the machinery of breath and syllable both prose and poetry reveal verbal tensions. It is these tensions which suggest what is dramaturgical in all good writing. These are the ingredients, I think, which constitute style. Put another way, the object-conscious voice creates style in fiction.

Fiction's voice is an idealization of speech's patterns. It is not speech per se, rather it is a kind of speech. In Eudora Welty's *One Writer's Beginnings*, her mother says of a neighbor: "She wasn't *saying* a thing in this world . . . she was just ready to talk, that's all." More than merely transcription the voice in fiction *says* by evoking pictorial things. Perhaps the keenest difference between speech, talk, conversation, dialogue, voice—and whatever—comes about in David Mamet's play *Glengarry Glen Ross*, when Moss and Aaronow, two low-level real estate swindlers, in a Chinese restaurant, *discuss* the theft of real estate "leads" from their bosses.

> AARONOW: You haven't talked to him.
> MOSS: No. What do you mean? Have I talked to him about *this*? (*Pause.*)
> AARONOW: Yes. I mean you are actually *talking* about this, or are we just . . .
> MOSS: No, we're just . . .
> AARONOW: We're just "talking" about it.
> MOSS: We're just *speaking* about it. (*Pause.*) As an *idea*.

Voice is shaped, given form, builds from experience a rhythmical arc of circumstance, finds a tension which allows for fiction's ultimate push and pull. It is shaped, less repetitive, more lyrical than ordinary conversation, of speaking, of talking. Yet a language needs a sense of utterance to be fiction. Conversation is not dialogue. Speaking is not saying; talking is not the voice of fiction. There is a cadence which the writer steals from the actual, shaping this rhythm into the voice of fiction. When tension enters into the equation of speech and voice, dramaturgical moments occur. It is the transformation of what is possible into what is. Actors transform words into living moments. So do writers.

Drama so often is what is *not* said. That is the quality which short fiction shares with the drama. There are ellipses, pauses, and silences, between which often the very substance of voice, if not language and words, is manifested. And drama joins fiction and poetry in its concern with being concise. Truth is only capitalized at the beginning of a sentence in fiction as in drama and poetry. What is more important than truth is being faithful to the rhythm of experience. Short fiction can lack character, plot, and theme, but these are replaced by figures like image, form, rhythm, and tension. Poetry, drama, and short fiction withhold—leave out. Part of the seeing voice is its silence.

The Influence of Poetry: Breath, Syllable, Energy

Charles Olson's observations about "breath" and "syllable" in his essay "Projective Verse" were articulations cutting to the bone of our civilization. Cicero described it as "breath, tongue, and syllable," and he probably learned it from Roman *histriones*, who learned it from the Greeks, who learned it from the dithyrambs. It goes back to animal mimes, probably, in pre-Christian Sicily, where poets wore a rabbit's foot for good luck and had only one way to convey their poetry— on the tongue, on the hoof. Breath is where voice originates, somewhere back in those Sicilian performances, and just as those poet performers drew breath, the fiction writer today must do the same.

Besides the grammar of a writer's voice, fiction draws upon breath for life. It is the unique way each person enunciates the syllable, whether spoken in the mind or from the mouth. Breath is what centers experience. A friend once suggested, because I smoke, that I study yoga. His feeling was that people smoked not so much because it was an addiction but because tobacco centered breath, just as yoga does. I have often thought that I would murder people if I didn't write. Not violence, not sociopathic behavior, but why most people who end up in jail end up there. Misplaced energy. After a good cardiovascular workout, jogging, rowing, swimming, bicycling, breath is centered. It is measured. Word pictures take on a cadenced appearance. Her rump in black and white shorts. The sycamores in the park. The waves on the water. The circles which the paddles make in the water. The white line in the roadway. That pit bull on a long leash. That helicopter. That puddle the shape of Texas.

I smoke most when I am writing, and if this friend's theory is correct, I do this because tobacco centers breath, without which the writer has no voice. One makes fiction by breathing fiction. This is done in the energy of a sentence, exploding outward until it becomes a paragraph, until it becomes a page of prose, until it becomes a chapter, until it becomes a book. Until it becomes. It is what Eudora Welty calls "the beautiful, sober, accretion of a sentence."

Syllable becomes a building unit in breath's progression from air into sound into words, into pictures, into emotional associations—into voice. In Asian countries where Chinese numeration is prevalent there is no fourth floor in many hotels. Whereas our Western superstition about numbers is a biblical one—Judas being the thirteenth disciple at the Last

Supper—the Oriental superstition is syllabic. *Sa.* The number four. Why? Because that syllable also means *death*, and you cannot utter that syllable for the number four without also saying "death." The Chinese word "sa" literally holds a word picture in its utterance, since it is an ideogram. Originally the character for "death" was drawn by making a skeleton and a person sitting next to it on the right. Ancient Chinese were buried in a sitting position. This is how the syllable for "four" became unlucky, and it is also why many hotels do not have a fourth floor.

The ideogramic nature of Chinese language reminds me that a voice which does not see will lack objects in its imaginary landscape. When prose becomes abstract and objectless, its domain becomes nonfictional. Two aspects of this objectless prose are essays and journalism. This is not a value judgment; it is an observation about the quality of the fictional voice. Interestingly, though, when fiction is only representational (realistic), it more resembles journalism today than poetry. Its purpose is only photographic and informational, another adjunct of communications. By making fiction voice-centered, the stress goes away from representational toward the presentational. It becomes gestural, human voice-activated, and the body is the soul because what you see is what you get.

The poet Louis Zukofsky wrote about a time in China when names were omitted from literature. There was no literary production for nine reigns, "because there was neither consciousness of the 'objectively perfect' nor an interest in clear or vital 'particulars.' "

I tend to agree with Faulkner that a fiction writer is a failed poet. But I also tend to think that maybe the poet is a failed dramatist. Someone ought to write a study of the public reading styles of contemporary poets and stand-up nightclub comedians, both of whom often share uncanny resemblances in their public uncertainties and how they use language. And I do not give an ascendancy to dramatists unduly; I am a fiction writer myself who can only claim to dabble in dramatics at this point. By the powers of the voice the poet and fiction writer often can create the illusion of social complexity while merely dwelling on aspects of self. The dramatist must get inside of others, and the only vehicle available for this discovery is the voice, its enunciations and its gestures and its silences. I am not alone in this assessment of dramatic values in writers.

Here is Eudora Welty again: "Characters take on life sometimes by luck, but I suspect it is when you can write most entirely out of yourself, inside the skin, heart, mind, and soul of a person who is not yourself, that a character becomes in his own right another human being on the page." But it is the writer's voice which makes this other. In writing of her character Miss Eckhart from her story entitled "June Recital," Miss Welty writes about the discovery of her voice: "in the making of her character out of my most inward and most deeply feeling self, I would say I have found my voice in my fiction." All of these discoveries are the result of syllables laid on syllables, like making a brick wall, the mortar of each word building, building.

How the breath and syllable move in a voice is by waves of energy, the motions of saying and speaking. This is colored by experience, its different rhythms. It was Ezra Pound who wrote that every experience has its own unique rhythm. The rhythm of experience cannot be understated because it annihilates that bony, grandmotherly notion that everything has been said, and therefore nothing new can be written. How it happens is what happens.

I used to think that the nucleus of the poem was the image. This was information I misread via Black Mountain via the objectivists back to the imagists. But from short fiction and drama I learned that the greater center—imagination's DNA—is the voice. This quality of voice in fiction is there at its extremities and its midpoint. You see it, you hear it, at fiction's origins and at fiction's present state. Its range today includes the extremes of best-selling coffee-table fiction, vitiated, compromised, anemic; and, at the opposite end of the rainbow, it is there in the ultraexperimental prose of midnight offsetters, mimeograph ranters, and handset, limited-edition lunatics. In the kingdom of fiction the seeing voice charged by rhythm of experience—that is what is meant by style.

Dramatic Influences: Depth Illusion

Our critical vocabulary about fiction generally is outmoded and/or inappropriate to the landscape of short fiction. This might explain why the critical assessments of a dramatist like Peter Handke are so often misreadings when his short fiction is addressed. Most of the vocabulary for interpreting fiction derives from Aristotle's *Poetics* in which his recipe gave an ascendancy to plot and character. The *Poetics* overlooks a fifth-century Greek dramatist like Euripides because he often ignored plot and character for the sake of finding the music latent in the natural voice. Yet the silence of Cassandra in Aeschylus' *Agamemnon* says as much about drama as any Sophoclean plot. It is by her silence that Cassandra instructs us about contemporary short fiction. This doomed shaman bypasses Aristotle for a cozier relationship with a later age where short fiction is born. It is around the time of Gutenberg, but her blessing is not to the invention of movable type. Cassandra locates the voice of short fiction, not in type, but circa 1420 in Brunelleschi's invention of perspective. With this invention we see the illusion of depth born in our culture. Surfaces expand. The landscape of the imagination thickens, even though its borders stay the same. The linearity of words is a world of surfaces, of flatness. But voice—including Cassandra's silence—creates the illusion of depth. Voice gives perspective to language.

I started to paint one summer in order not to drink. Anyone knows that a painter paints and then likes to drink afterward. There are even cases where the painter painted and drank simultaneously. We grow up hearing Cedar Bar stories of Jackson Pollock and Franz Kline. But because I am a writer, first, I become intoxicated with the *idea* of painting, I became intoxicated by this idea so much that I stayed sober one entire summer. But my dogs, trees, moons, women, children, chairs were all literal-minded, the line too simple, reminiscent of writing itself more than painting. Even a painter friend said it: "You paint like a writer." One day I found myself doing two things at once. I was drinking; I was painting. Still, I had not become a painter, I will never be a painter, because I am a writer, and when I paint, I paint like a writer. The point of this is to suggest that the best writers often *think* like painters; and the best painters possess that inherent visual sense which finally is an aspect of drama. Brunelleschi's invention did more for stagecraft than it did for painting; and it probably did more for contemporary short fiction than anything else.

How Voice Sees

Good writers see things. Even beyond the good sense to see words as things, many writers also painted. This list of writers-*comme*-painters includes D. H. Lawrence, William Carlos

Williams, E. E. Cummings, Henry Miller, Jean Cocteau, to name just a few writers who were passably good painters. Playwrights out of necessity often acquired visual skills, acting, directing, or doing set designs. Sophocles was known for his stagecraft as well as his playwriting. As well as introducing a third primary actor onstage he also invented new set designs, including painted three-sided sets called *periaktoi*. He gave up acting because his voice was weak, but his dancing ability was legendary, and all his writing for the stage was informed by a keen visual sense in an age which had but one criteria for the visual—perfection. The Elizabethan stage was fairly uncluttered by sets and props, but what there was of it no doubt was given touches by Shakespeare, writer, actor, and without a doubt a theatrical jack-of-all-trades. Molière, we know, did everything, from acting to directing to writing the plays, and so he had to have had his hand in set designs and other visual details of a production. Baudelaire's art criticism is excellent; so is Apollinaire's. In the last thirty years many American poets engaged in art criticism for magazines, and Frank O'Hara was also a major curator for the Museum of Modern Art.

William Carlos Williams is one of the best examples of a seeing poet, one who literally engages his spirit in the visual arts. Unlike his buddy Ezra Pound who sought the lush papal reds of Giotto, Williams was after American images in his own paintings and in his friends' works. Yet I do not think of Marsden Hartley or Charles Demuth when I read Williams' poetry. Instead his poems remind me of Milton Avery's paintings, their simple majesty, their joy, and their sense of American celebration. I was walking through the twentieth-century galleries of the Metropolitan Museum of Art and came upon a painting by Avery entitled *White Roosters*, and immediately these words from "Spring and All" flashed through my mind:

> so much depends
> upon
>
> a red wheel
> barrow
>
> glazed with rain
> water
>
> beside the white
> chickens.

and instead of "white chickens" I said "white roosters," both of them two syllables with similar idiomatic stresses. In both Williams' seeing voice and Avery's telling eye something like the simple, elegant lines of white New England houses is manifested. I mean that there is an architecture to sight and sound. These are structures, "the pure products of America," if you will, which finally are as mysterious as a Japanese house which Tanizaki might have designed, minimal, spiritual, functional (cf. Tanizaki's *In Praise of Shadows*). By comparison the "utterance" in a painting by Andrew Wyeth is sentimental and from the Poppers to the Super Realists the "voice" in the paintings is too intellectually mocking.

Williams' voice, like Avery's paintings, appears to me to be of pastels, bled thin by turpentine, often two-dimensional and childlike. It is stark and clear, reedy but tough. It is not so much two-fisted as it is wonderfully ambidexterous. The image of the world from which voice draws its energy blends pinks and blues into a circular universe dominated by white roosters or white chickens. Of course, the wheelbarrow is red. Williams *shows* us instead of *telling* us. But the seeing voice does not merely record objects in a landscape and render them into a linear vocabulary. It jumps from the throat, demanding utterance, as Williams does in another poem called "A Unison":

> The grass is very green, my friend,
> and tousled, like the head of—
> your grandson, yes? And the mountain,
> the mountain we climbed
> twenty years since for the last
> time (I write this thinking
> of you) is saw-horned as then
> upon the sky's edge—an old barn
> is peaked there also, fatefully,
> against the sky.

I dwell on Williams for the paradigm of a seeing voice because he is something of a miracle worker. Through his voice he offers, like a gift, the privileged sense of sight. And the gallery in which Williams offers the gift of the seeing voice is a varied collection of objects and sounds. At a painting by Edward Hopper—a visual artist whose bleakness speaks to us—it would seem that to think of Williams here is to speak only of contrary natures. But as Avery's paintings sparked one register of Williams' voice, Hopper triggers another. This time I am reminded of a poem like "These," in which Williams' voice is colored in deeper shades:

> are the desolate, dark weeks
> when nature in its barrenness
> equals the stupidity of man.
>
> The year plunges into night
> and the heart plunges
> lower than night
>
> to an empty, windswept place
> without sun, stars or moon
> but a peculiar light as of thought

And still later in this spiralling downward cadenced dirge, Williams practically alludes to Hopper when he writes:

> houses of whose rooms
> the cold is greater than can be thought,
>
> the people gone that we loved,
> the beds lying empty, the couches
> damp, the chairs unused—

I take Williams as a paradigm of the seeing voice because his range of utterance goes from the unbounded joy of white chickens and a red wheelbarrow to the dreary *film noire* interiors of "These." In between these colorations on the spectrum are all the sounds a dramatist or fiction writer needs to know, and see.

Fiction Itself

I use two mediums, drama and poetry, to reveal things about fiction; and I use two senses, sight and sound, to illustrate what I think is fiction's center, the voice. You can be raised on white bread with peanut butter and jelly and still be moved by Isaac Babel's evoking of borscht, herring, and vodka. Without the slightest difficulty, Seamus Heaney's poetry often triggers the smells of turf and potatoes. The presence of a samovar in a Chekhov play can make you thirsty. The liver cooking in Leopold Bloom's kitchen is still redolent at the opposite end of the century, just as the onion in the opening paragraphs of Gogol's "The Nose" cannot be avoided. *Our* nose smells it! Hemingway's prose makes us thirsty for alcohol; Proust's makes us hungry for a madeleine. These are sense impressions which undeniably are the result of fiction's sensory powers. Yet the dominant senses in this world are those of sound (from the mouth/on the ear) and sight (inner/ outer).

Poetry is an ultimate sound, and that is why this study of short fiction is bracketed by it. The drama is partly spectacle, a visual extravaganza; it is where the greatest depth illusions occur. But fiction is utterance, too, and fiction—even when inward and still—strives, like drama, for depth illusion. The best fiction lives within a push and pull with poetry and drama.

Finally, this thing about short fiction, its voice and all—I want to paraphrase from a short story by Flannery O'Connor—is as obvious as a pig on the sofa.

2

Exemplary Voices

IN TERMS OF BREADTH, influence, and range, no three writers exemplify this pursuit of voice in short fiction, as I understand it, as do Beckett, Kafka, and Borges. A personal addition—its silent mime, if you will—would be Isaac Babel to this trinity. As the master of the genre of silence Babel must be there like the kings' fool, a kind of monkey on their backs, pantomiming the greater wisdom of voice, its silence. This is a curious synod of fiction's high priests, especially for an American to essay, because none of them speak my tongue. When I read these four writers, I am not given their truest voice but rather a kind of paraphrase. Everything comes down to me via the prestidigitation of translation. I am reminded of the old saw that poetry is what is lost in translation, i.e., the voice is not translated. But in this dramaturgical setting for fiction I would like to suggest that the role of the translator is analogous to that of the actor to his character. I am talking about *collaboration*, the art of the theater, in other words. I read Beckett, Kafka, Borges, and Babel, searching for their voices in the manner of an actor searching for the business and purpose of a character. Speak the lines out loud. Get the text on its feet and move around the empty space.

Samuel Beckett: *Texts for Nothing*

The problems of reading Beckett in English are less severe because he is English-speaking at his rhythmical origin. He does not so much write well in French and English as he writes *brilliantly* in both voices. The care with which he translates his own work from the French, either by himself or with a collaborator, is by now legendary. (Read Deirdre Bair's biography.) I am told by several writers who have met this old master that Beckett speaks French with an accent, or as an uncle once corrected me when I said I could not understand his *accent*, he said, "I don't have an *accent*, Mike, I have a *brogue*." As voiceless as Beckett has striven to make his fiction his French still possesses, in its rhythms, his spokenness, his brogue. The major quality in evidence with Beckett's fictional voice, either in French or English, is its Irishness.

I begin with Beckett because he is a fiction writer, a poet, and a playwright. Voice is the overriding principle which operates in all the forms he has plumbed in literature. In his fiction, as in his recent dramas, one does not have to isolate voice in Beckett, because often that is the only quality in the prose which allows us to call it fiction. Rather than call it an extreme of this incidence, I prefer to make it the exemplar when I choose a work like *Texts for Nothing*. Here, nothing in the traditional sense of plot and character is evident. Only the voice of the author characterized—the closest he comes to characterization—is operating. As in the medium of radio, the voice of this fiction is disembodied, something akin to transmissions in the air which are recorded in a receptor. It is lyrical, energized even for all of its ennui; it traps a certain light in the landscape of its utterance. I call it fiction because there is that rhythm of experience operating within its borders, its incredibly confined space. And I call it dramatic because the voice changes, has peaks and valleys, push and pull, tensions and conflicts.

In the eighth chapter—which could as easily be called a *scene*—the voice says: "Only the words break the silence, all other sounds have ceased. If I were silent I'd hear nothing. But if I were silent the other sounds would start again, those to which the words have made me deaf, or which have really ceased. But I am silent, it sometimes happens, no, never, not one second. I weep too without interruption. It's an unbroken flow of words and tears. With no pause for reflection. But I speak softer, every year a little softer. Perhaps. Slower too, every year a little slower."

Not only is the voice the only quality in this prose which makes it fiction, but the subject of this voice is the voice itself. Its silence. Its pace. Its flow. Its cadence. Its rhythm. I cannot account for anyone's taste but my own, and for me this is what fiction is, a model of its destiny, an examplar, as I said, of its finest moments, the tradition out of which the present and future of the craft should consider itself. Why? Because Beckett isolates the supreme aspect of his craft, and with that alone, voice makes itself into fiction. Beckett is nearly pedagogical here in how he highlights that part of the craft which is most important, as though showing us by example what the thing is. Fiction is voice, Beckett says.

Because I am an American of Irish descent, I've always felt that much of Beckett and also Joyce, Flann O'Brien, and Yeats were second nature to me. Vladimir Nabokov refers to this as the "comparatively lowly kind" of imagination in the reader—that of empathy. A reader's greatest error, Nabokov writes, is when "he identifies himself with a character in the book." With Irish writers I practice a lowly form of readership. But I imagine that even Nabokov was this way with certain Russian authors. It is part of our ethnic natures, no matter how far removed we are from the origins, to empathize with certain works. Why is it, a director asked me recently at the rehearsal of a play I wrote, that all the actors are struggling with their lines except Ryan (an actor from Dublin)? The ensemble consisted of a group of very professional and highly imaginative actors, all of whom I respect and all of whom eventually mastered the lines. But Ryan, as I told the director, "he has the lines in his blood." Voice is ethnic as well as geographical and regional. Beckett's disembodied voice still has its Irish accent, I mean, apologizing to my uncle, I mean it still possesses its *brogue*.

Franz Kafka: "Home-Coming"

When I consider Kafka, I can find no place to empathize with his voice. He does not allow me to be a lowly kind of reader. I never dreamed of being an insect; I do not dream of mice. My own parochial background makes it impossible to understand many of the obsessions of his culture. Guilt is universal—that Beckett thing about the "sin of being born"—but Kafka's voice is laced with a guilt of another sort. You could not characterize the voice as being either Jewish or Middle European, though qualities of that theological and social atmosphere create a patina on his voice. What I hear in Kafka's voice is not so much alien as it is immigrant, that of a displaced person. Even within his own territory I listen to the conflicts of an exile—that glad-to-be-gone/wish-I-were-back-home kind of pendulum. I do not see that voice as being out of place in a landscape like New York City. In fact, since I've first read Kafka, I often pictured him in Manhattan, on the Upper West Side, sitting on a bench on one of the islands of Broadway, talking to himself. Or I've pictured him walking along the Promenade on Riverside Drive, again, talking aloud to himself.

Only another writer would be drawn to that private soliloquy. Kafka is not threatening; he is not dangerous, except maybe to himself. By that I mean that others would pass him by, not even noticing, but that another writer would stop, unafraid that K. might attack physically, though verbally rocks would fly. (As I write this, from an apartment located at 110th Street and Broadway, all I need to do is look out my fifth-floor window, westward, and see a bunch of street crazies who would be unanimously approved by Central Casting as accomplices to this imaginary biography of Franz Kafka.) I listen to people talking on the street because their lunatic energy is attractive. There is a black Korean War veteran who passes by my windows like clockwork every morning between seven and eight o'clock. He has one of the biggest voices of anyone I have ever heard, so strong that even in winter, with the windows closed, and the noises of the traffic, garbage trucks, and sirens interceding, this man's voice challenges everyone to listen. What he proclaims, in his scratchy, hyperlunatic, yet resonating, voice is a personal history of his Korean War experiences. I have heard him every day for ten years, and it is not merely this early morning hour in which he orates. All day long, up and down Broadway, straight-backed, walking in a regimented cadence like a drill sargeant, he moves, screaming about his campaign. If that man were a writer, I would think his voice an American equivalent of what Kafka's voice sounds like to me.

I do not mean that Kafka's voice is as strident as the street veteran's, but it is as *obsessive*. Kafka would be at home in this neighborhood among these other muttering travelers, because this is an area with no one clear ethnic voice. It is a concatenation of voices, and often you can walk north or south on Broadway for ten or more blocks without hearing a note of English. Instead there is this blend of Spanish, Korean, Chinese, Haitian French, Jamaican patois—as musical as any language on the face of this earth—Jews speaking Yiddish, Hungarian, German, Polish, Rumanian, and Russian, and street kids parsing the American idiom into the rhythm of breakers and rappers.

In this world Kafka would have a license to speak aloud, not understanding them, not being understood. There is this bench on an island in the center of Broadway, one block from here, on which I have imagined Kafka sitting many times. It is an intersection at which there is a Korean deli which sells knishes, a Puerto Rican topless bar, a Woolworth, an Arab drugstore, a Greek newstand, a Cuban-Chinese restaurant, and a Cuban restaurant called Ideál. The street people are Dominicans mostly, some Blacks, and some Puerto Ricans. From across the street I see Kafka's lips moving, but I cannot hear his voice. When the light changes, I venture into his sphere on the island. The voice, even in translation, is accented, comic and sad, obsessive, unique.

This is what Kafka is saying: "I have returned, I have passed under the arch and am looking around. It's my father's old yard. The puddle in the middle. Old, useless tools, jumbled together, block the way to the attic stairs. The cat lurks on the banister. A torn piece of cloth, once wound around a stick in a game, flutters in the breeze. I have arrived. Who is going to receive me? Who is waiting behind the kitchen door? Smoke is rising from the chimney, coffee is being made for supper. Do you feel you belong, do you feel at home? I don't know, I feel most uncertain." Etcetera. (From "Home-Coming" in *The Complete Stories*.)

Jorge Luis Borges: "Everything and Nothing"

I take Borges' voice in his fiction "Everything and Nothing" to be the final exemplary voice in the dramaturgy of style, because it is a prose that is as much about the author as it is about its putative subject, William Shakespeare. In fact, it is Borges *acting* as Shakespeare. The Elizabethan was an actor-writer, and it is worth noting that Borges becomes an actor-writer in this tale. How the blind see, though, is literally through their other senses, so that to speak of Borges' seeing voice goes without saying. This voice is muted and often transparent, but there still remains its trace in Borges' prose; it is what transforms this biographical essay into fiction. Of Shakespeare, he writes:

Instinctively he had already become proficient in the habit of simulating that he was someone, so that others would not discover his condition as no one; in London he found the profession to which he was predestined, that of the actor, who on a stage plays at being another before a gathering of people who play at taking him for that other person. His histrionic tasks brought him a singular satisfaction, perhaps the first he had ever known; but once the last verse had been acclaimed and the last dead man withdrawn from the stage, the hated flavor of unreality returned to him.

It is worth asking why Borges thinks of one of the greatest writers of all time as first an actor. We think of Shakespeare as a writer first. But Borges correctly suggests to us that Shakespeare—and therefore Borges himself in this dramaturgical instance—thinks of himself as an actor, not so much first as foremost. The exact choice of words is instructive to unmasking Borges' voice here. Both the actor and writer "become proficient in the habit of *simulating.*" Simulation is an artifice, a ruse, a false appearance; it is the art of *imitation*. The other telling word about drama and fiction's voice is that of "histrionics," a word derived from the Etruscan and later Roman word for "actor." The French *histoire* or story and our own English word "history" bear some etymological correspondences with this word as well.

In this short fiction we are given another exemplar of voice, even an apogee of what the dramaturgy of style in prose means. Here, through the medium of a voice, we learn about Borges as well as Shakespeare. We learn about fiction's dramaturgy. Like Sophocles' Tiresias, these verities about the seeing voice are offered by a blind seer. It was Oedipus' fate not to listen to the blind prophet; but it is our good fortune to accept Borges as being correct in this prophecy. I think if there is a road on which fiction travels, this is a major point where the traveling actor stops for nourishment before continuing on into the future.

Isaac Babel: The Godfather

To conclude with Isaac Babel is a personal, not a historical, choice. Back in 1968 when I met him in Los Angeles, Hubert Selby told me to read Babel, and I have read him ever since, regularly. More even than Flaubert, Babel lives and breathes Ezra Pound's dicta about poetry: the direct treatment of the object; every experience has its own unique rhythm; poetic concision/*dichtung*; and *le mot juste* (Pound via Flaubert). Babel's voice is a careful, painstaking merging of a fiction by its strongest poetic links to its clearest dramatical ends. Drama is about human tensions exploding into revelations. Words join actions to create ideas. All of this explains Isaac Babel, too. But to understand Babel the dramatist you need to understand something about the man, because his voice comes from the person. He was a Jew in a Russian army that was not known for its kindness to Jews. He was an intellectual; he was a Cossack. Imagine Martin Luther King in a frontline combat unit in the Central Highlands of Vietnam circa 1968, preaching the Lord but gung ho for battle. Here is Christ in camouflage battle dress utilities. Gandhi parachuting behind enemy lines with the Screaming Eagles, M-16 in his hand, six hand grenades fastened to his web belt.

Babel's voice broke every rule of his time and culture, and there is no reason to suspect that history has tamed and civilized him. As a Russian he owed it to his country to be massively imaginative, to carve out a landscape in fiction as dense and spanning as those in *War and Peace, The Brothers Karamazov*, or the shelfful of other Russian masters from the previous century. Even Chekhov was capable of being expansive in his prose and plays. Babel was something else. He could write about an Odessa gangster as soon as locate the typical in Russian idiom. His voice is unsentimental, tough, observant; he is not a bully or punk but rather a hard-nosed, intelligent man. I imagine that he would not have been out of place in a *film noire* gangster movie, and sometimes I think that Bertolt Brecht must have taken lessons from Babel on how to conduct himself in public, what aspect of voice to put forward. I often think that Babel must have been an excellent boxer. I have no biographical information for this detail, but I intuit it from voice in his prose and his bulldog neck in his photographs. From his grittiness, his observations of reality, the things in his stories, I think I would have liked him as a friend.

Part of the depth of his loyalty to himself and those he respected or loved is attested to by the powerful enemies he made. Babel's voice was not that of a big-mouthed tough guy; it was the voice of a pugnacious attitude. That voiced, yet unspoken, attitude would have been perfectly at home hanging out in Selby's Greek diner in *Last Exit to Brooklyn*, and not one of those hoods, toughs, punks, and dockworkers could have said *boo* to this gentleman. I think perhaps that Babel was always combat-ready. There is a false deadness, a vacant fury in the eyes of all combat veterans. We know that look from photographs of Vietnam veterans, Korean War vets, and those who fought in World War II. Babel's eyes learned to see in Russian campaigns through Poland and elsewhere. Americans like silent tough guys, and Babel is no exception to this romance we have. He exudes silence; he exudes toughness. And this attitude, as I say, made him powerful enemies, the Establishment of postrevolutionary Russia, the birth of the Soviet Union. To them he was a baffling, rude pantomime, and they knew right away that his silences burned like frostbite.

When Babel spoke it was not the voice of an egotist, nor was it the voice of a shy, unconfident man. His voice was imbued with self-confidence by a life of harshness and survival. As he said himself, he was the master of the genre of silence. Beckett's silences make us ponder; Babel's silences are hollow and assertive, that of a pugilist who knows what round he is going to knock out his opponent. This is a silence after rocket fire. Those wire-framed glasses made Babel look like a librarian, but his silence is not librarial. It is an actor's disguise, almost like Clark Kent's glasses to hide his true identity as that of Superman. Babel is a sublime warrior, a soldier, a fighting man, as was Sophocles, as was Aeschylus, as were the heroes of Homer's epics. There is not an ounce of Plautus' Miles Gloriosus or Shakespeare's Falstaff in Babel. His dramatic sensibility goes back to the time of the Romans, when an afternoon's entertainment included feeding Christians to lions (the Christian mimes) or performing a version of *Thyestes* in which the children (real children!) are chopped up and served for dinner. The emperor Heliogabalus declared that all acts of sex onstage must be believable. All acts in Babel's voice are believable without needing an edict. The rhythm of experience is chiseled out of every sound. The drama of a life is there. And his voice is all poetry.

"He buttoned his green frock coat on three bone buttons, flicked himself with the cock's feathers, sprinkled a little water on his soft palms, and departed, a tiny, lonely visionary in a black top hat, carrying a big prayerbook under his arm."

In a purification of Soviet life and art Isaac Babel's voice was sent into the exile of a nonperson. From the moment of that exile in the late thirties his voice was never heard from again. He did not exist. That is why Babel is the one pantomime among these exemplary voices. He creates the illusion, with his silence, that I actually hear his voice. I don't think Babel would be ill-at-ease in the world of the mimes, a spoken theatrical improvisation of which pantomime is the silent adjunct. Since its inception the mime was home to crook and actor, murderer and panderer, jugglers, mountebanks, minstrels, the circus, prostitutes and actresses. It was the only theatrical form which allowed women to play women's parts. (The Babel of "Guy de Maupassant" would have enjoyed such big-bosomed company.)

As jaded as mime's history often appears—the second oldest profession sometimes worked as a screen or cover for the oldest profession of prostitution—mime also accounts for the genesis of some of Western culture's most lasting characters. Both Miles Gloriosus and Falstaff have character origins in mime. This is also true of characters like Sganarelle in Mo-

lière; Keaton's silent creations as well as Chaplin's Little
Tramp; and Marcel Marceau's Bip. Beckett's characters like
Estragon and Vladimir, Lucky and Pozzo, with origins in
vaudeville, likewise can be traced to an origin in mime. And
so can a character like Isaac Babel's Benya Krik, the Godfather of Odessa.

After shooting Eichbaum's cows in a midnight raid, this
Jewish gangster is able to say, as though it were Al Pacino or
Marlon Brando in *The Godfather*: "If I don't have my money,
Monsieur Eichbaum, you won't have your cows. It's as simple as that." Where Babel's voice approaches the antiquity of
the mime is in its balance of humor and violence and the
broad sexuality of his characters. Even Benya Krik is human.

"During the raid, on that dreadful night when cows bel-
lowed as they were slaughtered and calves slipped and slith-
ered in the blood of their dams, when the torch-flames
danced like dark-visaged maidens and the farm-women
lunged back in horror from the muzzles of amiable Brown-
ings—on that dread night there ran out into the yard, wearing nought save her V-necked shift, Tsilya the daughter of old
man Eichbaum. And the victory of the King was turned to
defeat."

The voice of Isaac Babel is Russian Jewish, but it also has
echoes in another time, dating back to sixth century Megara
and the Atellan farce of Naples. Comedy itself originates in
the mimes and old phallic rituals. Why I connect Babel's
voice to this dramatic activity is because mime was nearly always fugitive. It was an art form as easily in favor as out of favor. It had none of the civic rigmarole that the tragic dramas
had. Mimes were vagrant, footloose sorts of people, ex-sol-
diers, ex-cons, ex-slaves, petty crooks, pimps, and gangsters.
(The word "mime" is used both for performance and per-
former.)

Isaac Babel is a fugitive writer. His voice dramatizes the fugitive element in our universe. Short fiction is a fugitive's game, usually too irregular to be merely a short story, it is not at home in most journals, whether commercial or experimental. Sometimes it finds its way into a small press. I imagine Babel winking to me at this observation. Imagine him saying, "Fiction, it is as good as any con game in this town." When a con man pulls a scam on you, he accomplishes the crime with usually one sensual thing. He is a good talker.

Prose becomes fiction when we are seduced by the voice of the writer into believing anything. We buy the landscape without realizing we'll never live there except in our imaginations. Coleridge called it the willing suspension of disbelief. But I think Babel, talking in the American idiom, might say it is more like taking somebody to the cleaners.

Part II

Voices of the New Muse

TO SPEAK OF LIKENESS in the voice of different forms is not to suggest there are no differences. While the ideal voice is concise, often the voice of fiction strays from areas of drama. I am thinking of fictions, concise, like poetry, and often lyrical, but not moving through dramatic arcs so much as starting on a note, high up, energized, and sustained there through verbal pyrotechnics, they almost resemble one long cadenza. Early examples are Joseph Conrad's *Typhoon,* and some good contemporary examples are Barry Hannah's *Ray;* the voice of Russell Banks' *The Relation of My Imprisonment,* though its structure is dramatic; Kenneth Gangemi's *Olt* with its list-obsessed voice; *The Axing of Leo White Hat* by Raymond Abbott; *Spanking the Maid* by Robert Coover, which has it both ways by being cadenzalike and yet essentially dramatic; *The Self-Devoted Friend* by Marvin Cohen, a short-fiction master by this point; *The War Outside of Ireland* by Michael Joyce; *Stolen Stories* and *Moving Parts* by Steve Katz; *Some Business Recently Transacted in the White World* by Ed Dorn; and *Cities* by Robert Kelly. Often these works, many of them published by small presses and now long out-of-print, are manic voices, even ecstatic ones, certainly word-drunk voices, voice-happy, from first to last page.

Mostly, though, short fiction shares dramatic affinities; this issue of one-note cadenzas is the exception to the rule. At its origin short fiction shows more resemblance than dissimilarity to the drama. A notable quality is not simply concision, but the technique of the voice to leave out, to omit, I mean, to disregard accumulations for the sake of omitting as much as is put in. This is a suggestive, rather than definitive, impulse. This suggestiveness—the impulse to leave out—is an old standby of drama's. Withholding information creates suspense, and this quality draws the reader or audience into the dramatic web. It is this quality in Herman Melville's "Bartleby, the Scrivener" which makes it both mysterious and a mystery. In less dramatic hands that story would be twice or three times as long, and interestingly, it would say far less. The only condition Bartleby offers by way of autobiographical information is his haunting refrain, "I would prefer not to."

I would prefer not to.

This is nearly the logo of short fiction, combined along with that dramatic instinct to exclude, to hide. I often have thought of the ideal bar where writers would hang out; it would be our place exclusively, like a rumpled Ivy League or British private club. As Faulkner suggested in an interview it probably would be good to have whores—why not? There might be rooms upstairs for naps as well as rooms for doing writing, nothing electric, big upright typewriters in plain, threadbare cells. Above the mahogany bar would be Bartleby's philosophy in big letters: I WOULD PREFER NOT TO. The barstools would have backs on them, for our aching backs in our backbreaking work. The beer would be icy cold, real cheap, and each of us would have a tab, like credit cards, with reasonable ceilings so as not to go drunkenly into the red. There might be a game room for chess and darts and cards, gambling at poker and gin being permitted here. In the bathroom, unisex, without urinals, only bowls, rows and rows of them, for peeing and barfing and otherwise, along one wall, there would be written:

MAKE IT NEW

It is a dramatic consideration, harking back to that theatrical term about "the illusion of the first time." Its greatest explicator was Ezra Pound, who wrote about it in "Canto LIII," beginning, "Yeou taught men to break branches."

> Tching prayed on the mountain and
> wrote MAKE IT NEW
> on his bathtub
> Day by day make it new

The cells upstairs might have other inspirational ideas and sayings; the game rooms could have their own mottoes. But the two essential venues in this ideal bar would be at the bar itself and in the head. Both are essentially dramatic inspirations, yet both are likewise signposts for fiction writers, probably the loneliest creatures in the Writer's Bar. Imagine this fairly dark, wood-filled elongated room sometimes inhabited by outsiders, groupies, but also agents and publishers and editors, and each time they ask the writer to *do* something, either he or she answers, "I would prefer not to."

The answer, of course, is tied up with Pound's injunctive in the bathroom: MAKE IT NEW. And since this is a writer's bar, some wag has written Pound's dictum in its original Chinese.

新
日
日
新

Before Pound gave it a voice in an American English cadence it says, FRESH DAY DAY FRESH. *Shin* or *Hsin* consists of an ax and a standing tree, the picture rendered into interpretation meaning that in order to make a new or fresh field, you must cut down the old trees. It is the same ideogram found in newspapers in Korea, China, and Japan, meaning "news" as much as it is "new." Poetry is news that stays news. Short fiction is prose that stays fiction. It is not so much a question of providing new information as it is creating that illusion of the first time. That is how drama enters into this poetics on short fiction. The illusion of the first time is an important issue in the Writer's Bar. It was William Carlos Williams who wrote that no news is found in poetry, but that men die each day for a lack of what *is* found there. What I am suggesting by this is that there is a progression from the drama into poetry into fiction. But in order to understand this progression completely it is necessary to go back to the origins of the drama.

It was Arion (625–585 B.C.) who organized the dithyrambic chorus, those hymns to Dionysos, the god of wine and fertility, this oriental deity being a relatively late addition to the Greek pantheon. These early poems were recited collectively by a chorus, and no distinction was made between poetry and dance, drama and fiction. Eventually a single character emerged from the group. This great theatrical innovator was called Thespis, from whom our word "thespian" derives. Think how often since that initial impulse fiction writers and playwrights have done the same, i.e., stepped from the group to create a singular, particularized voice. Originally the chorus entered the ritual space via ramps called *paradoi,* turning figures, Noh-like slow, until they came on the orchestra, a large circular space of pounded dirt, very similar to our own pitcher's mound in baseball. Behind them was an altar at which libations were poured for Dionysos. In earlier versions of these rituals—and this was a custom which was to continue into Greek comedy like Aristophanes'—the men wore large leather dildos strapped on at the waist.

How Thespis distinguished himself was not so much by the difference of his story—all of the chorus were telling the same story whatever it was—but by virtue of his voice. It is certain that in order to make this severing authentic Thespis had to concentrate and focus himself. There were one or two steps he took. With this simple gesture, unadorned but theatrical, Thespis changed poetry into drama, and also planted the seeds of what would become fiction. What made the difference, again, from his gestures being merely choral or poetic, was *voice,* singular, imitative, dramatic.

Fiction's seed is planted with Thespis, but it is not born until the time of Gutenberg and Brunelleschi with the linearity of movable type and the spatial illusion of perspective. Make it new; make it news. Before these inventions there never is a question of where a poem must occur, and that is on the tongue. By the fifteenth century the issue becomes whether the poem rests on the tongue or on the page. Sometimes the poem or the fiction gets tricked out on the page, but ultimately the cutting edge still remains with drama, where words must be spoken by human beings impersonating other beings. Poetry and fiction sometimes forget these lessons from Thespis, but the drama never does.

Spokenness is still the measure in our literary arts, and while voice is a slacker measure than the metronome's, its variable cadence is what gives us music. The sonnet is a brilliant little machine which more resembles clockwork than the human voice. How many times I've read a play by Shakespeare, not sure of a passage or line until it was said on the tongue, and if I were still unsure, putting it on its feet, going through the paces until—there it is!—all sense came about from the voice in concert with gesture. Voice is a physical instrument, not a mental one. Shakespeare proves this time and again. What ultimately distinguishes him from his contemporaries is his voice consciousness. This finally is a lesson for both poets and fiction writers from the drama. The more the spokenness of the human voice invades the page—the more the words approximate the wonders of poetry and fiction. Isn't this the reason why we admire Southern writers so often? Think how voice permeates Eudora Welty's and Flannery O'Connor's prose. It is as though Thespis were born and reborn, again and again. His singular gesture still is what joins the poem to the play to fiction.

Those ritual origins of drama are important to fiction for other reasons, too. Essentially, in a more primitive time, they were preludes to drunkenness and orgies. In a later time Aristophanes had great comic fun with the leather *phalloi*. And so back at the Writer's Bar, drinking a cold beer, I am thinking, not words, not voice, not writing. Let's imagine I've had a good day of writing and around five o'clock I've come to the bar for its happy hour. Instead of words I am thinking about sex, trying to come up with the sexiest woman in history to be the muse of this voice-centered short fiction. I think of some remarks I once read in Camus' *Notebooks* in which he said that abstention was good for writing, which reminds me of old-time prize fighters who abstained from sex before big matches. In one of the game rooms of the Writer's Bar is a photograph of Camus, and I cannot help observing how much he looks like Humphrey Bogart. Did Bogart abstain while shooting a movie? I doubt it.

Today many top-ranked boxers invite their wives to training camps before a fight. Other ways to peak a boxer's aggressions have been found instead of denying him his nookie. When I think about writing and sex, I assay it two ways, both as a form of activity in fiction (the requisite sex scene in popular novels) and as a personal need in every human. Thinking about those rituals to Dionysos, I would like to suggest that sex is good for writers, when they are writing, when not writing, any time of day or night. As I think about this, sipping a cold beer at the Writer's Bar, the room is not filled with anyone I know yet, I struggle to recall so-called sex scenes in fiction which turned me on. Some Henry Miller in adolescence. *The Ginger Man,* again as an adolescent. Grown up, I recall a sleigh ride in *War and Peace,* where the voice in the prose shifts from distancing into a passionate register, and clearly because Tolstoy is turned on, his voice turns on the reader. Yet nearly every poem I have liked has a sexually charged underpinning to it, even if the content isn't explicit about sex. There are poems by Robert Creeley, "My love's manners in bed," his poem about the woman on the roof with his wife in bed. Sappho has kissed many women poets in our age: Carolyn Forche, Ai, Denise Levertov, Kathleen Fraser, to name only a few. I mean that their poems excite.

The writer's voice in the theater is different, though, because it is transmitted through another human being. Nearly every woman in *The Sea Gull* is capable of arousing Dionysian lusts in a man. Aging Arkadina still turns people on; Trigorin, the writer, is still in her thrall. Nina turns on Trigorin, too, a sure sign that her youth is sexual. Even Masha has an earthiness which translates into sexuality. Drama's ritual expectations are still sexual at their origin, and the voice of fiction needs to do more than passively consider this origin. Since the beginnings of theater there were red-light districts intermingled with the legitimate craft. The early Greeks had it both ways by being legitimately sexual in their rituals. Comedy, of course, never abandoned these origins, and Lenny Bruce ultimately was the most classical of our actors because of this fact. I marvel at Richard Pryor's *Sunset Strip* movie for the same reason, how faithful his voice is to the ancient beginnings of drama by its gestures and words, its profanity and its sacredness.

I am not merely being like Heliogabalus, suggesting that all sex onstage appear authentic. That can be accomplished in the arena of a massage parlor on Forty-second Street. But the voice needs to be connected to the senses, sight and sound, touch and taste and smell. Actors coupling on stage don't really fill the bill as a return to the magic of drama's beginnings. Sam Shepard in *Buried Child* has a character put his hand down a woman's throat as a gesture emblematic of seduction. Harold Pinter has a seduction take place in *The Homecoming* over a glass of water. The voice of fiction needs those kinds of objects—a glass of water. A glass of water. In my mind Pinter has one of the most seeing voices imaginable. By comparison our fiction writers (male and female) are somewhat prudish, or worse, completely disconnected to the magic and ritual at drama's origin. The tendency is to be pornographic, i.e., perverted and/or violent rather than sensual. It is as though fiction's voice had become as abstemious as Camus' in his *Notebooks*. And I keep thinking the Writer's

Bar needs a muse, a new muse, one who will correct these problems at fiction's origin in the ancient dramatic rituals. Then it comes to me. Helen of Troy!

"Helen of Troy?"

It is the bartender talking.

"Yes, Helen," I say.

He opens another beer for me, presuming my day has been unduly rough.

"Why?" he asks.

I am muttering words like "cadenza" and "leaving out" and "concision."

Why?

"I would prefer not to," I say.

"I get it," the bartender says, walking away to wait on some writers at the end of the bar.

"Make it new," I say. Or I say, "The illusion of the first time." As the bartender comes past again, I say, "It all adds up to Helen."

Think of how many Greek dramas, starting with Aeschylus' *Oresteia,* in which Helen is central to the action. Yet she never appears. She is what is left out of the drama, while remaining its catalyst. She is both spectral and subtextual; all we know of her is her reputation. Talk about virtue in dirty underpants. Euripides' Helen is as charming as a hooker or inflatable Go-Go doll. She is like that creation of Tomas Landolfi in "Gogol's Wife."

Helen is everywhere and nowhere in Greek drama. Her biography is akin to Shakespeare's in Borges' two-page fiction, "Everything and Nothing." She is, and she is not. Even in Homer her "smoky-voiced" entrance is reserved for some brief descriptions of her, like Gandhi, grooving behind a spinning wheel. She prefigures tragedy, historically and imaginatively; she precedes the dithyramb and the goat song. Before Arion and Thespis, there is Helen. It could be suggested that she invented drama from her bedroom in Troy. Princess and whore, Helen is like fiction itself, adept at playing the goddess or floozy. Even her superficial biography is incredible. Here is an eight-by-ten glossy with her résumé on the back.

Daughter of Leda and the Swan (Zeus); sister to Clytemnestra (Agamemnon accuses her of being too manly at the beginning of the *Oresteia*); one brother a boxer, the other a jockey; kidnapped as a girl (the macho would suggest she asked for it); wife of Menelaus, Agamemnon's brother; and—Paris' amour. Helen is a beguiling combination of Playboy bunny and passionate intelligence like Lou-Andreas Salome. It is no wonder that writers as divergent as Poe and Shakespeare evoked her as their muse.

Her voice is composed as much of silence as it is of words. To be sure she eroticizes everyone with her subtext, her stage business, her bits. Consider her sister Clytemnestra, if you will. The difference between these sisters is really the difference between fiction (traditionally, generically) and short fiction. Clytemnestra is told she speaks too much by her husband Agamemnon. Helen is only remembered for her song, and maybe it is her silences which men think of as music. One sister says too much; the other says nothing, and yet this silent one is remembered for her voice. Even if we do not understand what Helen is saying in her "smoky-voiced" whisper, we have to presume it has to do with theater's origins.

I imagine that every Greek actor was thinking of Helen when they worked on their voices, the most important equipment for the stage. They would eat eels (for protein and energy), lettuce (to stay regular), and garlic (to open the throat). Outwardly these gestures were for Dionysos; privately they set their altars for Helen. But what a muse! She is not so much mother as she is mistress to the drama and fiction, and out of this role comes tragic necessity for the Greeks, and in our time—the tragic-comic muse, a beautiful woman from the soap operas. Helen is as easily a drag queen as she is a sensuous female. Strap a leather dildo on her and she'll dance a *kordax* as good as any hairy satyr.

All of this suggests that it is not poetry per se that is the highest art but rather the word itself. But it must be wed to (screwed into, in Helen's case) speech, the spoken—a voice. Poetry demands voice. So does fiction. Helen is that thing which motivates the rhythms of the voice into drama, into poetry, into fiction. How else explain a nation's madness over an infidelity? It is the type of event from which even the police beg off. A domestic matter, they say. It goes back to make it new. Make it news. News that stays news. Those Chinese pictures in the bathroom of the Writer's Bar and on the bathtub of Pound's poem. Helen is all of these things, and by her example fiction finds its voice.

If anyone is offended by these observations—be offended. They are meant to be offensive. Much that is contemporary in fiction is that, too. Characters in Steve Katz's stories peel off skin with razor blades and store lovers in closets. Fiction is not a polite form of discourse. Really, it is a big stretch of the imagination, offensive all the way. The history of the theater is like that, too. The greater tension in which drama (and fiction) exists is an enormous push and pull between the sacred and the profane. Those live sex acts, massage parlors, peep shows, and Triple XXX movie theaters interlarded with playhouses on Broadway—this condition was there with the Elizabethans, with the Italians in the Renaissance, with the medieval religious cycles, back to the Roman mimes, back to the Greeks, and back into Sicily. Theodora, a promiscuous mime artist, became the Empress of the Eastern Empire after she married Justinian, who no doubt thought she looked like Helen. Read Guy Davenport's translations of *The Mimes of Herondas,* playlets which would fit in well between strip acts in Las Vegas or Atlantic City. The high forms of drama often drew upon or were intermingled with its vulgar roots, the kinky, the outrageous, the disgusting, the bizarre, the venereal. When Robin Williams speaks to his penis in a stand-up nightclub act, he mirrors a comic situation which goes back to the magical beginnings of literature.

In late Roman times, with the ascendancy of Christianity, Helen as muse becomes problematic. Oscar Brockett in *History of the Theatre* writes: "The theatre was a favorite target of the Christians for at least three reasons. First, it was associated with the festivals of pagan gods. Second, the licentiousness of the mimes offended the moral sense of the church leaders. Third, the mimes often ridiculed such Christian practices as baptism and the sacrament of bread and wine." This is right out of an old Lenny Bruce bit about his tattoo, a routine which was not allowed on television because it was deemed offensive to Jews and Christians. All of the above taken note of, it is quite baffling to realize that Helen emerges in the rebirth of theater, not in some whorehouse, where her resurrection might be expected, but in the church itself. A trope, a mere scrap of dialogue, is inserted into the Easter liturgy. It amounts to a new voice, an energy, another seed, a kind of fiction, the old tensions surfacing again.

> ANGELS.   Whom seek you in the tomb, O Christians?
> THE THREE MARYS.   Jesus of Nazareth, the crucified,
>   O Heavenly Beings.
> ANGELS.   He is not here, He is risen as He foretold.
>   Go and announce that He is risen
>   from the tomb.

This miscellaneous trope is where Western drama as we know it today originates. From it springs to life, over the slow and steady roll of centuries, such names as Shakespeare, Molière, Racine, Ibsen, Chekhov, Brecht, Beckett, and the roll call of names associated with fiction, short and long, and the roster of poets from Dante to Yeats, from Eliot to Frank O'Hara. Helen herself does not give birth to fiction until a few centuries later, but she was in the back of that medieval church, silly hat on her head, pretending to be proper. Her smile that day had to be more mysterious than the Mona Lisa's. Because Helen is Helen, it will be impossible to say whether the father is Gutenberg or Brunelleschi. Fiction has its Mediterranean passions as well as its intellectually Teutonic inclinations.

As soon as Helen gets theater back into the business of the church it is thrown out on the steps and eventually winds up in the marketplace, secular, brewing, full of its ancient mischief. It becomes fiction. The stretch so far includes her jaunt in Troy right up to the gates of Hollywood. Today her breath reeks of liquor. She's at the end of the Writer's Bar, smoking cigarettes. Rumor has it she snorts cocaine. So what else is new? It's a kick, she says. When she speaks at the end of the bar, the writers *see* her voice. Drop a coin in the jukebox and she'll boogie like your sister Kate. Erotic, wanton, seductive—Helen is all of that. Nowadays Helen is self-reflexive, self-possessed, often singular in voice. Her breasts (firm, upturned, fruitlike) are ageless. She looks at herself with a hand-held pocket mirror. Often she sits alone in a dark corner of the Writer's Bar. From this vantage she teases, torments, strokes, bends, flexes, tenses her muscles, struts, draws in, ripples her abdomen, swivels her hips, gyrates. She pulls a flush line, and like that girl in *Flashdance,* she drenches herself in water. This is fiction? This is the seeing voice? This is drama? Or poetry? In a sense, yes.

Asked to dance, Helen answers, "I would prefer not to."

This gets a good laugh from all the writers at the bar, male and female alike. She's practically one of us.

When a young writer hands her a new fiction, she throws it back in this child's face.

Her face gets hideous, as though it were a mask.

"Make it *New!*" she screams.

Later she recounts Euripides' tale of her doings in Troy, explaining that she had been kidnapped and that this semblance—picture Gogol's wife again—was inserted into Troy.

"It was in my likeness," she says, wearing black on black, a veil covering her ancient eyes, "a breathing image out of the sky's air. He thought he held me but he held a vanity which is not I."

Not I, Beckett's voices.

Helen's voice.

Fiction's voice at origin.

"He held a vanity," Helen repeats.

Osip Mandelstam sits at the opposite end of the bar, drinking Polish vodka, and he calls down to Helen. I stare at Bartleby's statement over the bar.

Mandelstam says, "What's meaning but vanity? A word is a sound—"

I wish more fiction writers in this Writer's Bar would listen to Mandelstam. Actors already know what Mandelstam is saying; it is useless to look for meanings when rehearsing a play. Better to find a *purpose* for the characters, a character, your character, and from that maybe try to find objectives. What does this character want? If I ask this question of Helen, I think it is another drink, and so I'll buy her another drink. Like the stage itself, we sit in the Writer's Bar, proscribed, finite, blocked. Short fiction is like this, too. Some things work; some don't. There is a context for the fictional voice. This is my context, a fictional "I" framed by one of the century's greatest poets and one of drama's greatest floozies, a creature full of spectacle. Helen reminds me of a line which Edgar mutters in *King Lear* about doing "the act of darkness" with his mistress. Seeing Helen at the end of the bar I realize that short fiction is another kind of act, of darkness, sensuous, amorous, rhythmical.

I raise my glass to the Russian at the end of the bar drinking his Polish vodka and to this dark lady from antiquity, sipping her martini.

"To the illusion of the first time!" I shout.

"Here, here," the bartender says, sensing I am getting out of line.

Mandelstam does not look up; like Kafka uptown on Broadway, he mumbles to himself in his native tongue, making everything he says foreign to me.

From her expression I see that Helen likes this toast, and so I stumble down the end of the bar in her direction, ready to lay it on thick. I am thinking of David Mamet's character Richard Roma about to charm someone out of his money with some bogus real estate in Florida. Buy a piece of short fiction for your retirement years! The voice, the voice, I say. It is as much how you say it as what you say. This is where a younger con man is about to get taken by an old-timer like Helen. Like Roma to the rube Lingk in the Chinese restaurant, I'll ask the old gal what she is drinking. Here is my hand. If she asks my name, I'll tell her; I'll tell Helen my name . . .

Call me Ishmael.

The Voices

In the following chapters I begin with a discussion of poets, keeping to my argument about framing short fiction by it and the drama. What contemporary fiction does best, it seems to have learned from poets. For these reasons I spend a chapter each on the late Paul Blackburn, Joel Oppenheimer, and Gilbert Sorrentino. The last writer is a bridge into fiction because his background literally comes out of poetry before publishing a considerable body of fiction. I choose to begin with Blackburn because he is a poets' poet, and his influence is quite extensive in America's literary community, if not well known to a wide reading public. Joel Oppenheimer's poetry follows, because his work is highly representational of a poetry after Williams and Pound, and I do not think Oppenheimer has been given his deserved laurels for what he has accomplished.

My chapters on fiction writers are not meant to be a full chart of all the waters. Instead I am concerned, narrowly, with poetic and dramatic concerns via the voice in short fiction. Hubert Selby, Jr., heads off this section, because he is a major voice. He was personally connected as well to the writers in the preceding chapters, and what Selby knows about fiction he admits quite readily to having learned a great deal of it from these poets.

Following Selby, it might be logical to include a survey of the influence of Latin American and South American writers on the fictional landscape today, but I think this subject is more than well covered by other writers than myself. The Spanish influence, so culturally evident in our American cities, is a wonderful cross-cultural phenomenon, starting with Whitman and Poe creating non-European influences and culminating in a generation of American writers after World War I with William Faulkner's mythological territory dominating. Most often this writing is called "magical realism," but a better name for it might be simply "magic fiction." Part of its power and charm is how it transports us, not so much to the Spanish-speaking Americas, but to imaginary

worlds, where myth and ritual are as potent as guns and butter. I don't know any writers who begrudged Gabriel García-
Márquez receiving the Nobel prize for Literature; his way of
making fiction has altered the way all of us make fiction, and
even see the world.

Instead of Latin influences I have chosen to dwell on two
different aspects of the American fictional voice in regard to
Asia. First, there is a chapter about Vietnam War voices,
most of it written by Vietnam veterans, a powerful moral
voice in our fictional landscape. This is followed by a chapter
on the Asian immigration to America. Perhaps the best-
known writer about the latter condition is Maxine Hong
Kingston, whose *The Woman Warrior* and *China Men,* although
longer works of nonfiction, are strongly voice-oriented in the
sense I have applied that term here, meaning that she has a
high sense of poetry and drama. My concern is not with Chinese immigrant writers but with the more recent immigrant
voice from Korea, the land of America's other war after
World War II. I have visited Korea several times with my
wife and daughter, and we lived there in 1978. As I write this
I am recently back from yet another visit there. It is this interest in the Land of Morning Calm which drew me to the writer
I write about—Theresa Hak Kyung Cha. Perhaps she is the
greatest loss to account for in this study of short fiction, because shortly after her novel, *Dictee,* appeared, she was sense-
lessly murdered in New York City. I cannot presume to
calculate the loss of this voice in a short chapter.

The section on fiction writers concludes with what I think
is the best ongoing practitioner of short fiction in our country
today, and that is Stephen Dixon, whose career begins with
small press publications in the 1970s and continues today
with commercial, medium-sized literary houses and university presses. Story to story this "I"-obsessed writer seems

never to change his attack, which is frontal and straight to the heart. Yet each Dixon collection is different. His voice is one of the most distinct and uniquely resonant practicing at this moment—jittery, demystified, real, dramatic, poetic. Its present-tense obsessiveness is all about what I mentioned earlier regarding "the illusion of the first time." It is a voice which took me a long time to become familiar with, and I want to explore his writings for that reason.

This overall passage about voice concludes with a chapter on playwrights, Sam Shepard and David Mamet, and their debt to Harold Pinter. Shepard is a representative voice of the noncity American; Mamet's is a quintessentially Chicago voice. Both writers, I think, have learned a considerable amount of their craft from American poets and fiction writers. They conclude part two because I think as a future remedy against becoming stale and too singular, American fiction writers could learn a lot from these playwrights' dramaturgy.

3

Paul Blackburn

PAUL BLACKBURN'S most representative publication is still *The Cities,* which Grove Press published in 1967. He was only to live a few short years more, dying of lung cancer in his forties. Born in Vermont, Blackburn's voice had nothing Frostian about it. (I mean Robert Frostian, since his mother was Frances Frost, and Paul was raised by his grandparents, Amos and Susan Frost, no relation to the poet Robert.) He was not a pastoral or bucolic man but rather an essentially urban one. New York often was his most urban location, but he made journeys widely, especially scholarly jaunts in Europe for research on his Provencal troubadour poetry translations, of which Ezra Pound was an admirer. I am told that Blackburn read his translations to Pound, and the Old Buzzard, given to silence after his release from St. Elizabeth's Hospital, grunted his approval of these Peire Vidal renditions.

I begin with Blackburn because he is the most Poundian of his own generation, yet he could take the rhythms untrapped out of Pound's influence and work it in a measure as spoken and colloquial as William Carlos Williams. In fact, Blackburn's voice is a wonderful synthesis of these great American poets. I don't mean to suggest that Blackburn was an imitator. The nature of his voice was to assimilate multiple influences into the steady range of his own intentions. If anything, he is the writer most imitated, not the reverse. In the 1960s, because his poetry was so voluminously published in small press magazines, it was not uncommon to find Blackburn's work carrying an entire issue of a magazine, his work sandwiched in between a bunch of contemporary and younger writers riding on his shirttails.

Blackburn always wore a cowboy hat and had this Fu Manchu beard, and his dark eyes behind his glasses reminded me of Lao Tzu. He smoked strong European cigarettes, and living above McSorley's Old Ale House on East Seventh Street, he was frequently found downstairs drinking ales by the fistful, two and four at a time, because McSorley's does not like to serve their ale in odd numbers. Every Monday evening you found him at St. Mark's in the Bowery, either taping or moderating the Open Reading. Somewhere in the course of that Monday night circus, in which anyone who wished could come in off the street and read their rantings, Blackburn would pull out his black, springbound manuscript and read a new poem. He was prolific in his poetry and generosity, the latter almost to a fault. His ear was never closed to any young poet who wanted to talk with him.

When I started by saying Blackburn's *Cities* was his most representative publication, I did not mean to suggest that this was the height of his articulation. Because he was so prolific and also did not have the same publisher for his works, the wide range of his work was often unavailable or hard to find. I can recall perfectly wonderful poems read at St. Mark's that to this day I have not seen published in book or magazine form. This matter recently was rectified with the publication of his *Collected Poems* (ed. Edie Jarolim [Persea, 1985]), which shows the dynamism and range of that deceptive voice.

His voice was deceptive because it appeared effortless what he accomplished with it. First, it was deceptively colloquial; and second, it was deceptively artful. Its artfulness took in the entire tradition of poetry as laid bare by Ezra Pound, i.e., a tradition that is three thousand years old. That part of his voice was highly allusive, yet this scholarly side of Blackburn never intruded into the emotional world of the poem's immediacy. You could read him without knowing that a poem was a sirventes or some Provençal ballad form. At the colloquial level I think that critics perhaps did not understand what he had done, because what was on the page appeared so easy to accomplish.

> The lights
> the lights
> the lonely   lovely   fucking   lights
> and the bridge on a rainy Tuesday night
> Blue/green double-stars   the line
> that is the drive and on the dark alive
> gleaming river
> Xmas trees of tugs scream and struggle
>
>   "Midnite"
>   (*Brooklyn Narcissus*)

The hip voice, of which this poem is an example, streetwise, beboppy, worldly elegant, is often not a compassionate voice. That is because to be hip is not a native attitude but rather an acquired stance. The voice of hipness is often an energized cliché of a subculture, not a refreshing insight into the overall culture. Blackburn was a child of the Beats, of jazz, of the Lower East Side, a poet doing with his voice what Jackson Pollock did with paint—let it explode and find its inner life. In all the little magazines of the late fifties, you read of sameness of voice, a derivation, a bunch of loonies out to out-Kerouac Kerouac and make a jukebox thunder beyond Allen Ginsberg. But Blackburn's voice is different. His voice is hip *and* compassionate, and that tension gives his voice its special edge.

The hip resonance aside, Blackburn's voice is peopled with his knowledge of other writers, sometimes the rhythm reminiscent of Pound's *Cantos,* sometimes with the delicate lucidity of William Carlos Williams' American idiom lyrically punched out and shaped onto a page. (Blackburn makes his poems ride off the margin more effectively than nearly any poet of this time whom I can think of.)

> Here, at the beginning of the new season
> before the new leaves burgeon,   on
> either side of the Eastern Parkway station
>   near the Botanical Gardens
> they burn trash on the embankments, laying
> barer than ever our sad, civilized refuse.

The breath is nearly prose's, but the syllables belong to poetry in "Meditation on the BMT." The rhythm of this experience is urban, Brooklyn, to be specific, while the impulse of that rhythm is nearly pastoral, urban man's flash of nature: "at the beginning of the new season/ before the new leaves burgeon." The measure is American idiomatic, slant rhymed (season/burgeon); alliterative (beginning/before/burgeon); musically repeated (new/new). Notice, too, the chantlike rhythm of those first four lines of prepositional phrases (at/of/ before/ on/of/ near). Finally, there is a dramatic progression from the ideal (pastoral) to the real (the urban). The last two lines bring us full-circle to where the poet hears and sees with his voice in Brooklyn: "they burn trash on the embankments."

You can take nearly any passage or fragment from a Blackburn poem and give it over to such analytical scrutiny, and it holds up finely, as carefully put together, piece by piece, as any academician's bloodless prosody. That really is not what I want to remark, though. You can take or leave such particulars in any poem. What is most important is how the voice of the poem goes to the heart, not the head. Blackburn is not sentimental, but then most nonacademic poetry of his time was not that either. Much of the poetry of the fifties and early sixties was filled with an inverted sentimentality, that hip surface, cool and unsquare, with-it, and archly against the grain. Call it the sentimentality of the coffeehouse. But because Blackburn's voice sees, he is ultimately after none of these effects. His voice is there to juxtapose the real with the real, those nearly burgeoned leaves with the burning trash on the embankments. Both images are of this city in Brooklyn. That juxtaposition of the two reals of the city are also found in William Carlos Williams' poetry quite often.

The next stanza of Blackburn's poem brings out several tendencies, all of them in that Poundian vein he often mined. It is a harsh, sharp-edged rhythm, rocklike, like Pound uses in his translation of "The Seafarer," but it is also Whitmanic, and even Homeric, especially since it is a list.

> 1 coffee can without a lid
> 1 empty pint of White Star, the lable
> > faded by rain
> 1 empty beer-can
> 2 empty Schenley bottles

1 empty condom, seen from
1 nearly empty train
empty

empty

empty

But Pound's and Williams' poetry is not the only influence in Blackburn's voice. His voice is his own voice, as I said, but it was filled with echoes from the broad traditions of a world of literature. Two good examples of Blackburn's breadth of voice are gathered in his translations, *Peire Vidal* (Mulch 1972) and *Lorca/Blackburn* (Momo's 1979). Again, from Pound, he learned that a translator needs more than an academic knowledge of what the poem says in another language. You need a sense of its rhythm in the original, but more importantly you need a sense of adventure and invention in the language to which the poem will be rendered. Adventure and invention Blackburn had in abundance as a translator. (I once saw a textbook translation which Blackburn did of *The Cid,* but obviously some academic mind found it unorthodox, because I never saw it available again.) Some other poets who shared Blackburn's sense of adventure in translation were Louis Zukofsky (his Catullus) and Charles Olson (using Rimbaud in his own poems).

In the introduction to the Vidal translations, George Economou writes: "Paul Blackburn chose for his major work as translator the poetry of the Provençal troubadours. It was a choice that was good for poetry, good for the troubadours, and good for him. It was a choice made out of a special affinity for them. Because he had the gifts and desire, he *became* one and all of them, as with genius and learning he gave their poems his own voice and new life in a new language."

Renaissance Italians anthologized troubadour poems and ballads, often adding literary prose by way of biographical sketches. These were called *vidas*. They included *razos,* or comments, showing the genesis of poems. Through these scholarly conventions Blackburn brought Vidal to life. "He fell in love with all the pretty ladies in sight, and was suitor for all their loves: all told him to do and say whatever he wished, so he believed himself the lover of each of them, and that each was dying for him. All of them deceived him." In "Razos" Blackburn frames the poems with more prose inventions: "He entered the room and went to the bed of ma domna Alazaïs and found her sleeping. Kneeling before her, he kissed her on the mouth: she felt the kiss and thought it was Barrals, her husband, and rose laughing. When she looked and saw that it was the mad Vidal, she began to cry out and raised a great clamor." Here is one of Peire Vidal's own *cansos* about the incident:

> I entered her house one morning
> and kissed her like a thief
> chin and mouth

And elsewhere he says:

> I would have been more honored than any man born,
> had that stolen kiss been granted me
> and given nicely.

And in still another *canso,* says:

> Love beats me with the sticks I cut myself:
> for one time, in a high and regal room,
> I stole a kiss of which my heart remembers.

In other passages of the book, Blackburn lets the poems
stand in their own context. With the poem on the page, even
in translation, I cannot help but read it as though with musical accompaniment, a stringed instrument, as probably Vidal
himself sang his poems. Also, in Blackburn's translations, I
get this sense of others whom Vidal influenced, from St.
Francis of Assisi, who sang the troubadour ballads in his
youth, to Dante, who was a great admirer of Vidal. And this
progression works through Ezra Pound on up to Paul Blackburn himself.

> MORE THAN A BEGGAR I dare not
>   grumble,
> more than a poor man who sleeps in a rich man's hall
>   who doesn't dare complain
> though his complaint be great, fearing
>   his lord take offense, I
> dare not grate against my mortal pain
> though having for reason her disdain toward me
> whom I've wanted more than any,
>   at least that!
>   and yet dare not cry mercy—
> I fear so to have her angry at me.
> (*"Plus quel paubres que jatz el ric ostal"*)

In one of Blackburn's own poems entitled "Sirventes" you
see the poet as Vidal. The voice is American Blackburnian,
but the form is ancient—the *sirventes* is an Old Provençal form
whose main theme is usually personal abuse, literary satire,
moralizing on the evil state of the world, politics, and current
events. *The Princeton Encyclopedia of Poetry and Poetics* says:
"The tone is mostly satiric, and gross vituperation is common."

> I have made a sirventes against the city of Toulouse
> and it cost me plenty of garlic:

and if I have a brother, say, or a cousin, or a 2nd cousin,
I'll tell him to stay out too.

> As for me, Henri,

> I'd rather be in España
> pegging pernod thru a pajita
> or yagrelling a luk
> jedamput en Jugoslavije,
> jowels wide & yowels not
> permitted to emerge—
> or even
> in emergency
> slopping slivovitsa thru
> the brlog in the luk.
> I mean I'm not particular

Later in this same long poem Blackburn invokes Peire Vidal:

> That mad Vidal would spit on it,
> that I as his maddened double
> do—
> too changed, too changed, o
> deranged master of song,
> master of the viol and the lute
> master of those sounds,
> I join you in public madness,
> in the street I piss
> on French politesse

With Vidal Blackburn brings that poet's sense of adventure to the poem, re-creating anew. Because the poems are ancient, his invention is really reinvention, to resuscitate Pound's dead art of poetry. But when Blackburn translates Federico García Lorca, the adventure is with a writer nearly

contemporary and with whom Blackburn has shared affinities. Lorca's *duende* becomes Blackburn's *duende*.

> "Of those four men with mules
> going down to water,
> the one with the dappled mule
> robbed my soul.
>
> Of those four men with mules
> heading down to the river,
> the one with the dappled mule
> is my husband."
>
> ("The Four Muleteers")

The figures of words, its faithfulness, is carefully rendered.
Meaning, Blackburn's invention corresponds to Lorca's in-
tent. Elsewhere, the poet in Blackburn submerges the translator, and the literal voice is given over to the figures of
another voice, a correspondence, in a new language. First, I
will give Lorca's poem in Spanish, and that will be followed
by Blackburn's translation:

> Ya se ha abierto
> la flor de la aurora.
>
> (¿Recuerdas
> el fondo de al tarde?
>
> El nardo de la luna
> derrama su olor frío.
>
> (¿Recuerdas
> la mirada de agosto?)
>
> ("*Eco*")
>
> Dawn's flower has already
> opened itself
> up.

> (Remember?
> the depths of the afternoon?)
> The spikenard of moon diffuses
> its cold smell.
> (Remember?
> the long glance of August?)
> ("Echo")

A Lorca purist might find much to grouse about, but essentially Blackburn is doing what he always does so well, trapping the voice of another writer into the voice of himself. Blackburn never smothers another writer in the web of his own voice. Just as in his own poems in English, in the American idiom, in that beat of the cities—he embraces. Whitman would not be out of place at Blackburn's table. Ezra Pound literally was not. Nor was William Carlos Williams. Nor were Robert Creeley, Gilbert Sorrentino, Joel Oppenheimer, and numerous other writers.

Let me conclude by focusing on Blackburn's later work, written before his death and published posthumously. One of these is his *Journals,* because I am interested in setting down aspects of this poet's voice which cut across the different mediums he wrote in. In fact, the journals have as much, or even more, interest to the movement of the dramaturgy of style from poetry into prose. I don't think you can conclude from either the journals or from a book like *Halfway down the Coast* that he was hard-living, say, like Kerouac or Neal Cassady were. And yet his spirit is very much of a fabric like theirs. Like Frank O'Hara in his poem "Steps," Blackburn did "smoke too many cigarettes," and like Kerouac, he probably did drink too much. His quietness was intense, I mean, and *carpe diem* had to have been one of his mottoes. Besides, I think, he was generous to a fault with others. He didn't squirrel himself away, but rather made himself available, to anyone, to everyone. I did not know him well, but certainly we met a good number of times when I lived on the Lower East Side, and once on a rooftop on Second Avenue, we gave a reading together to about twenty or so friends.

"That was very good," he said afterward, a typical Blackburn stance, the voice reaching out, giving, giving, not just in that human being, it's all over the poetry, in his journals, I am talking about a voice with the fullest sense of others, all grace and encouragement. When Blackburn died he had amassed one of the most extensive audiotape collections of other writers' reading their poetry. Why? It was archival, to be sure, but it was also archetypical of Blackburn. He was into how others spoke; he had sympathy and understanding for voices which were not his own. No doubt there was also a kind of gypsy thing, and you can be sure if you read something of interest to him, like a thief in the night, Paul incorporated it into his own poetry. Blackburn's voice was a great synthesis of many voices, ancient, modern, contemporary.

Halfway down the Coast, though published after his death, was written mostly during a Guggenheim year in Europe (1967–68). His cancer would not be diagnosed for three more years, but many of these poems foreshadow that later condition, if not physically than psychologically. This book is a good place to begin with Blackburn's later voice. The coast is a verdant, poetic terrain, like Apollinaire's coast between Mobile and Galveston. It is coastal also in the sense that the reader can get "next to" his voice immediately. Once there, the vistas are magnificent, not dwarfing. As I said, Blackburn's utterance does not smother, it embraces. He is not overly refined, not rarefied in how he makes poetry; but it is heady like mountain air. These poems are healthy in the sense that they are full of life, resonance, the arc of experience, its rhythm and pulse. When you read these poems, even without knowing the poet, there is a sense that he is still *there,* downtown or wherever. *Yo,* lets *salsa!* The voice is one of life without apology, unfolding, winding down. There is little posture, except maybe to some, that hip tone. From the opening poem, "The Surrogate," the voice is driven by an intelligent whimsy:

> She stole ma hat
>> ma hat . was in the lounge with ma jacket
> The jacket she dint take it, but
>> ma hat, she tukkit, clean
>> outa the place

to the more philosophical ending of the last poem, "Backsweep/Black":

> Time
> gone now
> and again
> recurs

Blackburn's seeing voice is photographic, capable of absorbing singular observations. The sound of what he sees is nearly always lyrical. In a book as late as *Halfway down the Coast* what is to be remarked about that lyricism is its sustained energy, kind of an infinite patience with the pattern of a life. The energy is never too fast not to see. He shares this pace with one of his mentors, William Carlos Williams, that is, the shape stays highly emotional yet focused. Again, the shape is deceptive, seemingly effortless, its allusiveness understated. The complex forms are rendered with a sly intelligence. There is almost a practical communism here, because the poet embraces everyone and everything, but it is not generalized—he is a writer of the particular—it is not soppy, too broad, or trivialized.

This gets down to how his own voice developed, of how he had this gift to overhear the cadences of common speech, and turn that speech into poetry. This is not only a storyteller; the voice is as much that of a listener. Blackburn does not put-down; he elevates others' voices. It is a voice which keeps declaring its love for people, for things, for life itself. In his lapsed Catholic way, he loved giving unto others. What he was given for his own largesse were stories, anecdotes, the speech of a time. He was never without a notebook; it was sort of his trademark, for he was that kind of writer. If it catches your ear, write it down immediately, don't wait. Many obscure men and women were immortalized, in that way, in his poems. Common utterance was elevated to its perfection in his work.

When the poetry is rolling the voice *suggests* natural speech, but it ultimately is more perfect, less repetitious, more rhythmical than natural speech.

> what softness we run toward
> and the rock of wool pulled short the
> mountains stand
> under the forks of rivers
> The bowman lays it out and keeps us
> down
> no names
> that gives us not our death,
> O swift current, O buffalo.

The poem was written for the ear to enjoy, yet its simple content is multiple. In the preceding quote from "Baggs," there is enough allusion to satisfy a Chinese and Pound scholar ("Song of the Bowmen of Shu"); a Jesuit scholar ("Our Father"); and a native American scholar ("O swift current, O buffalo").

The voice of the dying Blackburn is not different than the living one. His voice was charged from beginning to end as though the next moment were to be the last. Is he morose? No, he is goofy and exuberant until the end.

> Listen, Death
> Beth, see, it's
> not so bad . . .

Or the poem, "As It Ends":

> I want you all to know
> I love you very much
>
> O, shut up, you are a dead man,
>   for Christ's sake!

This possibility of death, of the voice no longer uttering, of the voice no longer seeing, taking in, sorting, sifting, shaping new poetry—it is suggested throughout this book. In *The Journals* this possibility becomes a reality in Blackburn's voice.

The Journals consists of poetry and prose begun in 1967, when Blackburn was still energetic, to 1971, when the poet died of cancer in Cortland, New York. This has a special value for me, because I attended two years of college at Cortland, a state university with a heavy sports and physical education concentration, a little upstate community probably with more cows than people. (In a town several blocks long, when I was there from 1963 to 1965, it had twenty-seven bars.) A couple of us, after meeting Joel Oppenheimer after a reading he gave there, packed it in and moved to the Lower East Side and wound up in Joel's workshop. Blackburn would have loved this: because a bunch of us who wrote poetry hung out in the Hollywood Bar, we called ourselves the Hollywood Poets. All of us were former jocks turned poets. What a sight!

Beer chugging, frat parties, panty raids, all the rigmarole of a small college are not to be found in *The Journals*. Instead, as the book progresses, the idea of death is superseded by the daily elements of physical decline and the actuality of dying. Yes, Blackburn's voice changes. But what is remarkable about the voice is its thirst to experience and to know, to cherish the real. His poetry and poetics are mature, not maudlin, the energy and intelligence are still there, but now a human courage informs every breath and syllable. It is consummate Blackburn. The energy of his intelligence refuses to wane, even with cancer.

Lastly, Blackburn was a poet at ease in many languages and places, and his unique application of macaronics is equal to his other mentor, Ezra Pound. As a native son to many languages, Blackburn readily uses Spanish and English within the American idiom, and *The Journals* even has a poem ("Rue de Lois") written in colloquial French. Other poems blend in and out polyglotwise. There are references to the Provencal, to travelogues across America, to places in Spain, Italy, and southern France. Toward the end of *The Journals* Cortland turns into the Mediterranean ("April 19, 1971: the Southern Tier"). Blackburn's penchant for languages, usually after a few Fundadors, brings out some polylingual puns:

> burger joints, a movie, & even a gas station, ES-
> So es . y no es . si-saw. So.
> Off they go, back to Memphis,
> > tank full of gas and a
> > pocketful of rye.
> > > (November Journal 1967)

The strongest aspect of Blackburn's final voice is not its poetic range but its qualities of human emotion, its directness of object treatment, its fidelity to the rhythm of experience. Its human progression is a sad one, from full life to carcinoma, but Blackburn is the last to color it sadly. Early in *The Journals* entries are of a fully lived life, covering places in Europe and throughout the United States. There are meetings with Ezra Pound ("old eagle"), Julio Cortázar, friends in France and Spain. One entry is about the death of an old Spanish waiter. Another entry is about visiting the poet Robert Kelly (who was the fine editor of this posthumous work), and while there, Blackburn's wife receives a telephone call about the death of her father. As other deaths come to surround the poet, he comes to realize that he likewise is terminally ill.

As I said at the beginning of this, Blackburn was a poet of cities, so that it is more than ironical that his final days were spent in the country, teaching in milk and apple territory, the hippest person in town being probably your John Deere tractor salesman. He could have moaned this fate, but instead, like everything else he noticed, Blackburn turned it into song. Instead of indulging cancer dreams, he deals with his growing pain as though it were a toothache or what he himself refers to as a pain in the shoulder. Here is how a dying man sees the world:

> Cities & towns I have to give up this year
> on account of my cancer: Amster-
> dam, Paris, Apt, Saignon and Aix
> (Toulouse I'll never loose), Perpignan and Dax,
> Barcelona and south
> > (or the other way,
> > Catania . I warn ya)
> The hell, I read a review of a reading in January.
> They loved me in Shippensburg, Pennsylvania.
> > (17. IV. 71)

By May 1971 in "The Blue Mountain Entries" the dying poet writes a touching sonnet about the excuses everyone has for not making his reading. To complicate this frustration he forgets to buy batteries for his cassette recorder. (If you want to know what an objective correlative is, it is Blackburn with his tape recorder.) The disappointment, given his condition and his unusual devotion to being the keeper of the words, must have been immeasureable. But he ends the sonnet with this wry remark: "It's a good reading."

The June entries contain references to his lack of strength and loss of weight. In mid-month his physical energies collapse and he is unable to build a fence in the backyard. The voice is full of its tension, though. Superhuman mental vigor accompanies the physical deterioration. That voice still gropes for things to evoke. There is still a beauty in the spoken which Blackburn wishes to spring into form. That self-effacing hip posture, the love of drink and poetry and life—these things do not abandon him. I mean, he does not abandon them. The choice is his alone.

The last entry is dated July 28, 1971; Blackburn will die on September 13, 1971. Never one to pass up a deadpan, humorous, tragic-comic line, even at his own expense, Blackburn ends his journal:

"Bigod, I must have been full of shit."

4

Joel Oppenheimer

IN ANOTHER LIFE Joel Oppenheimer would be a base-ball player. His nonfiction book about the Mets suggests this strongly enough. I imagine that his ethnic background would be Irish, probably raised in the Bronx, perhaps right across from Yankee Stadium, but to spite the Steinbrenners of the world, he would play for the Mets. He would be their pitcher, with a fastball like lightning, and in his later years— he'd develop a knuckle ball, to save his arm.

In another life Joel would never get gray, as he did quite early in his present life. He would drink, but have no problem with it. If he married multiple times, as he did, it would get better and better for him, as it probably does in this life as well. Instead of Oppenheimer his name would be Shaugnessy, as in his poem, "The Beer Hall Putsch" from *The Love Bit*:

> songs we sung oh
> shaugnessy, songs we
> sung locked in
> immutable oh man rhythms

But Joel was Jewish, and he was born and raised in Yonkers—all things he is proud of—and he went off as "the dutiful son" (the title of an early volume) to Cornell University, the sciences, engineering, but dropped out, and he wound up studying printing and poetry at Black Mountain College. From then to now, his mentors remain steady: Olson, Creeley, Williams. He will pay lip service, even high praise to Ezra Pound, but don't believe a word of it. Oppenheimer is the son of William Carlos Williams. Even in Paul Mariani's biography of Williams, Joel is referred to as one of Williams' sons. So was Amiri Baraka (LeRoi Jones). So was Gilbert Sorrentino. (Ah, I have laid an egg by mentioning a verboten name in Joel's cosmology!) But let it be for the time being.

Like Williams, Joel often referred to his own poetic charges as his sons. Mind you, he has five—count 'em—authentic sons, growing and grown. But after so many years of being the director of St. Mark's Poetry Project, of being the poet-in-residence at City College, of being the guest poet at hundreds of colleges, Joel acquired many additional sons. Yet he is more avuncular than anything else, I mean, he is one of the boys, if you will. This is both his charm and the reason, perhaps, his reputation is not as fully appreciated as it should be.

Of all Williams' sons, of all Creeley's and Olson's students—Joel Oppenheimer is the most faithful to their testaments.

In another life Joel might be a knuckleball pitcher, but in this life he is a poet, and all his pitches are as straight as arrows to the heart. The kind of arrows with a rubber suction tip. There are no tragedies in Oppenheimer's world. He is a poet of domestic particulars, of flowers bought, of flowers given, of loving gestures, of irresolvable differences in the interrelationships between men and woman, men to men, father to son. The hierarchy of his occasions—and he is the first to say that he is an occasional poet—is nearly Confucian, if the Chinese sage were also an anarchist, which Joel pacifically is.

His poems are neither bitter nor overly tender but rather like a jazz singer's bittersweet melodies. The voice, coming out of its time and its place (the late fifties/ the Village), strives to be hip, but finally is too vulnerable to be simply a know-it-all's posturing. It is not overly tender, yet certainly it is tender enough.

> thus for the warm
> and loving heart the
> inmost and most
> private part shall ever be
> sweet eros' dart.
>   ("Triplets")

Like King Lear, Oppenheimer's voice is that of man more wronged than wronging. Yet it is more comic than tragic. The human being behind that voice is as much into trivia— on what date did Babe Ruth hit his sixtieth home run?—as it is into making art. Oppenheimer's art is as fond of afternoon soap operas and gossip as it is at ease with Catullus' love poems. Baseball has as much ascendancy in the register of his voice as does the sirventes.

The sons of Williams may have pushed Oppenheimer to the side, vying for the good doctor's laurels, but the simple elegance of what he says, and, more importantly, how he says it, is undeniable. This is a poet's poet as well as a people's poet. More fans know him as the baseball poet in New York than readers know him as the poet in New York. More newspaper readers know his column in the *Village Voice* than that his poems are as finely written as anyone's around. To speak of his poetry, which is considerable, if not in its range then in its articulation, you need to rehabilitate the poet from the various popular cultural heaps on which Oppenheimer has sat, the baseball nut, the barfly of the Lion's Head back in the sixties and early seventies, the journalist, the poetry teacher, the trivia expert, the Civil War aficionado. But this is a worthwhile excavation, because Oppenheimer's role as the dutiful son is most efficacious as a contemporary poet.

To begin, like Shakespeare, Oppenheimer is not an inventor of forms, he is an articulator of the given, a poet who works refinements on what already is. The breath and syllable of his poetry transparently connect to Black Mountain, to Olson and Creeley, back to the objectivists, to William Carlos Williams. This lucubration is nearly too easy a task. Yet there are differences of voice certainly worth noting. First, it is a matter of geography. Oppenheimer, unlike his mentors, writes out of a specific locale which is New York City, and more specifically—downtown. He is, as they say, as he would like it known, a Greenwich Village poet, even for a time, one of the Village's fixtures.

Part of this role is cliché; part of it genuine. The cliché is that poet drinking himself to death in a corner of the bar. But luckily for him and for us, that was put to rest. The poet went dry a decade and a half ago. As one of his cronies at the Lion's Head said to me, "Joel wasn't even a *good* drinker." But Oppenheimer disputes this: "A quart or more a day of bourbon qualifies as a good drinker in my book!" But this stereotype of the drinking writer demanded more than booze. Joel looked like a poet too, that is, from Central Casting. In his thirties, he was prematurely gray, bearded, beat, long-haired, disheveled, washed but appearing unwashed. There was a strong resemblance to the old Ezra Pound after St. Elizabeth's Hospital. In those days to play a poet obstructed the actual writing of poetry. The wetter the poet got, the drier his output became. The lyrical beauty of his early poetry (*The Dutiful Son, The Love Bit*) was put on waivers.

Oppenheimer's genuineness came out in the clarity of those early poems, and during his nonwriting period, in his extensions toward younger writers in his poetry workshop at St. Mark's. I met him when I was seventeen years old, as was mentioned in the chapter about Paul Blackburn, in Cortland, New York. Years later, having heard a few hundred other poets read, his voice is still unmistakable. The Gauloises cigarettes, the Old Overholt bourbon, the biblical cadence (more Song of Songs than anything else), the simple dexterity of line he learned from Williams and Creeley, and the dance of the syllable he learned from Olson—these are part of Oppenheimer's resonance.

His poems are examples less of MAKE IT NEW as they are of let it be. The energy of the moment comes from the simple wonder of the moment. I know that I learned a lot of my own fiction's prose cadence from Oppenheimer's poetry. I think of the first stanza of an early poem like "For the Barbers":

> tenderly as a
> barber trimming
> it off i
> sing my songs, like
> a barber stropping
> a razor, i rage.

What I learned was to get prose's dialogue out of a he said/she said syndrome, putting it into some rhythmical immediacy with the rest of the words.

> let/s put it this
> way, if you had a
> bullet, why don/t
> you write
>
> your friends yr cousins
> with the blunted soft
> lead end jack london
> said the
>   'best to use'
> and no erasure
> necessary.
>   ("A Postcard")

It does not matter if Jack London ever said that, but that Joel probably said it. That just adds to the fiction in his voice, its mythical dimension. In another poem from *The Love Bit* entitled "Blood," the vocabulary of the poem, added to its outward thrust, adds up to a poem which is also a kind of short story, including a narrative, characters, and a fictional voice.

> How, ever else to
> do it? But with
> love, and a new way
> to comb my moustache?
>
> Or she said: you
> and your old
> man, sitting here both
> in your underwear!

The cadence of this poem is distinctly Joel's, but the lesson from which it comes is in a direct line to Creeley on back to Williams. There is a Creeley poem, more virtuoso, but no more voice-centered, no more human in its intensity. Creeley's poem is entitled "I Know a Man," and in its short, tight, electric span, I can detect at least two titles of other books inspired by it, Gilbert Sorrentino's *The Darkness Surrounds Us* and Jeremy Larner's *Drive, He Said.*

> As I sd to my
> friend, because I am
> always talking,—John, I
>
> sd, which was not his
> name, the darkness sur-
> rounds us, what
>
> can we do against
> it, or else, shall we &
> why not, buy a goddamn big car,
>
> drive, he sd, for
> christ's sake, look
> out where yr going.

Or consider this poem by William Carlos Williams:

> "No dignity without chromium
> No truth but a glossy finish
> If she purrs she's virtuous
> If she hits ninety she's pure
>
> ZZZZZZZZZ!
> Step on the gas, brother
> (the horn sounds hoarsely)
>   ("Ballad of Faith")

Oppenheimer also learned from Williams about how to plant things in a poem, literally to let the flora sprout in the midst of one's emotional charges through language:

> i wish all the
> mandragora grew
> wild, screaming.

> and in the cattails,
> pussywillows, etc.
> wind soft as
> eastern standard time.
>
> ("Blue Funk")

Like Creeley *and* Williams, Oppenheimer is a gracious poet, a man of infinite grace, either in that Yeatsian sense of grand gesture or as a kind of state one aspires toward.

> no matter our passion i
> could not forgo offering
> coffee, and could have kicked
> myself not thinking of
> cigarettes sooner. that's
> the indecency, compelling
> an order to exist, because
> there was one one time
>
> ("The Obscene Graces")

And like his teachers and forebears, Oppenheimer propels the voice with the underpinnings of music. In Williams there is "Bunk Johnson"; in Creeley there is that tight, finely intellectual sound of bebop, especially Charlie Parker on saxophone. With Joel Oppenheimer it is just the blues, mam. It is not instrumental; it is sung, raspy in his own raspy throat.

> flowers of love the
> dollar bills float
> down
> all the perfumes
> of the orient stink up
> my sweets, as if we
> dragged her thru. look
> look at the essence of
> her bosom and her snatch.
>
> ("Short Blues")

Or take perhaps Oppenheimer's best known of these blues riffed poems:

> from the heart of a flower
> a stalk emerges; in each fruit
> there are seeds. we turn our
> backs on each other so often,
> we destroy any community of
> interest. yet our hearts are
> seeded with love and care sticks
> out of our ears. but there is no
> bridge unless it is the wind which
> whistles our bare house, tearing
> the slipcovers apart and constantly
> removing the tablecloth covering
> it (the table) like a shroud (the
> shroud of what the table could mean,
> if only we were hungry enough to
> care), and we cut ourselves off
> because we discovered each man is
> an island, detached. man, the
> mainland is flipped over the moon.
> all i have to depend on is effort,
> and the moon goes round and round
> in the evening sky. my sons will
> make it if they ever reach age,
> but how to take care i dont know.
> it doesnt get better. on the other
> hand, even with answers, where
> would we be, out in the cold, with
> an old torn blanket, and no one
> around us to cry
>   ("Leave It to Me Blues")

The voice is seamless. In fact, I could not think of where to excerpt in this poem to make my example, and so had to quote the entire poem. That is Oppenheimer for you. His music is sonorous, elastic, fluid; almost, I want to say, like early Miles Davis, muted and cool. Even more than Paul Blackburn's music, Oppenheimer's is full of spokenness. None of the machinery of the poet is visible. I consider Joel's use of American idiom as subtle as Williams', at times even more muted than the Old Master's. It is quiet yet assertive, never pushed in its rhythm, the poet untraps it as though it were as easy as opening the birdcage and letting the bird fly about the room.

Held up to Williams and Creeley's poetry, the influences are apparent in Oppenheimer's poem, but you have to look more carefully for the differences, those qualities that make Joel Oppenheimer's voice uniquely his own—and his voice *is* as unique as any poet around. First, the voice is less allusive, I mean, literally stripped of literary references. One of the few references you'll find in Oppenheimer's poetry, barring the constant echoes back to Williams and Creeley, is the one found in "Leave It to Me Blues," the shrouded antithesis to John Donne's line, with Oppenheimer's counterstatement going, "each man is an island." Mostly, though, the object is laid bare, with reference to other objects, not an idealization or a perfection of that object either but rather the object imperfectly satisfying to the seeing voice of the poet. It is, as Oppenheimer says himself, a celebration of the occasion in a life, the resonance of that moment the fact that it is this and nothing else but this.

> lemons, lemons arranged
> in the green and brown
> bowl, the grapefruits
> heaped in the corner.
>
> ("Anniversary")

It is Oppenheimer listening to the father, because he is a dutiful son: "Say it, no ideas but in things." But how he focuses on things is with his own point-of-view in his own voice, his downtown, formerly-from-Yonkers, printer's dirty-fingered, rabbinical, beatnik-hipster's voice. His own voice, not a New Jersey doctor's (Williams) or a Harvard dropout's (Creeley's), but an educated, working-class, American Jew-from-New York's voice, *kvetching* but not whining, humorous, with as much scat as scatology in it.

Both Williams and Creeley write beautiful love poems, and so does Oppenheimer. But their approaches to the feminine are probably as different as their individual tastes in the feminine. Joel's horny-voiced love poems are more in the tradition of Henry Miller, although like Williams, he can be equally Catullian. Creeley's love poems, on the other hand, seem more in the fashion of English love poems a few centuries earlier or even courtly as perhaps the troubadours were. Oppenheimer has written more poems about tits and ass, literally, than perhaps any living poet. These synecdoches of women, running through his poems as obsessively as even his hierarchical images of sons and fathers, have allowed many to misread the softer intentions of the poems' lyricism. (I saw women walk out of readings in the seventies when Joel read from *The Woman Poems,* whose compulsive voice is given over to this metonymy.) But more than being sexist, these are the honest impulses of a man's voice as he charts his bafflements and wonders about women.

> a bosom of
> green buds,
> ass like a
> valentine.

And in an early poem like "The Torn Nightgown":

> and i wondered then in the night
> if all wives had such badges.
> and bitterly, if over each
> set of stretch marks, over
> each veined breast, each brown
> nipple there floated soft and
> white a torn nightgown.

But as Oppenheimer told me when we first met over twenty years ago, his book *The Dutiful Son* consisted of love poems written in a happy marriage, whereas *The Love Bit* contained poems about the dissolution of that marriage. To a poet of domestic particulars, to a man whose voice thrives on the occasion, a marriage is perhaps the grandest (its thriving) and worst (its breakup) relationship of one's life. And Oppenheimer wrote in his bio for *A Controversy of Poets*: "My verse seems concerned for the most part with the inter-personal relationship: man-to-woman, man-to-man, man-to-child; otherwise I drink, love, and play games." This is true, for rarely do you find his voice projected inwardly, as though in singular meditation. His voice projects outward. He always seems to be addressing his poems to one particular person. And his strongest projections are those reserved for women he is fond of, he loves, worships, or has fallen out with.

In 1954 Oppenheimer could write:

> every time
> the same way
> wondering when
> this when that.
> if you were a

> plum tree. if you
> were a peach
> tree.
>
> ("The Lover")

But by the mid-1970s, divorced again, still the father of many sons, in the blood and in the poems, an avuncular sage, in the full blossom of his bachelorhood, and dry, on the wagon, he could wonder:

> twenty years ago i
> knew about love. now
> i am tired. i study
> primary needs.
>
> ("Gettin' There")

Oppenheimer's voice caressed the figure of women in his poems, whether ecstatic (*The Dutiful Son*) or bittersweet (*The Love Bit*). By the seventies the poems of women became *The Woman Poems,* not the poems of an occasion, not a celebration. Invariably these poems are addressed to a mythic woman, something totemic, nightmarish, below the conscious. The replacing of the real with the mythical has its advantages and disadvantages in this poet's voice. What is lost is the Rabelaisian, Villon-like stomping through a life. The scatology is given over to intellectual and psychological discovery. Instead of scat there is recitative, word talk. What the poems gain from their antecedents is a deeper honesty, a greater obsession, and revelation. So this is who I really am? these poems keep asking.

> as i was sleeping
> mother i saw your
> four forms in her

> body. i saw the
> good mother her
> mouth, the death
> mother her asshole,
> ecstasy in her
> tits, and the
> stone mother buried
> deep in her cunt,
> the teeth waiting.
> this is not a good
> dream mother.
>
> ("Dream Mother Poem")

Less Williams-like, Oppenheimer said of these poems of the seventies that they were influenced from hearing Robert Bly read his essay about the Tooth Mother. Then, too, this decade was one where women as political forces emerged concretely and firmly.

> i have fathered
> four sons, they surround
> me in an age of
> women, they will
> have to fight like
> hell to find the
> action, i have laid
> something very heavy
> on their heads. the
> youngest, perhaps,
> will survive into
> the new world.
>
> ("Father Poem")

His "Discovery Poem" begins with a prayer: "lady, sister, lover, mother/woman," and moves into the discovery:

> i want to fuck you as
> li po tried and died.

The poems of the seventies contain a progression in their voice from the dirty old man (a favorite stance of Joel's) to that of an old man, I mean, old before his time. The dirty old man is still there, i.e., read "Dirty Picture Poem":

> when i asked you how
> you could pose naked for
> them and not for
> me you said it
> was art.

Or later in this long poem:

> i wonder did your
> nipples erect for cold
> water as once for
> me, or lie flaccid
> like me. even dreaming
> of such sights i cannot
> raise a hard-on.

The voice of *The Woman Poems* is a moribund, frightened one. All celebration has been syphoned from its well. I think of some later Billie Holiday recordings in which she sounded too stoned to talk much less sing. It is more habit than art. And yet I see them as a necessary purging for Oppenheimer to inhabit the next stage of his poet's life. In "Discovery Poem" Oppenheimer says that sex comes before poetry, that that is his hierarchy; yet for all the tits and ass, cocks and scrotums, panties and high heels—and space, not prudery, does not allow me to quote all of it—there is little eroticism in these poems. The equation is more one of sex and death, though moments of Oppenheimer's former exuberance and celebration and whimsy creep into these poems toward the end of its tract.

> why didn't i
> let you blow me in
> the bar one time?
> why couldn't i
> fuck you in the field
> that warm spring day?
> what clothes will
> you wear in heaven when
> i meet you with an
> eternal hard-on?
>
> ("Fantasy Poem")

Earlier I mentioned what I learned from Oppenheimer's poems. I was speaking about a way to say it, with energy that is muted through the corridor of the human tongue. But there are other qualities of voice worth mentioning. For instance, Oppenheimer's frank use of argot is not only refreshing but necessary. In my own mind, probably the result of a parochial education, I've seen the reservoir of speech located under this layer of mulch. In order to get to the truest feelings of the deeper vocabulary, the writer draws upon the language of this rotting surface. That surface primarily consists of the verboten, our curses, our profanity, our scatology, our argot, our vernacular. Call it what you will. But it exists, and needs also to be gotten through to reach our deepest feelings with words.

The Woman Poems, of one note nearly throughout, are less failures of Oppenheimer's voice than they are experiments. In them he attempts to wallow in the rot of the mind's surface where all the sewage is in order to break below the surface. I imagine a kingfisher in these poems. How that bird perches— the one I saw on Cape Cod once did—high up in the trees, then plunges straight down, below the mulch, the rotting leaves, the scummy surface, into the deepest water. And when it comes up again, its beak is filled with a wiggling bass. These poems were necessary for Oppenheimer to find the bass.

But I do not want it to seem that I am apologizing for these poems. I am not. They stand, if difficultly, quite well on their own terms. And I believe not enough poets or other writers are willing to expose themselves so barely with such materials. In a recent chapbook entitled *The Progression Begins* (an unnumbered issue of *# Magazine*) the old man comes back to the territory of the dirty old man. It is a long poem about feet. In it I hear the old Oppenheimer as well as the Oppenheimer who worked himself out of the dulls of *The Woman Poems*. As I said, that last book was necessary for the poet's voice to move forward. As though explaining his dark journey in those poems about woman, in the first section of this new poem, Oppenheimer writes, vis-à-vis seeing a shrink:

> what i remember is i was
> always forcing myself into
> the cellar of my being
> because instead i wanted
> to ride always upward

By the fourth section of this poem I can hear the old Oppenheimer—I mean, the Oppenheimer of old—speaking. It is the voice, so the story goes, of the poet, when asked by a library who wished to purchase his papers and books for their collection, who gave them that along with boxes and boxes of his old skin magazines. Maybe this is apocryphal, yet it carries the essence of this wonderful man in its tale. Here is where the old man gets dirty, the uncle comes back out, the poet who is as comfortable with a good dirty joke and skin magazine as he is with the poems of William Carlos Williams.

> itchy feet
> are not the same
> as itchy palms
>
> i don't like to walk
>
> travel doesn't interest me
>
> but i've been cursed
> with itchy feet

How like Joel Oppenheimer's voice those lines are!

5

Gilbert Sorrentino

HUBERT SELBY, JR., has called Gilbert Sorrentino "the Pound of his generation," and there is good reason for this appraisal. Like Pound, Sorrentino is a literary factotum, a jack-of-all-literary-trades, having been editor, publicist, tastemaker, reviewer, essayist, vituperative critic of the conventional, champion of the new, as well as poet and fiction writer. His recent publications have included his *Selected Poems,* several works of fiction, and a collection of his essays and criticism, *Something Said.* It was Sorrentino who acquired and edited Selby's *Last Exit to Brooklyn,* then single-mindedly promoted it to what Sorrentino thought no doubt a dim-witted and ignorant literary world. (Cf. the rejection letters in the front of *Mulligan Stew* to get an idea of GS's opinion about the publishing world's intelligence.)

One could easily write an essay—even a book—about any one of Gilbert Sorrentino's literary activities, but even separated, his various hats interchange, and to talk of his fiction, one must consider his poetry and critical writings, or even his editorial work and his various literary crusades. Additionally, nowadays Sorrentino is professor at Stanford University, and if that were not enough, he is exceedingly erudite, his thoughts and ideas carrying a broad influence. It is not groping after empty phrases to say that he is brilliant. He is. But like Pound this brilliance is problematic, has inconsistencies, and is flawed. Pound had a tragic flaw, which history has shown us to be his infatuation with fascism and anti-Semitism. Sorrentino's flaw is not political but rather interpersonal, a wrathful judging of others. Imagine an omnipotent god declaring that he who is without sin should cast the first stone. Then cut to a boyish Sorrentino running around Literature's neighborhood, breaking a lot of writers' windows.

Sorrentino's work *is* flawed by commentary; telling instead of showing (an idea he debunks in his critical writings); judgments, prejudicial remarks; two-dimensional characterizations, vindictiveness, vituperation, sneering insincerity, and misanthropy. But like Augustus Winterbottom in *Tillie and Gus* or Egbert Sousè—accent grave (rhymes with wave) on the 'e'—in *The Bank Dick,* two W. C. Fields inventions, these qualities are what provide Sorrentino's comic genius.

Like Fields might do, let's start in a bar. This is not any bar, though. Once upon a time it was a real bar, though it was long gone by the time I heard of it. How writers like Joel Oppenheimer, Fielding Dawson, and Gilbert Sorrentino talk about it, this bar is nearly mythical in my mind. I am referring to the Cedar Bar, where the abstract expressionists like Jackson Pollock, Franz Kline, and Willem de Kooning held court nightly, and these young writers rubbed elbows with them. Art and Literature. They are terms which stick on the tongue like blackstrap molasses. The best of us are content to talk about Art and Literature without doing anything about it. But bar talk is not Literature; the voice may resonate but it rarely sees. Some time after the phenomenon of the Cedar

Bar wained, Gilbert Sorrentino removed himself from his barstool, and he went home. I am not spreading rumors when I say that many of his friends and colleagues stayed on. But these two big—and too big—words, Art and Literature, are what became Sorrentino's themes.

There must have been a particular day in his life, sitting in the Cedar Bar, when Gil Sorrentino grew tired of his friends' talking about writing, and having made his own personal commitment, however eccentric, to Art and Literature, he let the bar talk stay in the bar, and he went home to write. Let us imagine him playing a record, something experimental and Hungarian, by Bela Bartok, the violins beautiful and en-nervating. The music in the background, he sits at his desk, looking almost like a pianist or maybe even Puccini before composing an opera, let's say *Madame Butterfly* or the incomplete *Turandot*. It is a pose both buffo and serious. Others in his household have been instructed not to disturb him; he is busily working. On his desk he flips the pages of an old Sunday color funnies, dwelling on Moon Mullins and Kayo, Mamie Mullins and her drunken-loutish husband. I suppose the old friends in the bar never forgave Sorrentino for this brilliant inspiration, using two rhythms of experience to shape his mature fiction—the funnies and the Cedar Bar.

Back in another bar, because the Cedar is no longer there, one writer complains of the caricature of himself in *Imaginative Qualities of Actual Things,* while another claims to be insulted by the portrait of himself as the driver in *The Sky Changes.* A third writer, though he never met the author and is twelve years his junior, claims to be maligned as a minor character, a poet *manquée.* But if the truth be known, I think it was that Gil became sick of bar talk, its occasional light, its repetitions, its bits. Bar talk breeds flies. I am writing here about a man who decided to write, instead of talk, about writng, but that this talk about writing became a major subject of his writing. In this sense he is the best of that spoiled and lousy bunch still left in the bar, waiting to be inspired, waiting to be discovered, and neither getting accomplished. These are sad, broken people at whom Sorrentino pokes fun. Imagine a beer being thrown in my face when one of these old renegades reads this. If a writer reads books, writes books, edits books, reviews them and promotes them, lives for them in his world—what more can you ask from him?

In those halcyon days of Art and Literature in the Cedar Bar, it is interesting to speculate on Sorrentino's importance in its flow. His early poetry is representational of its period; that is certain. His magazine *Neon* published all the new writers worth publishing outside the university world. His own poetry was published in magazines like LeRoi Jones' *Yugen,* and his tendential, vitriolic reviews of people like Lowell and Snodgrass were also published there. If not the most important character in this heady circle, like one of Dante's greater sinners, he inhabited an inner circle with the poets. But even then, writing in what amounted to nonacademic utterances, Sorrentino was the strongest formal voice in that crowd. By that I mean that his form was tighter on the page and less natural on the tongue, though still with its spokenness apparent. It is a comparative situation, for Sorrentino's poems were more voice-centered than the established poets' voices, but they were not clearly as voice-centered as Blackburn's or Oppenheimer's or Creeley's. Like a character from a Racine play, I imagine that the young Sorrentino came down to the footlights, took a pose, and *recited* his poems, half tragic, half comic, a purely operatic presentation. The early poems seem to have no interest in the dance of life at the eye's periphery. They are head-on, sometimes assaultive, sometimes stentorian, finally a kind of formal experimentation.

"I've nothing to say to them," Sorrentino writes in the first poem of his first book, *The Darkness Surrounds Us* (1960). "I've nothing to say to them. And I won't write." It comes at the end of the poem in a flat, declarative way, nothing ironical except for the lapse of time from when it was written until the present. Having nothing to say to them, Sorrentino went ahead to publish more than eighteen books of poetry, fiction, and essays, a fact which makes that early statement eminently ironic.

His novels, while having nothing to say to them, are filled with portraits and comments about *them*. In his fiction Gil Sorrentino skewers characters with his voice. He lambasts poetasters, pillories unfaithful wives, vilifies friends who wasted their talents, and he becomes especially nasty to artsy-fartsy types. The fiction writer's voice is judgmental, contemptuous, full of commentary, full of telling instead of showing. Pity the character who gets on Sorrentino's shit list, for this is a writer obsessed with lists and we must presume that that particular list is one of his most important. But let me come to the uniqueness of his fictional voice via his poems.

Sorrentino's poetry is less judgmental, but only by degrees. Like the prose its finest register is the vituperation. The differences are ones of focus between the fiction and poetry. With the fiction it is a focus on an imaginary landscape, the world of the characters. But Sorrentino writes his poems for himself. His poetry combines a voice that is both speaker and listener, which explains its striving for purity of expression with a formality of utterance. In some respects, I think this is what he means by "the perfect fiction," the title of a later poetry book. The poems are cloistered, a closed system, even a hermetic machinery, without reference to anything outside their own movement and pulse. Sorrentino will not write for them, but he will write about them (the fiction) and for himself (the poetry). Yet this writing for himself is not necessarily about himself; it is not autobiographical, I mean. The formality makes the writing about self an intellectual investigation.

It is useful here to backtrack into antiquity by way of explaining the evolution of Sorrentino's voice. As I said elsewhere the roots of drama are oldest in the comedic forms, working from Aristophanes back through the mimes into the hillsides of Sicily, where the animal mimes first developed comic types, the portly coward, the dirty old man, the foolish doctor, the lovers, the complicating fools and servants. All of these comic types were to flourish through several eras, lasting into the millennia, first in the *commedia dell'arte,* bursting through all of Europe on the operatic and comedic stages, going through the Elizabethan stage, and working their way through vaudeville, silent films, and today on situation comedies on television. Two aspects of this theatrical form are highly relevant to Sorrentino's fictional voice—improvisation and the use of stock characters. Even this form's various names seem appropriate to Sorrentino's Art: of the profession, improvised comedy, off-the-cuff comedy, erudite comedy, and comedy by suggestion.

Another important aspect of this comedy, exemplifed by Aristophanes' voice, is that its barbed satire was not there to tear down so much as it was to conserve. The impulse to make fun of things is more a conservative one than a revolutionary one. It is a type of nostalgia, really. The urge to barbarize the new is a sentimental one. This is true with Aristophanes; it is true with Plautus; it is true with the *commedia dell'arte;* it is true of television programs like "Saturday Night Live," in which a kind of homage is paid to people made fun of on its program, including Dan Ackroyd's impersonations of Tom Snyder and the actor for Crazy Eddie commercials. It is an homage which Eddie Murphy pays to James Brown, Gumbi, and black jazz musicians. I think the conservative strain of the comedian is also contained in Gilbert Sorrentino's voice. What savagery waits in its coil is propelled by a conviction to go backward in time, not forward into the future. It is sentimentality wearing the masque of bristling sentiment. This is a voice with a stance, a posture, not one pushed forward by genuine emotions. It is all comic opera.

These qualities of Sorrentino's voice which reflect the history of comedy in our civilization are more hallmarks of the prose, not the poetry. In the poems the comedy is blunted by an intelligence, the student and pedant capable of lecturing for hours about the roots going back through Creeley and Olson to Williams and Pound, which stops on the way for Zukofsky and Oppen. In fact, Sorrentino's poems do not so much contain a voice as they do project a range of intelligence. Like a kind of precursor to pop art, much of the early poetry is filled with references to comic-strip personalities, including Major Hoople, Skeezix, Mamie and Moon Mullins. These poplike images are combined with his relationship to the world of Art, with many poems referring to or about painters like Franz Kline (*Black and White,* 1964), Philip Guston (whose final paintings were whirling with comic-strip imagery), and Dan Rice. But the early poems more often trap particulars instead of shedding light.

> I am no tree
> no dogwood, nor
> red sumac, not
> even crabgrass

The voice is allusive to other poets, including his contempories like Blackburn, Oppenheimer, and Creeley, with echoes back to Williams. It is a voice which sees, yet it does not reveal. Finally, it is a kind of voicelessness, which ultimately gets exaggerated further in later poetry when Sorrentino progresses toward a Mallarmé-like poem of language. The photographic becomes painterly. It is a voice floating at the surface of things. What is seen gets replaced by what is imagined.

In early poems like "The Fights" and "The Totem" voice often gets replaced by erudition. It is not until Sorrentino projects a voice into a fictional landscape that it begins to become its own voice, shedding influences simply by imitating them, mocking them, dropping them, and moving on. Like James Joyce, Sorrentino's fictional voice often is a kind of zany, intellectual ventriloquism, a kind of stand-up comedy of impersonation. It is a voice made of two comic traditions, the first being that Sicilian one I mentioned earlier, and the second is an Irish one, via Joyce and Flann O'Brien. (Sorrentino is of Irish and Italian ancestry.) In an early novel like *Steelwork,* traces of the two traditions are there in the voice as well as the content. In a mid-career work like *Imaginative Qualities of Actual Things* the comedic strain is a combination of stock characters and improvisation, back through the commedia clear into the animal mimes of ancient Sicily. With *Mulligan Stew* and *Aberration of Starlight* it is infected with Irish wit. But what Sorrentino does to the humor of the Irish voice is to possess it, as though by a seizure, letting his intelligence foreclose on a writer like Flann O'Brien. Voice, characters, and the whole shebang from Joyce and O'Brien are gathered and collected, and Sorrentino submerges them into the voice of his own intentions.

It should be noted, though, that the exploitation of other voices is likewise a major quality of James Joyce. But then a Borgesian question arises: If Sorrentino co-opts Joyce and O'Brien, does he become these writers? Or do they become Gilbert Sorrentino? It is a situation something like Pierre Menard being the real author of *Don Quixote*. Besides these questions, other questions arise about whether Sorrentino has co-opted too much from Joyce and O'Brien in a book like *Mulligan Stew*, and has failed to provide his own voice. With a work like *Imaginative Qualities*, though, these literary speculations are irrelevant. The allusiveness of the voice is apparent, but so is the inventiveness and even the genius of this writer's voice. I think it is a question of degrees in which at his best Sorrentino is mimetic; and at his weakest when he is merely imitative. But I need once again to go back to the poetry before proceeding any further with the fiction.

While the prose runs a circuit from the brilliantly mimetic to the not-so-brilliant imitative, the poetry tracks along in a fairly set pattern which includes the tradition of the American idiom going back to William Carlos Williams. A statement which Sorrentino made over twenty-five years ago, still seems to hold true, but with some additions which I wish to dwell on shortly. He wrote: "Three great literary markers are Pound, who taught me that verse is the highest of arts and gave me the sense of tradition, Williams, who showed me that our language can produce it, and Creeley, who demonstrated that the attack need not be head on." To these names I would also add Jack Spicer's, about whom Sorrentino wrote one of the best essays in *For Now* magazine several years after the remark above. But that is not the end of influences for this writer and his voice. Quite early on in his career Sorrentino expressed his love for French writers—Rimbaud, Baudelaire, etc.—which became more pronounced as his career went on.

Early Sorrentino absorbed writers like Rimbaud and Baudelaire into his vocal strategy. The midpoint Sorrentino calls upon the voice of Apollinaire. Later Sorrentino seems to be preoccupied with a pure utterance reminiscent of Mallarmé, and sometimes this influence is his least efficacious. Where the French influence works best is with the dazzling verbal pyrotechnics of *Splendide-Hotel,* a work which rides in a world between poetry and fiction, and whose voice is rocklike certain, authentic, and full of Sorrentino's invention, arch, domineering, abrasive, erudite, judgmental, refined, even operatic. Often his later poetry seems less influenced by his roots going back from Creeley to Williams to Pound than it is coming out of W. H. Auden and John Ashbery. The voice is technical, virtuoso, overly crafted, resembling a Fabergé egg. It is a voice which annoys and interests simultaneously.

It appears to be a voice hiding something, or at least not willing to reveal anything by its formal utterance. For all of Sorrentino's intellectual range—and the breadth of his intelligence is considerable—there is an air of impotence more than omnipotence. In many respects it betrays Pound's injunctive about the direct treatment of the object. That is because the voice often dances around the object. There is almost a rejection of things as a source of revealing feelings. The voice does not so much see as it does assay things. There is a touch of *il Dottore* in it, I mean, a kind of theatrical cant and pomposity. It is the voice as hollow pumpkin. His recent novel *Blue Pastoral* suffers from a similar lassitude in the voice.

Much of this distancing comes about from that more formal nature in Sorrentino, and it was there from the beginning. A book of poetry like *The Perfect Fiction* (1968) is absorbed by, and is about, craft and technique. The volume consists of one long poem made of a kind of American *terza rima,* though it is devoid of Dante's fondness for the vulgar tongue. This is not a poem of the street but rather one of the garret, of mind more than voice; of breath and syllable, yes, but somehow lacking the rhythm of experience. Because of the interconnecting nature of the work, it is impossible to give a brief example here. It is mentioned because I think with this book Sorrentino begins to locate his own voice which finally emerges in the prose. In this book you can see Sorrentino's affinities with Black Mountain, and to some degree Pound, begin to dissolve. They are not sloughed off so much as they are given a different location in his hierarchy. This is the beginning of the journey from Black Mountain to France, all of it done in an armchair, i.e., the author never leaves New York. Somewhere over an imaginary Atlantic Sorrentino's finest poems emerge, all of them in his best collection *Corrosive Sublimate* (1971). A good example of what I mean by this is to be found in a poem entitled "Coast of Texas 1–16," an Apollinaire-inspired poem.

> Although the sky
> was bright blue and clarity
> the exact love
>
> That blank city allows
> at times: so that it
> did not seem I was
>
> In Hell
> I was in Hell. O
> love. That impairs my song.

That last stanza also contains a rhythmical homage to Jack Spicer, especially in a poem like Spicer's "Billy the Kid":

So the heart breaks
Into small shadows
Almost so random
They are meaningless
Like a diamond
Has at the center of it a diamond
Or a rock
Rock.

I am suggesting that a sea change occurs, and Sorrentino moves away from the concerns of poetry into the world of fiction. Two novels, *The Sky Changes* and *Steelwork,* are already in print, but it is a question of a man moving out of shadows. With the poetry Sorrentino is overshadowed by writers like Robert Creeley; with the prose he is overshadowed by his childhood friend, Hubert Selby, Jr. But then with *Corrosive Sublimate, Imaginative Qualities of Actual Things,* and *Splendide-Hotel,* all of them published within a few years of each other, Sorrentino has become his own man, his own writer. He has found a voice, and that voice will cast its own shadow out of which younger writers must move or languish within. I would like to suggest that this is an awesome transformation, assertive, willful, full of Sorrentino's ferocity and venom; it is even heroic when viewed retrospectively.

The years are 1971–73, clearly this writer's banner years. Through the 1970s his reputation, based on these three books, I think, was to burgeon, although his output—quite voluminous—will not achieve this personal best again until the publication of *Aberration of Starlight* in 1980. It comes as almost an afterthought to his much heralded *Mulligan Stew* (1979), critically his most acclaimed work, but as I said earlier, finally too derivative, while also being nearly unreadable in its density and one-note comedy. One reads the *Stew* out of loyalty to the author more than out of any pleasure in the text. *Starlight,* by comparison, is Sorrentino's most touching achievement, a work which goes to the heart, something the author is not accustomed to giving the reader. Clearly it is Sorrentino's most autobiographical voice, and its illuminations literally are bathed in starlight, i.e., a wonderful nostalgia and sentimentality, which the author brings off quite naturally.

The next morning he saw that his mother's eyes were red and he knew that she had been crying. Things were very strange at the house when they all had breakfast, his grandfather seemed very loud and happy, and talked about how the weather was changing, fall was definitely in the air, almost time to get back to the old grind, but it would be a relief. He even spoke to Tom the same way, all smiles and jokes, but it gave Billy the creeps. His mother sat very quietly, picking at her breakfast, and leaving her second cup of coffee half-drunk. For some reason, everybody else was as loud as his grandfather, but their voices were phony and reminded Billy of how the kids in school talked when they put on a pageant for Open School assembly.

A story entitled "The Moon in Its Flight" also emanates outward with a voice made of that rhythm of experience tightrope walking a delicate balance between nostalgia and the harder edge of technique.

There are two other aspects of Sorrentino's literary career which need to be noted in order to understand the full dimensions of his voice. They both are aspects of a similar wellspring in the man. The first is his critical acumen, not merely manifest in his book reviews and essays but pervasive in his voice, too. The second was his editorial work. This latter aspect is a traditional occupation for many writers in Europe, i.e., working in a publishing house. Eliot did it. Today writers like Philippe Sollers and Italo Calvino do it. In America writers like Toni Morrison, E. L. Doctorow, Scott Spencer, Joyce Johnson, Jonathan Galassi, to name a few, were or still are editors. Most of Sorrentino's editorial work was done at Grove Press, and he worked with authors like Hubert Selby, Jr., John Rechy, William Burroughs, and Samuel Beckett, that is, all of Grove's major literary names. Being an editor provides several perspectives on publishing which other writers don't understand or enjoy, mostly that knowledge of what houses don't want and of what maybe they might take. The rejection slips at the beginning of *Mulligan Stew* are as much comments on the editorial process as they are about the depressing world of a struggling writer.

Sorrentino's critical savvy is part of this profile as an editor, allowing him to discern new voices that perhaps another editor would turn down because a frame of reference with other writing could not be found. I had the opportunity to witness both the intelligence and the skill which Sorrentino brings to this task, because he was the editor of my first novel which Grove contracted for but eventually never published. (That is a long story best kept for another tract, and it has little to do with Sorrentino, and more to do with circumstances and the times.) Part of that author/editor relationship with him was like going to lectures on literature; each time I visited him in his office on University Place, he would have some new author for me to read or he would vituperate for hours about the uptown establishment. His verbal flourishes and energy often reminded me of Lenny Bruce. Something of the man, in this case, the editorial man, is there in the fiction, too. I would characterize it by saying that one does not talk with, or engage in dialogue with, Sorrentino but instead becomes his audience. His best verbal form is the monologue.

Where he is most selfless, it seems, is in his critical writings, and that is because, again, like Pound, he is capable of releasing his own prejudices to evaluate writing on its own terms. As I said earlier, his essay on Jack Spicer is the finest I have read on that writer. Sorrentino also wrote the publicity explaining *Last Exit to Brooklyn* to reviewers. Most recently, he wrote a short essay about the Irish writer Ralph Cusack's *Cadenza* in *Adrift,* the Irish-American experimental magazine edited by Thomas McGonigle. His nonfiction book, *Something Said,* consists of forty-seven essays, ranging from a long one on William Carlos Williams to shorter to medium-length essays on Louis Zukofsky, William Bronk, Kenneth Rexroth, Lorine Niedecker, Paul Blackburn, Hubert Selby, Charles Olson, Ross Feld, George Oppen, John Hawkes, Paul Bowles, and Ross Macdonald. There is a wonderfully vicious essay on John Gardner entitled "Rhinestone in the Rough," which begins: "John Gardner is of the puppeteer school of novelists."

Because Sorrentino is a writer engaged in the life of the imagination as his subject, I don't think it unreasonable to consider his intelligence and erudition as part of the rhythm of his experience, and therefore the voice in his fiction. Often it is the most admirable quality of all his imaginative qualities. This voice of sensibility is strongly evident in his *Selected Poems* (1981), in how the writer excludes, rearranges, lets some tendencies come forth and others recede. Seemingly disparate movements coalesce or *correspond,* a Baudelarian idea which Sorrentino uses in his critical writings. Again, that early idea of being written for himself, not for *them,* is still an issue. Seen as a totality, the poems share the same virtues and faults as the fiction; they are cantankerous, self-effacing, brilliant, defensive, even vicious, the voice is full of judgments and pronouncements, the voice is of the commedia's *zanno* (the complicating servant) grown up to become his own *Dottore.*

> I have this enormous faith in dead forms
> Especially the catalogue that gets you nowhere.

Shortly after these poems appeared, his novel *Crystal Vision* (1981) appeared, and if not a culmination, it is a melding of different voice strategies into running conversations outside a magical candy store in Brooklyn. The nostalgia of *Starlight* combines with the acid of *Imaginative Qualities*. If it is not another apogee, it is a good representation. Its strength comes from how Sorrentino culls from the rhythm of experience, but then he renders this experience with a voice that is of an imaginary world. This is fiction, I mean. Again, there are Old Comedy standards, improvisation and stock characters, the Arab this time becoming *il Dottore*. Here they are in a section called "In Sheepshead Bay."

Must we again tolerate with benignous good nature and bon-homie in the extreme these clichéd and unfounded mindless cracks about Italians? the Arab says.

Mindless my ass, Bony Ruth says.

Excusez-moi? the Arab says. I failed to auriculate your *mot,* cadaverous one.

Bony Ruth is often called "M.B.," or "Mosquito Bites," a cruel sorbriquet that refers to the size of her breasts.

What a character, she says. Ugh.

Anyway, Ticineti, is there any way you can help me out with this kid of mine? Connie says.

A phony touch of delirium tremens might straighten the lad out, he says.

I'll bet you half a buck Ticineti didn't say "lad," Bony Ruth says.

I'll have to chime in agreement with you, osseous one, on that, the Arab says.

To say that nobody in Brooklyn speaks like this is so obvious that whoever says it should be hit on the head with a dead fish from Sheepshead Bay. This is a voice whose words are written in the blood with the breath and syllable of an ancient source. Its comedy comes from *lazzi* (comic business) found in the collective unconscious—the dream of Harlequin bonked on the head with a frying pan or baseball bat, a slap-stick, I mean, that baton which old-time comedians wore, and used, when nothing else got a laugh. This is the land-scape of the improvised *canavaccio,* and even the setting at the candy store—that's show business from antiquity!

It all goes back to that first poem in Sorrentino's first book of poems, *The Darkness Surrounds Us.* This is a writer with a lot to say, and to be said on his own terms. Twenty-five years later Gilbert Sorrentino still has nothing to say to *them.*

6

Hubert Selby, Jr.

A FTER WRITING A REVIEW of Selby's last novel, *Requiem for a Dream*, for the *Nation* magazine in which I said that he was our best living fiction writer and should receive the Nobel Prize, the literary editor returned my copy with the following note:

> Dear Michael,
> I'm sending it back because it seems inflated beyond what anyone could believe, and in that it does the book a disservice. I know you believe this, but I don't think it helps to suggest that the fellow deserves a Nobel prize and whatall. That simply sounds silly—praise his daring, his unconventionality then ask for all the conventional prizes and hype him with the conventional praise—best American novel, etc. The rest of it I like—when you get down to talking about the book.
> Let me know if you will let it go in without the frosting.

I wanted the review published, but I could not think where to tame the prose into what the editor wanted. Part of the problem is that she did not want to believe something which would be news to her. Selby had been around nearly twenty years. No other critics were writing of him this way. Therefore, I figured she had reasoned, Stephens is being hyperbolic. Another part of the problem is that I had read the book and she only read my review of the book, so that her opinion about Selby as a writer was based on her previous notions of his work. No one in their right mind would question the power of his first book, *Last Exit to Brooklyn*, and while it had not been given critical attention since it was published in 1964, urban colleges throughout this country used it in their syllabi.

The editor's skepticism of my objective tastes perhaps had to do with Selby's previous novel, *The Demon*, which had not done well because it was not as realized as his other writings, including the second novel, *The Room*. Still, there was nothing I could rewrite in the review, which began and ended by saying, "*Requiem for a Dream* is an American masterpiece". Did I believe it? Yes, I did. Do I still believe it? Yes. I thought and thought of a strategy to come up with in order to save the review without watering down my feelings about the novel. Granted, I am better in letters than on the telephone or in person, because in the latter cases I come on too strong and defensively. I did feel as though my back was pinned to a wall. Selby is still controversial to the established literary order. But so were Isaac Babel and Herman Melville, Selby's admitted mentors. I decided that I would take a deep breath—and because I was living in New Haven at the time—telephone the editor at the *Nation*. As the telephone rang I reviewed the conditions under which I would articulate my opinion for saving the review intact.

Selby wrote a kind of underworld prose, his voice of the American dream's underbelly, not its "frosting," the editor's word of my opinions. He did not verify any middle-class, book-buying public's notion of their own world. The problem was one of misreading, I thought. Too often critics have assigned Selby's prose to the last breaths of naturalism, whereas in fact his fiction comes from other dramaturgical sources. Cubby once told me—his friends call Selby that—that he did not create his characters in any conventional, naturalistic sense, rather, like Sorrentino's characterizations (but in a different light), he dealt in *types*. And Selby literally sees his novels dramaturgically conceived.

"They are morality plays," he said.

Yes, they are that, as I hope to show in this essay. But meanwhile I had about three to five minutes to convince this editor at the *Nation* of my veracity with regard to the review of *Requiem for a Dream*. I decided to leave out any references to the history of the theater. I decided to be measured, and ultimately convincing. Finally, I knew I had to give up something to get something. At the beginning of the review I offered to remove the following:

"In this his fourth novel Hubert Selby, Jr., combines novelistic genius, lyrical integrity, master storytelling, high moral obsession, profound human feeling, and natural linguistic grace to produce what is certainly the greatest American novel of the century. It is a book whose central metaphors—heroin and television—are wrought in heroic proportions, with a relentless moral fervor driving the prose into literary realms that were inhabited previously only by nineteenth-century prose masters like Dostoyevsky, Tolstoy, Conrad, Flaubert, and Melville, and in our century by Joyce, Beckett, Faulkner, Mann, and Proust. It is a millennium beyond the erudition and moral outpouring of just about any contemporary American author, including our Nobel laureate Saul Bellow, the brave and nobel efforts that John Cheever strove for and sometimes achieved in *Falconer*, and the cadenzas and literary virtuosities of John Updike."

Hyperbole?

When the review finally was printed with the revisions made, I received a telephone call from the editor. After the review appeared she read the novel herself. I'll always cherish this revision of her own opinion about Selby. She said, "Michael, I don't think you praised him enough."

Naturalistic fiction stresses plot and character, but since Hubert Selby is not a naturalistic writer, it is best to approach his fiction through voice. But, first, if I am to hold this author as some kind of ideal of what short fiction is and can be, I need to make clear that his writing fits into my definitions of what short fiction is. As was stated in the first part of this study, this type of fiction draws as much from poetry and drama as it does from the annals of the novel and short story. Within its poetic dimension it is concise, rhythmical, object-centered, and energized. Its dramaturgical values consist mostly of that seeing voice. It is "short" not by virtue of its length— which is why Selby's novels can be discussed within its borders—but by the strength of its pictorial exactness as well as something which can be read in one sitting (ideally). From *Last Exit* to *Requiem* Selby's writing epitomizes these qualities of short fiction. The source of his creative instinct literally rests with other contemporary poets, including Gilbert Sorrentino, Joel Oppenheimer, LeRoi Jones (Amiri Baraka), William Carlos Williams, and Ezra Pound.

His childhood friend was Gil Sorrentino who first read Selby's attempts at fiction. Joel Oppenheimer was once Selby's roommate. (They had to be as unlikely a pair as Marlon Brando and Wally Cox; or kind of a hip version of *The Odd Couple*.) William Carlos Williams both read and encouraged Selby in the fifties. Robert Creeley first published Selby in *The Black Mountain Review*. The title of Selby's first novel was an afterthought, I am told, suggested by Sorrentino. Originally it was called *Love's Labours Lost*. Shakespeare was more on Selby's mind than James T. Farrell or Theodore Dreiser.

As for his seeing voice, I talked to Cubby several years ago about how he created his characters and he pointed out something about his dramaturgy for which I will be forever grateful. He said that if I think about it carefully there are few descriptive sentences or paragraphs in his writing. He does not create characters from the color of their eyes, the color of their hair, their noses and mouths, or the clothes they wear. Instead, he said, "I hear their voices speaking to me, and I evoke them, I mean, I create characters, from *how they speak*." He gave Georgette as an example in *Last Exit*. "Everything she says," he told me, "is sibilant, full of S's." How we *see* Georgette is not by descriptions, but by her voice. Especially those S's, the voice given sight by those utterances. In other words, Selby creates characters dramaturgically.

"Look. Look. Do you see there? A swan. O how beautiful. How serene. The moon follows her. See how it lights her. O such grace. O yes yes yes I do Vinnie, I do . . . Vincennti . . . See. See, she glides to us. Us. For us. O how white. Yes. She is. Whiter than the snows on the mountains. And they are but shadows now. But she glistens, shimmers. The queen of birds. Yes. O yes, yes, Cellos. Hundreds of cellos and we will glide in the moonlight, pirouetting to THE SWAN and kiss her head and nod to the Willows and bow to the night and they will grace us . . . they will grace us and the Lake will grace us and smile and the moon will grace us and the mountains will grace us and the breeze will grace us and the sun will gently rise and its rays will stretch and spread and even the willows will lift their heads ever so slightly and the snow will grow whiter and the shadows will rise from the mountains and it will be warm."

As this passage toward the end of "The Queen Is Dead" shows, we know Georgette not by narrative description, or even the usual conventions of the naturalistic tale, but through the author's seeding the voice of his character into the prose. The only way we see Georgette—and I see her quite clearly—is by her voice. We read plays this way, not usually novels. But *Last Exit* is not really a novel per se but rather a work of short fiction, a series of interrrelated voices, with the point of view shifting, section to section. How we see Georgette is similar to how an actor sees a character in a script. The voice is its center (words on a page), and these are physicalized, made gestural, put into the empty space of the stage in order to create the drama. Selby is not unconventional in how he makes fiction; he is uncanny.

Instead of going to the younger forms of the novel, dating back only a few hundred years in our language, his voice searches the storehouse of drama for his props. To say he is not unconventional does not mean his voice is conventional either. But it does suggest that Selby works within a given tradition. Melville and Babel are never abandoned. Instead, these influences are enriched by other literary sources. The idiom in which Selby's voice operates is American via Pound and Williams, i.e., the poetry of natural speech. But this idiom goes further back to sources like Dante's "vulgar tongue." And it constantly harbors Pound's suasions that there is a proper way to say something, an exact way, even a science to it. Flaubert's *le mot juste*. Selby is exact in his choice of words through every tale of *Last Exit*. What Wittgenstein wrote is appropriate to poetry in a voice: beauty is replaced by correctness in our time.

All of this leads to one important observation about Selby's writing: you enter the landscape of his fiction by way of his voice. If you go by way of character and plot, the journey is opaque. Olson's "composition by field" is more accurate to Selby's world than Forster's *Aspects of the Novel*. You come into Selby's fiction through breath, syllable, line. The fiction of *Last Exit* is more "projective" than naturalistic, because its energy derives from the impulses of speech. Readers were drawn to Selby's writing initially because of its content, its graphic details; but the electricity in his writing will not satisfy a nature after the merely pictorial. What really arouses a reader of *Last Exit* is how the breath pants, the syllable lurches, the tongue sees. Pornography literally means "whore's story." Part of *Last Exit* is a whore's story, but none of it is pornographic. Since the voice is an instrument, its only culpability is when its tones are not resonating. By itself the voice is a set of notes and silences like music's. It is an abstract sound. It becomes a literary vehicle only when it sees, but what it sees comes out of the rhythm of experience. Sight cannot be corrupted by pictorial details. Yet what sight culls, yes, there are moral choices in this kind of selection, and how the voice emphasizes those things, yes, this is part of the writer's responsibility, too.

But Selby, as he said, is writing morality plays with his fiction. The origin of these dramas is with religion, the evolution of liturgical tropes. Traditionally, the most lurid and fascinating station in the morality cycle was the portable stage representing Hell. Selby therefore is being historically accurate in what his voice chooses to highlight visually. If I were going to find the source of Selby's style, I would suggest going back to the birth of the Second Age of drama, circa the tenth century, right into the liturgy of the Christian ritual, and take it from the *Quem quaeritis* trope outward. Brunelleschi himself was considered one of the great innovators of these theatrical machines used in the liturgy of the Christian church, including the use of hundreds of flashing lights and special effects. From as far back as the twelfth century in France there are descriptions of these Hellmouth machines in front of which one segment of a morality play would be performed. What follows is a description from an Anglo-Norman play entitled *Jeu d'Adam*:

"Then shall the Devil come, and three or four other devils with him, bearing in their hands chains and iron shackles, which they shall place on the necks of Adam and Eve. And certain ones shall push them on, others shall drag them toward Hell; other devils, however, shall be close beside Hell, waiting for them as they come, and these shall make a great dancing and jubilation over their destruction; and other devils shall, one after another, point to them as they come; and they shall take them up and thrust them into Hell; and thereupon they shall cause a great smoke to arise, and they shall shout one to another in Hell, greatly rejoicing; and they shall dash together their pots and kettles, so that they may be heard without. And after some little interval, the devils shall go forth, and shall run to and fro in the square; certain of them, however, shall remain behind in Hell" (*A Source Book in Theatrical History* by A. M. Nagler).

Eventually this type of drama evolved away from the church into a secular enterprise. But even midway in this journey to what ultimately becomes our world of theater today, there were ingenious religious dramas which really were plain dramas after all. Certainly, an early English characterization like Mak, the sheep stealer, in *The Second Shepherds' Play* is practically a prototype of Selby's characters, and even his dissembling reminds me of those early Selby characters like Vinnie and Harry who forever hang out in the Greek diner in Brooklyn. If you think about it carefully, giving it a deeper visual association, the Greek's serves as a theatrical backdrop for nearly all of the action of *Last Exit to Brooklyn*, as though it were a kind of contemporary Hellmouth.

Selby's strongest affinities with his moral dramas—the morality plays of his fiction—and those in antiquity are found in the origins of the English drama. *Everyman* personifies all of us. *Last Exit* personifies the nobody in us, that utterly and spiritually bankrupt human of the urban variety. The Greek's diner sits on a kind of pageant wagon in our minds. The dives in Brooklyn and Manhattan also roll in and out like floats in a gruesome Rose Bowl parade. The types which Selby creates are not fully blown characterizations, but instead, like Medieval pageantries, they are representations of our different moral aspects. They are personifications of human qualities more than being human. The only thing that motivates them into anything resembling human activity is the author's voice behind them. There is something marionettelike in their movements, and even their violence is as stylized as a samurai movie. And yet this drama is not completely inhuman. What moves us is how voice alone transforms this drama into a living moment. I do not mean to suggest that Selby does not shake us up, because he does, almost furiously. There is more than a bit of Calvinist preacher in Selby's voice. In fact, that is his voice as he leads us before the next station in his drama, and this one is Hellmouth again.

In another conversation with the author, Cubby said that he writes "about pathologies." He was referring to the fact that his four novels dwell on this human aspect in his morality plays. He did go on to say that his future writings after the first four novels will attempt solutions to these pathologies. But I am not going to address that remark until later in this essay. For the moment, let us imagine, like the invention of the morality play itself, that Selby's voice moves us, first, from the liturgy of the Christian church out onto the steps of the church, then into the square, and finally into a secular world of the drama. It is important to keep in mind the overall push and pull of drama from its Greek origins outward. There is always this conflict between the sacred and the profane, of the religious and the sexual, and that the greatest dramatic tension occurs at the midpoint between these extremes.

Selby's fiction often uses biblical quotations to frame it. In keeping with these historical juxtapositions of the sacred and the profane, *Last Exit*'s sections are framed by quotations from Ecclesiastes, Genesis, Job, Song of Solomon, and Proverbs. In terms of biographical information it is not irrelevant to mention that Selby was once a heroin addict, then had a drinking problem, and was reborn a Christian. To the casual observer this last transformation may seem incongruous. He *is* the author of *Last Exit to Brooklyn*, one of the most controversial books published in the last half of the twentieth century. But, believe me, those biblical quotations in *Last Exit* are not incidentally placed. It is simply that Selby perhaps has a profounder religious sense of being damned than most writers operating in the contemporary world today, and I would include writers in countries like Poland where religion permeates even one's sense of socialism. Like so many other voices in our American literary landscape, Selby is very much a Puritan thinker. And he is a thinker. Only his thoughts are not made out of abstractions. His vehicle of thought is that probing voice in the landscape of these moral fictions.

But having touched on some dramaturgical origins in Selby's fictional voice, I want now to return to sources of the poetry in his fiction, another way to comprehend this writer's work. Again, it is not only of biographical interest that this writer was associated with contemporary poets from the beginning of his prose career. How he writes prose is directly related to those relationships with poets. Even a visual perusal of Selby's fiction—I mean, scanning the pages without reading the words—shows markedly different stylistic procedures than other prose. As in poetry there are line breaks, caesuras, breath pauses, enjambments. There are those stylistic flourishes found in his roommate Joel Oppenheimer's early poems, using a slash instead of an apostrophe, for instance. It comes back again to what Olson said about "projective verse." Selby does not so much write sentences or paragraphs. He dwells on words, and even within the prose these words are broken down further, to breath and syllable. And when Olson wrote of this phenomenon of poetic articulation, he did not mean it to be exclusive to contemporary poetry.

"The dance of the intellect is there," Olson writes, "among them, *prose or verse*" (my italics). Olson calls this "the swift currents of the syllable," as good a description as we'll find to delineate a voice like Selby's. The syllables of this fiction do not scan, but then neither do "open" poems. Their meter is the human breath, its spurts and pauses. For instance, the opening of the section entitled "Tralala" is as rhythmical as any poems by Selby's associates.

"Tralala was 15 the first time she was laid. There was no real passion. Just diversion. She hungout in the Greeks with the other neighborhood kids. Nothin to do. Sit and talk. Listen to the jukebox. Drink coffee. Bum cigarettes. Everything a drag. She said yes. In the park. 3 or 4 couples finding their own tree and grass. Actually she didnt say yes. She said nothing."

Selby's voice orchestrates the particulars until through his voice's rhythm we see. The language is as precise as a scientific manual, nearly a recipe in how it orders experience, moving into the arc of the story.

FUCKYOU FLATFOOT   GO AND FUCKYASELF
YASONOFABITCH   IF YOU MEN DONT BREAKITUP
WE/LL RUN YOU ALL IN   NOW GET BACK FROM
THAT RUNWAY   YEAH, SURE, AFTA WE BREAK
THOSE FUCKINSCABSHEADS   DERE TAKIN THE
BREAD FROM OUR MOUTHS   IM TELLING YOU
FOR THE LAST TIME, BREAKITUP OR I/LL TURN THE
HOSE ON YOU   WHO PAID YAOFF YASONOFABITCH
(*Last Exit*)

It is fiction by breath and syllable, but it is also dramaturgical, all voice, its significance found only in the human body, inhabiting a theatrical space. But it must be realized that the dramaturgy of the time in which Selby writes also includes the movies. Imagine that this really is how the characters in *On the Waterfront* would have talked, if there were no censorship in those days. I mean, this is what Budd Schulberg wanted to say, but could not. The dramatic values of this heightened speech are not lost on the writers of a movie like *Raging Bull*, where the character of Jake LaMotta (Robert DeNiro) speaks like a Selby character. There is unquestionably an energy in street talk, but it takes a writer with Selby's poetic breath to give it life and form. James Cagney in *Public Enemy* is as much an influence on Selby's style as Isaac Babel is. But then if you consider what Babel did to prose, it could be supposed that Cagney learned from Babel ("My First Goose") as well:

" 'Landlady,' I said, 'I've got to eat.'

"The old woman raised to me the diffused white of her purblind eyes and lowered them again.

" 'Comrade,' she said, after a pause, 'what with all this going on, I want to go and hang myself.'

" 'Christ!' I muttered, and pushed the old woman in the chest with my fist. 'You don't suppose I'm going to go into explanations with you, do you?'

"And turning around I saw somebody's sword lying within reach. A severe-looking goose was waddling about the yard, inoffensively preening its feathers. I overtook it and pressed it to the ground. Its head cracked beneath my boot, cracked and emptied itself. The white neck lay stretched out in the dung, the wings twitched.

" 'Christ!' I said, digging into the goose with my sword. 'Go and cook it for me, landlady.' "

The dramaturgical influence of movies is borne out in an early Selby fiction called "Double Feature," which is about two punks getting drunk in a movie theater in Brooklyn. The frame around the story seamlessly interweaves with the movie in the picture frame in front of Chubby and Harry, the two drunken characters:

"From making comments upon the action on the screen they progressed to prediction and then to direction; urging the girl-shy male star to kiss her, she wont bite . . . tittering, laughing, reaching for the bottle (clink) watching the wine being poured into the cup (plop, plop, plop), putting the bottle back (clink)—whatzamatta with that guy, is he nutsor somethin? If I had a broad like that runnin afta me I/d— swaying, wine sloshing in the cups; laughing, swallowing, bubbling, choking, wine splashing on their noses, dribbling down their chins, dark spots blotted by pants and shirts— reaching (clink), only a few drops left, watching the last drop plop into the cup, still one left (clink); two empties; good show, eh Chub? cups refilled (getting soft and soggy, dented, dont squeeze too tight, please dont squeeza the banana— held by the bottom in the palm of the hand); wheres the otha ones—all gone—no more haha—no (clink) more (bottle resting on his lap)—come fill me with the old familiar juice— HUH HUH—she slinks, semidressed, toward him, hair over the side of her face, hips liquid, rubs his cheeks then pushes her hand thru his hair, down his neck and back, sways in front of him, all virtues and charms (almost all) displayed, the voice throaty, begging . . . he asks her what she wants— OOOOO whattza matta? ya craze?"

As these two friends get drunk in the movie theater and eventually the police arrive and grill them in the manager's office, there are two real friends soberly writing poems and stories. That is, Hubert Selby and Gilbert Sorrentino, who have known each other since they were teenagers. Early on in Selby's writing career he would show his work to Gil, and as Cubby has said, "I used to go home literally crying, but it worked. I took his criticism seriously, and I kept improving each time Gil looked at the writing. I think of Gil as being like the Pound of our generation." In an interview in *Vort* magazine, Sorrentino said, "It was through Williams that Cubby got published, you know. . . . Cubby finished his story called 'Love's Labours Lost,' which is the first part of what is now called 'The Queen Is Dead,' but at that time was the only part he'd done. . . . 'Love's Labours Lost' was published in *Black Mountain Review*. He sent it to Williams, Williams read it, and he wrote back and he said, I'm absolutely knocked out by this story. This is the most incredible story. You're certainly *never* going to get this story published. You have to remember this was 1956: it was hot stuff, very potent stuff. Williams said, I know some very crazy guys down in North Carolina and this is their meat. So he sent the story to Jonathan (Williams). Jonathan read it and sent it to Creeley. As soon as Creeley got it—I heard later from Max Finstein—he said Creeley started to jump up and down and said this must go into *Black Mountain Review*. That's how Cubby was first published—through William Carlos Williams."

It was through this publication that Gil and Cubby met the Black Mountaineers as well as LeRoi Jones. They, along with Joel Oppenheimer, all got together at the Cedar Bar. It should be understood that at this time, Selby was the only prose writer among poets and painters. The only exception to this would be Fielding Dawson, who wrote fiction and painted, too. Gil was writing more poetry than fiction. The others were mostly writing poetry, too, though Jones would write fiction and plays eventually. Selby's voice corresponds very much to someone like Jackson Pollock, the creative density and violence of the gestures, the theatrical values of those colors. I would imagine that he met Pollock at some point during this period, though I've never asked him or Sorrentino about this. When Olson writes in his essay "Projective Verse" that "the poem itself must, at all points, be a high energy-construct and, at all points, an energy discharge," he could as easily be referring to Selby's prose or Pollock's paintings.

                                                            Just fucking
squeeze them, the ugly cocksucking bastards, pounding across the
cell from the wall to the door, the door to the wall, the wall to the
door to door to the wall, the wall to the door, to the wall, the door
                                                            then stopping
in front of the mirror and looking briefly at the pimple then squeezing it as hard as he could, his eyes tearing and wincing from the needle-like pain in his cheek, crushing the pimple between finger

tips until a few drops of fluid oozed out. God DAMN that hurts,
squeezing his eyes shut and shaking his head.

(*The Room*)

Like a poet, Selby breaks his prose line by breaths—the reason for that separation between "the door" and "then stopping." It is also how a painter like Pollock painted. The force
is an instinct, not a logical equation. There! It is done. But
the voice needs to be in exact contact with breath and syllable
by way of one's biology, how the heart pumps its rhythm,
how the blood flows. While the voice in *The Room* has correspondences with the voice in *Last Exit*, its arena is different.
The setting in the empty space has changed.

Last Exit's setting is nearly Brechtian, whereas *The Room* is
a voice in an empty room, in a jail cell. Its dramaturgy more
resembles that of later Beckett plays like *Eh, Joe* and *Not I*.
Where Selby's voice has gone in *The Room* can be found by
going back to the author's childhood friendship. Selby's first
book is dedicated to Gil Sorrentino; Sorrentino's book,
Splendide-Hotel is dedicated to Selby. The wheel turns; the
world turns. Sorrentino's little book is about Rimbaud and
Williams. If you crossed these two men, you'd probably get
Hubert Selby. And that is where Selby's second novel is—
with its philosophical echoes in French existentialism, specifically Camus' *The Fall* and Sartre's *Nausea*. And some spirit of
Rimbaud overrides the voice, too. That is because Rimbaud
is a writer of *being*, not *meanings*, and *The Room* shares this
quality. In the process of developing a play for the stage this
issue of meaning becomes almost entirely irrelevant. I mean,
it rarely is brought up in the exchange between actors. This is
likewise true in any voice-centered writing. Meaning has

more to do with economics (professors' salaries) than it does
with literature.

Because of its psychological nature, naturalism does transport meanings in its prose. But, as I said, Selby is not a naturalistic writer. In fact, he culminates it, not with a whimper,
but a gang bang ("Tralala"). Because Selby uses his voice to
write about theatrical types, as it were, it is inappropriate to
use any psychological formulas to evaluate his writing. His
prose has more to do with myth and ritual, i.e., the main-
stays of drama. In a work like *The Room* the voice of the prose
sees in a more inward fashion than his first book. The journey into sight is more in the sphere of revelation—I see the
Light!—than in spotlighting objects in an exterior universe.
What remains from the external world is the rhythm of experience, which is the music which guides us inward to the
death's head of his character. In the morality plays of the
Middle Ages one of the dominant figures on the stage was
that of the Dance of Death. Selby traps much of that rhythm
in the voice of his second fiction.

But
you know it isnt. You know that it only seems to be, and it only
seems to be because youve become accustomed to it. And when
they turn all the lights on it will be so bright you wont be able to
open your eyes all the way, then after a while it will seem like its always been that way until they turn the lights out and only the night
light is on and suddenly it will seem very dark until you become accustomed to it and then it will seem bright just as it did before. Its
always the same—you get used to one thing, then it changes. Get
used to another, and that changes. over and over. always the same.
(*The Room*)

It may appear that Selby has gone against the American
grain by drawing on so intellectual an influence as French
philosophy. But as those sources were there early on in friend

Gil Sorrentino (cf. Sorrentino's prose passage in book 5 of Williams' *Paterson*), likewise we can presume that Selby had been exposed to them early on as well. In fact, this push and pull between French and American writers goes back to Baudelaire's infatuations with Edgar Allan Poe, a writer whom Georgette, the drag queen, in *Last Exit* is fond of quoting, especially when she is high on benzedrine. The melodramatic terrors of Poe's fiction are there in *The Room*, i.e., Selby's second novel is as American as apple pie and urban violence. Even a modest perusal of Poe's "The Pit and the Pendulum" suggests strong parallels can be drawn with it and Selby's *The Room*:

"My cognizance of the pit had become known to the inquisitorial agents—*the pit*, whose horrors had been destined for so bold a recusant as myself—*the pit*, typical of hell, and regarded by rumor as the Ultima Thule of all their punishments. The plunge into this pit I had avoided by the merest of accidents, and I know that surprise, or entrapment into torment, formed an important portion of all the grotesquerie of these dungeon deaths. Having failed to fall, it was no part of the demon plan to hurl me into the abyss; and thus (there being no alternative) a different and milder destruction awaited me."

Both Selby's and Poe's voices are made of rhythms from the Dance of Death in the morality plays of the Middle Ages. In fact, much of Poe's fiction is set against the backdrop of such dramatic action. It is a dance, again, before that mansion known as Hellmouth. In both instances these American writers possess seeing voices. Their voices are dramatic, but their seeing in that sense makes them dramaturgical. The voice alone is a poetic thing, but once it locates itself in an action, the dimension expands to a dramatic level. Olson's beginning of *Call Me Ishmael* comes to mind: "I take SPACE to be the central fact to man born in America, from Folsom cave to now. I spell it large, because it comes large here. Large, and without mercy. . . . It is geography at bottom, a hell of wide land from the beginning."

Poe and Selby meet, of all places, at Gilbert Sorrentino's *Splendide-Hotel*, where Arthur Rimbaud is proprietor. When they check in for the evening, Selby suggesting it is Brooklyn, while Poe insists they are in the Bronx, Rimbaud interrupts them by saying: "I have swallowed a monstrous dose of poison.—Thrice blessed be the counsel that came to me!—My entrails are on fire. The violence of the venom twists my limbs, deforms and prostrates me. I die of thrist, I suffocate, and cannot scream. It is hell, eternal punishment! See how the fire flares up again! How nicely I burn. Go to it, demon!" (*A Season in Hell*).

What follows is my "inflated" review of Selby's last novel wherein I also mention his third novel, *The Demon*, but only in passing. For whatever reason, Selby's voice seems distant and removed in that novel, and it is not short fiction but rather has all the "fattiness" of best sellers.

Requiem for a Dream is an American masterpiece. Besides that, it is hip, sweet sounding, and spiritual, combining, as it were, the Holy Bible, qualities of *Naked Lunch*, Kerouac at his beboppingest, Snyder and Ginsberg at their most transcendental, and Selby himself at his funkiest. It is Selby's fourth novel, his most famous being his first, *Last Exit to Brooklyn*, and, although scholars and devotees of the first novel will find it hard to surpass that effort, *Requiem* is Selby's best work, maybe even the finest novel of a generation.

Selby can't be categorized easily. His writing has been studied in most urban universities for more than ten years now but his books sell by the millions in drugstores, airports and newsstands throughout America. He has been labeled, erroneously, the last of the naturalists, a descendant of Dreiser, Norris, and Farrell, but when professors teach Selby, they suddenly realize that he came out of the tradition of American poetry, which goes, as Charles Olson said, from Williams on out. What is most shocking to the academic mind but somewhat reassuring to Selby's other admirers is that his work holds up under strenuous analysis, continues to live and breathe after literary autopsy, and compares with the best literature. In our century, Selby's work is studied alongside that of Joyce, Beckett, Faulkner, Mann, and Proust. True, such praise comes largely from urban intellectual centers, while in the heartland, well, they are baffled, still.

The story of *Requiem* is simple enough: Harry Goldfarb, junkie, and his companion, Tyrone C. Love, junkie, want to put together a bankroll and buy a "pound of pure," argot for an uncut bundle of heroin. The subplot involves Harry's mother, Sara, who wants to lose weight in order to appear on a television quiz show. As the action on the street grows meaner and more serious, Harry and Tyrone get more strung out, and Sara discovers diet pills. The novel begins with Harry locking his mother in the closet, so that he can pawn her TV set to buy "a taste." It thunders along in bunches of mountainous paragraphs. Harry and company get high in the morgue, surrounded by iced corpses; Sara is called up and told she is being considered as a contestant on a quiz show; Harry falls in love with Marion, another addict. By the end of the book Sara is in the back ward of a mental hospital, and Harry, less one arm infected by a dirty needle, is in a Southern jail along with Tyrone after an abortive attempt to set up a connection in Miami. Marion, with her dreams of opening a coffeehouse and art gallery, is turning tricks for a big-time dope dealer. And, yet, in spite of this degradation, the novel ends with transcendence, a crescendo that is something of a Blakeian illumination.

Selby echoes Dante, and like Eliot and Beckett he draws upon the Old Testament. Like them, Selby is able to step into the breach of the underworld and walk about observing Hell. Selby's self-lacerating souls seem to inhabit the deepest regions of the Inferno. They are the Violent-against- Themselves, the Violent-against-Others, and the Violent-against-Nature. In *Requiem*, the descent is not guided by Virgil, though, but by heroin itself, the antihero of this mystery. Heroin is both guide and persecutor, Antichrist, salvation and damnation in one glassine bag of mortal powder. Like the souls in *The Inferno*, the characters in Selby's new book move from skin-pop to skin-rot, from love of self and others into the damnable *bolgias* of the loveless, godlesss, the torturedly alone. Selby is relentless in his investigation of this descent, as particular and obsessive as either Beckett or Eliot. Like Dante, Selby deploys street slang, common speech, argot, and scatology to create high poetic art. With Selby, however, the poetry is American speech, and it seems to derive from the greatest American poetry—Whitman, Pound, Williams, Olson, and Selby's boyhood friend, the poet and novelist Gilbert Sorrentino.

In its use of the American idiom, *Requiem* corresponds to Melville's *Moby Dick*. Both writers are basically renegade Puritans, men whose moral indignation was tempered by American experiences. Both make known great truths which reach beyond the confines of language. In place of Melville's whale, Selby has chosen to work with two images, heroin and television, and by way of these metaphors, he creates a super-text which forces the language (poetry and TV quiz show/commercial/sitcom parlance) to rise above the story and, like poetry, to resonate with extra significance. Both Melville and

Selby learned prose from poets—the former from Shake-speare and the latter from Williams and Pound. *Moby Dick* and *Requiem* are great fictions which weld action to metaphor and give utterance to something previously possessed of impenetrable silence.

What puts Selby's new novel in its own class is its energy and vision. *Last Exit* and *The Room* were visionary and energetic too, but the former is really a collection of fictions, while *The Room* resembles a French philosophical novel. *The Demon*, Selby's last novel, has great blocks of prose energy but is marred, at times, by its violent sentimentality. *Requiem* is a consistent and energized vision, from first sentence to last, and it is also Selby's most obsessive and unsentimental book, even though some reviewers have chosen to misunderstand Selby's choice of pop-culture and sentimental TV jargon. *Requiem* is also Selby's most tendentious and moral work, the endpiece of the four novels, Selby said recently, completing a cycle of pathological study, showing the disease without offering a cure. The new cycle, he has said, will offer solutions as well.

While many contemporary novels have attempted to make heroin the central concern of their works, few writers, other than Selby and Burroughs, have made the metaphor work. Robert Stone began *Dog Soldiers* well, but the moment the dope scene left Saigon and the heroin dreams were acted out in California, the book, for me, fell apart. It seems impossible to make a sweet vision out of heroin, but Selby has managed to create a bebop symphony from it. There are two composers, Mahler and Coltrane, who are mentioned by various characters in the book and, rightly enough, *Requiem* is written like a fusion of their sounds. That alone, the music of this book, suggests the durability of what Selby has forged here. He really is one of our cultural assets, and his latest work could prove to be one of the great American novels of the century.

That review was written several years ago, and with a few minor changes, I would say it still represents my opinion about *Requiem for a Dream.* (Those interested in style might notice, tangentially, the difference here and elsewhere as I write, and a piece of copy after its been run through editorial fingers at a magazine.) The only addition I would make to that review, because it came out of a conversation with Selby afterward, is the point I made earlier about his fiction being like morality plays. The characters, in morality play fashion, seem to be Heroin, Television, Bad Deeds, Jew, Black Man, Junkie, Whore, Mother, American Dream, American Nightmare, and—as with the other books—the Dance of Death is part of the performance.

I would elaborate certain references made to other writers, for instance, Selby and Melville learned from poets, and what they learned is that words explode. With Dostoyevsky he shares that panoramic sense, a vision seeded with compassion, a passion for particulars, minutiae, literary detail. Selby is ultimately a highly moral writer, not unlike Eliot in the severity of their Christian thoughts. And like Flaubert's *Madame Bovary*, Selby takes an ersatz language (TV quiz shows) and makes a richly textured poetic text from it.

In Selby's voice characters become embodiments of moral and immoral urges. The locus of this voice is in the Christian universe. Harry Goldfarb is a Jew—and that is no casual detail in *Requiem*—because Selby's Christianity is biblical, i.e., Old and New Testament and because Christ was a Jew. (I used to make a point of explaining to my Catholic students at Fordham University, where I once taught, that Jesus never converted to Catholicism; that he returned to Heaven a Jew.)

Part of Selby's voice consists of Cotton Mather. Good, Evil, Control, Lack of Control, Grace, Guilt—these are Georgette's, Harry's, Vinnie's, Tyrone's, Marion's, Sara's other names.

"I don't rely on outward descriptions to reveal character," Selby said at the New School several years ago. "Rhythm creates the character."

It was at this gathering when Selby talked about his four novels being about pathologies without cures, and that his future work would introduce solutions to these pathologies. It is a remark like that where Selby's fundamentalist Christianity is most apparent. Pathology is solvable, therefore one finds salvation through rehabilitation. It goes back to Everyman's best buddy, Good Deeds. But solutions, finally, are the most dangerous area into which a moral writer ventures. What comes to mind is a bearded Tolstoy in his later years, the demigod extending his munificence to the lowly, whether reader or peasant. This track of literary morality leads eventually to gospellike pronouncements like those of John Gardner's *On Moral Fiction*. Selby would have to consider whether he would join Gardner were he to solve his characters' pathologies. What I am saying is, I am not sure a fiction writer has a right to tamper with the rhythms of his characters at all.

The seeing voice is not a moral thing. Ultimately it is simply a working force beyond social or moral issues, more aligned with the order of the universe. Voice operates by its own laws. When it sees, it is fiction. Seeing, it evokes. Were it to stop and comment, which is what a solution to a pathology would inflict on fiction, it no longer shows but tells, i.e., it is nonfiction then. The plenum of the imaginary world has been punctured. For instance, this inserting oneself between voice and sight—the commenting author—is partly the reason for *The Demon*'s weakness. The natural rhythm of the voice is subverted and its natural energy strays. There seem to be solutions everywhere in *The Demon*, especially its ending when Harry seeks to kill the cardinal in St. Patrick's Cathedral.

What is conscious in fiction is its breath. Moral solutions are a kind of artificial respiration, helpful maybe sometimes, but always unnatural. Conscience in fiction is a rhythmical concern, i.e., how faithful am I to my own breath and syllable? Even within *Requiem* Selby nearly comes up with solutions for his characters, especially Sara and Harry himself at the end. But because the energy of the voice is firm, it stays unbroken. This urge toward problem-solving was not unnoticed by Seymour Krim, a critic who championed Selby from the beginning of his career. It is like that adage: the intelligent man raises questions; the lunatic has answers. I hasten to add that madmen and saints have a lot in common, and Selby's idea to solve fictional problems in the future comes out of, I am quite certain, a saintly instinct. Yet Selby ought to heed another moral writer's example. Graham Greene knows, novel to novel, that people want sinners more than saints in their reading. A guilty, fallible Christian with an unsolvable life.

I once piqued Allen Ginsberg because I said that saying he was a Buddhist is like someone saying they are Protestant, because each has so many sects, each is a given condition in their cultures. Who is not a Buddhist in the Orient? And who is not a Protestant in certain areas of America? Which brings up another point about Selby's Christian voice. There is a broad set of differences between Catholics and Protestants theologically, and within Protestantism the variations are legion. Catholics are born with mortal sin, that is, they are sinners, from start to finish. Also, their religion allows for forgiveness by the act of confession. These ideas permeate a good deal of the voices in our time, from Robert Lowell to Thomas Merton, from Graham Greene to Evelyn Waugh. It is manifest in the writings of Flannery O'Connor and recently in Mary Gordon's novels. To sin is human; human beings sin. It is a construct of the Catholic writer's voice. What I am getting at is that Selby's Christian voice is Protestant. It has the wrath of God in it, even a touch of Divine Election. This is proven by one simple detail. Catholics generally are ignorant of the Old Testament, why, I am not sure, but they are. Protestants seem to know and appreciate it more. Catholics are most familiar with the Gospels, because of exposure to them in the Mass. Selby's Christian universe is that of the Old Testament. Forgiveness has nothing to do with the voice of this God. But Good Deeds might help.

Years ago in Los Angeles, when I first met Selby, he told me to read Babel and Chekhov, because "he (the latter) loved all his characters," Cubby said, and Babel "was able to forgive and be unjudgmental." I hope those writers' words still echo in Selby's ear, and that he will come upon his fiction as he always did, without judgment, the music in sight, the sight going into his tongue, and from there the words explode onto the page, that old rhythmical energy of his fiction.

Lastly, it should be noted that while this writer has had a considerable influence on my generation's writers—his example shows up in Richard Price's first and best novel, *The Wanderers*, as it does in several Vietnam War fictions; in my own work, in Chuck Wachtel's *Joe the Engineer*, in Tom McDonough's *Virgin with Child*—Selby never has received a single award in his lifetime, neither large nor small, locally or nationally. It amounts to a conspiracy of neglect how the literary establishment has ignored Selby's achievements. I know of a small press run by a couple of writers who were trying to raise money to publish Selby's stories, and had not been able to. I know he's written another novel, and yet a book has not come out in many years. (The exception to this is a collection of his stories which Marion Boyars published in 1985.) After he published *Last Exit* he lived for a long time on the West Coast. It was in the late sixties when he got clean of heroin and alcohol. He had one lung removed because of tuberculosis; he is diabetic; he cannot be in a room where people smoke. In the late seventies and the early part of this decade, he lived outside New York City, then moved to Greenfield, Massachusetts. The last I heard he was back on the West Coast, working in a gas station; now, I understand, writing a film script. No one I know has heard from him in quite some time. It reminds me that our country gave Melville the same treatment. We are a nation of ingrates at times, with a record of disgrace toward our native genius, especially the literary ones. We pamper writers with a tenth of our great writers' talents. This disregard of Selby has been so consistent and so prolonged, I could imagine some representative of a genius foundation pulling into his gas station and offering him a lifetime of leisure with a fellowship to write, and after filling up the tank, checking the oil, and giving him his change, Selby, like Bartleby, would say:

"I prefer not to."

7

Vietnam: The American Ronin

I REMEMBER WATCHING, ritualistically, a week of "Million Dollar Movie" on television as a kid, watching and rewatching, night after night, a war movie called *A Walk in the Sun*. What purpose, what passion those soldiers had! They understood what was at stake, they understood each other, and they understood the chain of command. I am talking about the good soldier. Like their Eastern counterpart, the samurai, these soldiers understood the hierarchy of a world at war, they knew right relationships, that of master to pupil, of regular soldier to officer, and maybe the only thing better than those soldiers was John Wayne himself. The first movie I ever saw in the Gates Theatre on Broadway in East New York was *She Wore a Yellow Ribbon*. I am talking about strong quiet men, which reminds me of a remark I heard the fiction writer Asa Baber make at a conference on Vietnam War literature.

"When my son asks me, Daddy, how do wars start?" Baber said, "I'm going to tell him—*quietly.*"

How he whispered that last word, as though to give new coloring to *The Quiet American* and *All Quiet on the Western Front.* As Kurasawa himself knew, this quiet type is a cowboy or soldier in Western culture and the samurai in the East. Same-same. From Homer to Ireland's Fenian Cycles, right up to the almost present, it was this strong quiet type which dominated the literature of war. It is, as Ezra Pound knew perfectly well, a downright Confucian thing. This man of courage also knows right actions, and he sees the world in terms of what preceded him and what follows. He is more epical than dramatic, a distinction worth keeping in mind. He is Achilles; or he is Odysseus; or he is Finn Mackool or Cuchulain, one minute a fair-skinned, shy, quiet soul, the next minute, dropping his ogam stick, he goes into warp-spasms, and he annihilates a horde of ten thousand, including the slaughter of their cattle.

As I said, he is also John Wayne, even before John Wayne became this persona. He wears a white hat. He rides a white horse. He respects things and others. He is courtly with women, but vigorously manly with women of reputation, most of it regarding ill repute. He is outraged by injustice and evil. He is part of a noble process. The last of his kind died out at the end of World War II, though sometimes he was resurrected during the Korean War, and the myths of his exploits lingered for a decade and a half longer. What remains today is his legend.

What happened to this samurai type can be explained by an Arab story a friend told me a lifetime ago in San Francisco. It is about three travelers who come to the gates of a city at night, only to find it closed. The three travelers are an alcoholic, a pothead, and an opium smoker. First, the alcoholic attempts a solution; he bangs on the huge door; he fumes and curses. Finally he falls down, exhausted, frustrated, still boiling. The pothead has a cooler solution; he suggests that the three of them spend the night outside the gate, sleeping in the open air. But it is the opium smoker whose solution is most ingenious; he suggests that they slip through the keyhole.

The answer to what happened to the samurai comes from a Nchaioui proverb, which Paul Bowles used for the title of a lovely book of four stories: "A pipe of Kif before breakfast gives a man the strength of a hundred camels in the courtyard."

By the mid-sixties dope was an American way of life, even an institution among the young, and that hazy perspective made John Wayne look like the biggest dufus on the planet. But this new perception of the Wayne type, even that proto-type in movies like *The Longest Day*, was not universally shared by young Americans. There were still enough straight people around between Berkeley and New York, Los Angeles to Boston. To America's heartlanders John Wayne still meant something real, palpable, a representative of that un-dying myth of the warrior, the cowboy-soldier, the samurai as he was understood to the West.

John Wayne is perhaps the single most evoked name in the literature of the Vietnam War. Mind you, it is not always flat-tering. A type of wild-assed soldiering was considered to be "John Wayning it." A young soldier might have visions of John Wayne early on in many of the more conventional of the Vietnam War novels, dreaming of personal glory while in flight or in a troop transport ship. But once these young Americans—the average age was nineteen—came in at Dan-ang or the airstrip outside of Saigon, this perception of John Wayne soon altered. As the novelist Larry Heinemann (*Close Quarters*) said in a letter: "I always understood John Wayne as a put-down; as a parody; a joke, a folk myth the likes of Pe-cos Bill and Paul Bunyan . . . John Wayne always meant a pushiness, a foolhardy self-destructiveness. The John Waynes of your platoon were best got rid of by the most direct route, because dumb guys never lasted. The most valuable man was not John Wayne, but the calculating murderer who could be depended on to produce results, and not just run around like a chicken with its head cut off."

As Heinemann suggests, eventually the strong quiet young Americans, even the Duke's fans, lost their bearings. Call it what you want. Some said, *Dinky-dau* (crazy). Years later a VA shrink might call it posttraumatic-stress-disorder. Other wars called it combat fatigue or shell shock. Whatever you wanted to call it, it meant simply that a quiet American—of the nonspook variety—went into a combat situation franchised, without delusions, and full of patriotism, but over 365 days of a tour of duty and a lifetime recovering from that tour, many of the voices to emerge from the Vietnam experience were more raving than quiet, and they were no longer pupils of a master.

"Most veterans I've come across," Heinemann said to me, "strike me as ex-patriots in the double sense of the word." He also noted that the soldiers who were establishment but not particularly franchised or patriotic, "the go-alongs," he calls them, were conscripted (like himself) "with soul-deadening dread as though they were submitting to punishment—and I mean a wild thrashing with the buckle end of a belt, mind you. . . . By and large draftees were under no illusion of patriotism, and the guys who volunteered learned of their betrayal soon enough." Patriot or go-along, the ideal world of John Wayne disappeared. The noble samurai world disappeared. Instead patriot and go-along alike became masterless samurai in Vietnam, i.e, right action and the hierarchical orders disappeared. When the center did not hold, the rough beast to emerge was the ronin, the masterless samurai, a warrior from the East who entered the mind and body of the Western grunt, the boonierat, the trooper, the swinging dick.

Untethered from a master, the ronin is not a master himself. But how did this happen to a good old American boy, who like Bruce Springsteen sings, was born in the USA? French literature from Malraux to recent examples like Marguerite Duras' *Lover* show that Southeast Asia is a landscape which is unfathomable, a kind of labyrinth from which the observer never exits. Something about this landscape, lush, tropical, steamy, does not invite you in, but instead possesses you, your imagination, your mind and body. The French knew this for one hundred years, but when they left they forgot to tell the Americans. Joseph Ferrandino—a fiction writer and the literary consultant for the Vietnam memorial in New York City—as he writes: "Vietnam has many elements in common with other wars." But how then did right action and the hierarchical orders disappear? Ferrandino goes on to explain how the conventional warrior became a ronin by circumstance and the conditions in-country, this transformation almost immediate.

"Very few soldiers went to Vietnam as part of an organized unit. The soldiers neither trained nor travelled together. There was little or no chance to develop relationships under relaxed conditions. There was little or no group identification other than a mailing address in common. Strangers were thrown together in an intense situation. They shared this situation on an intimate, yet impersonal, basis. Each man arrived in-country alone; each one left the same way."

Ferrandino points out that perhaps the most insidious element of this circumstance about Vietnam, which made

it unlike any other American war, was the fact of the unde-
fined enemy. He writes: "The VC in the body count looked
exactly like the friendly Vietnamese barber back in the base
camp."

This is how a warrior first glimpses himself something other
than what he first perceived; some otherness pervades him.
But having once known what a warrior is—having strived for
that realm which the master preached—the ronin decides on
a new strategy. In place of honor, valor, bravery, in place of
courage—he decides to stay alive—to survive. What the
ronin learns, as Ferrandino says, he "learned, under fire,
that survival is the only rule."

Many young men went into the military, either drafted or
as volunteers, and especially in that last category, considering
themselves as though sons of John Wayne. They were pupils
studying with a master; they hoped one day to become samurai. As the poet W. D. Ehrhart told me in a conversation,
they were "franchised, establishment, and patriotic." They
were also what William Carlos Williams would call "the pure
products of America," and like that description from
"Spring and All," they went crazy. They were always patriots, from beginning to end, and they have kept that ideal
even into later years of disillusionment; but they did become,
many of them, disenfranchised and antiestablishment, and
their largest majority, if not as nonwriting civilians, then
those veterans who took up the pen are mostly writing in bittersweet resonances of the voice.

With his roots gone, the masterless samurai can be a disordered and dangerous man. Yes, he is still a great warrior.
Don't think for a minute he is not. But he roams through a
fugitive world. Like Isaac Babel, a soldier in another age, he
must live with impossible contradictions, and this was accomplished mostly through "the genre of silence," a literary
form of which many of these writers are masters. Frank Mill-

er's ingenious cartoon creation *Ronin*, a futuristic ongoing tale of this figure, often resembles that dispirited world of the Vietnam War veteran. His ronin is armless and legless, a kind of experimental mind, who occasionally transforms himself into a centuries old ronin when he gets into rages. Miller's ronin lives in a futuristic urban world of such rot and decay, of postmodern dregs, as though everything had turned into a firebase. More than postmodern, though, I think it really the imagination of America after Vietnam; it is really post-Vietnam.

Like the samurai, the ronin can be a poet; in fact, in a voiced consciousness, in this literature, in these novels, the American ronin often possesses the voice of a poet. And his grief is a poet's. Through a range of that poet's voice, many of the ronins have transformed themselves into samurai. Reading many of these transformed warriors, something quite amazing happens. Suddenly you find yourself rootless, untethered, even disenfranchised and antiestablishment and patriotic. It is as though the American ronin had possessed you, turning the reader into the masterless samurai. If we read these novels and poems and see these plays, it is for that reason—and I do read Vietnam War fiction with a great hunger to know, even resembling at times a reader with an addiction to this voice. Others may devour mysteries and thrillers; I have found my obsessive genre to be Vietnam War literature, not the histories or the political analysis, but the imaginative worlds created by the voices of the imaginative writers. Reading them, that pervasive rootlessness of a generation, mine and theirs, is put to rest momentarily. I am no longer the wandering ronin, or that part of me which feels that way is succored. I have attached myself to a master.

I mentioned earlier that the history of the samurai type in our literature goes back to Homer, and invariably he is a voice in the collective tones of the epic. It is a distinction—

about epic and drama—worth holding on to. The hero does not have to be particularized, for it is his actions which resonate, not his individual personality. It is a story in a narrative form, whereas the drama is a rhythm of experience which heightens by leaving out as much as it puts in and it is a voice built from tensions, push and pull, and often unresolvable actions. Nearly all the imaginative writings about the Vietnam War are dramaturgical; they are texts set in a theater of action, spectacles, even, and their highest thread of energy— particularized—is found in the voice.

Let me start with John Clark Pratt's compilation entitled, naturally enough, *Vietnam Voices*. The author/compiler is a retired lieutenant colonel with the U.S. Air Force who "flew 101 combat hours in nine different kinds of aircraft," and who wrote one of the few experimental novels about the experience, *The Laotian Fragments* (1974). He also is a professor of English at Colorado State, an eminent scholar, and as knowledgeable an authority, both of the literature and history of this war, as nearly anyone around today. His massive volume *Vietnam Voices* is given a subject index for political science/history, but really it is more than that. I have heard Pratt himself refer to it as "The Super Fragments," meaning that it is an experimental work, like his novel, and an extension of that voice into a broader arena. It is over seven hundred pages of primary documentation, from the literature, from the Defense Department, from the Vietnamese, north and south, from novelists and poets—from nearly every source imaginable. Its contents are offered as a Senecan tragedy with a prologue, acts 1 through 5, and an epilogue. Its bibliography alone consists of years of exhaustive research, most of the literature housed in a Vietnam collection at Colorado State.

As in his novel *The Laotian Fragments* and in his super fragments *Vietnam Voices*, Pratt sets the voice of this experience in a context, which he says "is a combination of fact and fiction." It is. The nonfiction uses fictional techniques; and the fiction borrows from facts, is often transparently autobiographical. Most of the novels are realistic, action-oriented memoirs, chronological in detail, clocking 365 days in-country, and they start with heroic innocence, quite often, as I said, evoking John Wayne early on. They most often end in disillusionment, fractured states, and that ronin's consciousness of being rootless and untethered, masterless samurai. Pratt's own novel is one of the few bright exceptions to this tendency. Its voice is steely and cool, distant, analytical, and it owes a lot to French experimental writers like Robbe-Grillet.

The voice is ironical, most of the "documents" compiled by York Harding, who is the figure which Pyle, the quiet American of Graham Greene's novel about Vietnam, refers to as his mentor and the author of the Third Force theory in Southeast Asia. Harding is a presence more than a character in Greene's novel, and he keeps his spectral eminence in Pratt's novel as well. His role in *The Fragments* is to document the life of Major William Blake, MIA. Like the later scholarly work *Vietnam Voices*, Pratt uses a combination of fact and fiction for his novel, combining intelligence summaries, diary entries, message traffic, news releases, and poems to create a kind of voiceless voice.

If there is a rhythm of experience in the novel, and I think there is, it is that cool, lofty perch from which pilots look down at us humans, and in this instance, pilots who mark bomb sites with tracers or who swoop in to drop their payloads, napalm, missiles, bombs, it is all a lot of spaghetti and green salad and bright sparks below, i.e., Pratt has the exact perspective in his narrative strategy to capture the rhythm of experience in that analytical voice. This is what the *seeing* voice takes in from ten thousand or thirty thousand feet or higher, a vantage from the clouds that only William Blakes are given.

It is worth noting here another experimental writing, this by Kenneth Gangemi entitled *The Interceptor Pilot*, in which the lofty coolness of the plexiglas and metal-enclosed seeing voice makes its fiction by telling the story in the form of a screenplay, another kind of cool and lofty distancing. Gangemi's tale is about Professor Wilson, a former combat pilot during the Korean War, who defects to the Russians in order to become a fighter pilot for North Vietnam. It begins:

"The beginning of the film is set at a Naval Air Station somewhere in the western United States. . . . It will be a western landscape of sagebrush and semi-desert plains and striking mountains."

Both Pratt's and Gangemi's cool voices (Gangemi is a former pilot with the air force, too) suggest how the samurai first lost his voice and later became a ronin. His first dissolution came about because of technology. The samurai no longer faced other samurai or no longer faced other human adversaries; he was coming up against machines, first tanks, then planes. William Crawford Woods documents this dissolution in his novel, *The Killing Zone*, (1970) a work set in New Jersey. There, at a boot camp, recruits are put through their paces in preparation for Vietnam, but somewhere along the way a computer enters into their training, live ammunition is inserted into its programming, and the atrocities start even before these characters leave the world. Not only is the ronin masterless; he also must go into combat against inhuman and nonhuman things. That is another reason for his untethering. John Wayne never flew jet planes. In Vietnam he flew helicopters.

To illustrate how Pratt combined fact and fiction in his novel, it should be pointed out that *The Laotian Fragments* had to be cleared by the government before publication. But lest I romanticize this juxtaposition out of hand, let me say that he is not alone in his estimate that those who experienced Vietnam and then wrote about Vietnam invariably had to combine fact and fiction in order to accomplish it. Pratt's novel is full of scholarship, and his scholarship (*Vietnam Voices*) is full of fiction, both his own and other Vietnam and Southeast Asia writers. As Philip D. Beidler writes in *American Literature and the Experience of Vietnam*: "Mainly, Vietnam would always be a place with no real points of reference, then *or* now. As once in experiential fact, so now in memory as well. It would become the task of the Vietnam writer to create a landscape that never was, one might say—a landscape of consciousness where it might be possible to accommodate experience remembered within a new kind of imaginative cartography endowing it with large configurings of value and signification. In this way, what facts that could be found might still be made to mean, as they had never done by themselves, through the shaping, and ultimately the transforming power of art."

Fact and fiction: Magritte's painting of a pipe with the words—"this is not a pipe"—written on the canvas.

Fact and fiction: Old woman, old men, mothers, children, young men, run from a burning village. The sound of AK-47's and M-16 rifle fire in the background. The sound of choppers in the background. Cobra gunships relieving their payload of rockets and mortar and automatic fire. A medevac helicopter dusting off the wounded. Then a voice superimposed behind these images: "This is not a war."

These are nothing but facts I offer above. Still, it is worth considering them. A person who sees, though, can maybe recount facts; a voice that sees can bend facts into fiction. Consider this description of the land in Vietnam from Tim O'Brien's *Going after Cacciato*: "He knew from long days on the march that there was nothing loathsome about the smell of the paddies. The smell was alive: bacteria, fungus and algae, compounds that made and sustained life. It was not a pretty smell, but it was no more evil or rank than the smell of sweat. Sometimes, when there was no choice, he had slept in the paddies. He knew the softness and warmth, later the chill. He had spent whole nights that way, his back against a dike and his feet and legs and lap deep in the paddies. Once, on the very hottest day at the war, he had even taken a drink of paddy water, and he knew the taste. He'd swirled the water in his hands, letting the biggest chunks of filth settle, then, because his thirst had been greater than the fear of disease, he'd swallowed."

There is an old Korean story about two monks journeying to China, but as they went into the northern mountains, one monk traveled on, the other did not. He did not need to go to China, because China was in his mind. Reading a passage like O'Brien's makes us realize that if you read this literature carefully, if you read the right examples of the literature, fact and fiction merge, there is a pipe and the words that say, This is not a pipe. There are the images of war, palpable, emotionally rendered, there is that paddy, not only sighted, but inhabited, smelled, heard, tasted, as O'Brien makes us do in that passage above. In his study of the literature about the war, Philip Beidler writes that "one truly did not have to go to Vietnam to bring the experience home in literature." But I think one has to read this literature in order to get a sense of Vietnam. As Asa Baber said, it begins quietly. But then it explodes. This is not a fact; it is fiction.

Let me frame the fiction of Vietnam by its poetry and its drama. The facts are there already, and I don't need to bring

them out. By its very nature Vietnam War literature inter-
mingles constantly with fact. Instead of fact, let me begin
with a representative voice from the poetry, that of W. D.
Ehrhart. He is a familiar presence to anyone who saw "Vietnam: A TV History" on the PBS networks in 1983. As a
principal interviewee of the fifth episode Ehrhart appeared—
aviator glasses, long hair, mustache—the essence of what has
come to be thought of as the Vietnam-veteran look. His measured voice, flat and countrylike, though, was anything but
typical, either of veterans or writers today. That voice may
possess matter-of-fact rhythms, but often that quality
masques a content which bristles with intelligence and finally
is downright startling. What Ehrhart experienced is amazing
enough, but the human tendency is to forget these things; Bill
Ehrhart forgets nothing, yet there is little bitterness in his
charged, emotional landscapes. His most recent work, *To
Those Who Have Gone Home Tired: New & Selected Poems* (1984),
is proof of that voice's deceptiveness, openness, and emotional
range.

I do not think there is *a* voice from the Vietnam War years,
but as I said, I think Ehrhart's is a good representation, and
what he represents with that voice is the disenfranchised,
antiestablishment patriot, the ronin, I mean. If not a master
to follow, the American ronin has a library of references to
help him along, including voices from Thoreau and Thomas
Paine. Even in the varied and rich spectrum of Vietnam War
voices, Ehrhart has qualities which are quite unique, part of
it being the medium in which his voice sees. What I mean is,
he writes poetry, and that is an unusual form in which to ex-
press the rhythms of this experience.

The standards by which Ehrhart's voice operates are those
of good contemporary poetry, including concision, the image-

laden line which is regulated by breath and syllable, open-field composition, and language charged with energy and emotion. In a poem entitled "Hunting," he writes: "The thought occurs/ that I have never hunted anything in my whole life/ except other men." There it is! His voice sees not so much by way of the imagination, but through observation of recalled things and events, thereby evoking feelings through those trapped objects. In "Hunting," for instance, Ehrhart happens upon his observations by conjuring the experience of taking aim with a weapon.

> Sighting down the long black barrel,
> I wait till front and rear sights
> form a perfect line on his body,
> then slowly squeeze the trigger.

The poet's work is not to comment and judge, and mostly Ehrhart does neither of these in his poems. He observes; then he conjures. His job is to evoke and show, and these things Ehrhart does in abundance. He is out to find the rhythm of that experience—I mean that overriding experience of combat which is there as a subtext even in poems not directly dealing with the war—re-creating it through sight and sound. Oddly enough, this strategy is one of the few that literally makes sense when it comes to Vietnam.

> The long day's march is over.
> Ten thousand meters through the bush
> with flak jacket, rifle, helmet,
> three hundred rounds of ammunition,
> three days' rations, two canteens,
> hand grenades, a cartridge belt;
> pack straps grinding at the shoulders,
> feet stuffed in boots that stumble forward
> mile after hill after hour . . .
>   ("Another Life)

In that last movement, abstract space merges with literal field of experience, and then it bleeds back into abstraction (time).

This kind of observation of detail belies some recent notions that Vietnam War writings are all generic, of a kind. By placing these voices into a genre—even I used the word—it is a facile way to ignore, first, their content and, second, and maybe more important, their esthetic values, that seeing voice. While Ehrhart is a Vietnam War writer, I am not sure it helps us to discover his voice by "labeling" him that. He is that, okay, but he is also that and something else—something more. Much of his poetry, while informed by the war, is also about other seeing things. Ehrhart seems to be walking point for us into the future, i.e., his and other voices are cutting new paths in our literature. They are leading the way, I mean, not dancing to a different drumbeat. It is not so much morality, which Ehrhart and other writers on this subject have to some degree more strongly than other contemporaries. But I am not sure moral voices in our imaginative writing is what we desperately need. More than morality, though, these voices present a new way of *seeing* things by way of voice.

In the case of W. D. Ehrhart, his later and new poems still contain political contents and resonate with the voice of his moral outrage, but the images are more ironical and humorous. A poem like "The Reason Why" is about the Russians taking over the world: Afghanistan, Nicaragua. "tomorrow/ New Jersey. Atlantic City!"

Sweet
Jesus, all those elegant casinos
in the hands of Reds. That's why
we need missiles. MX missiles.
Cruise missiles. Pershing missiles.
Let'em try to take the Boardwalk;
we'll blow their godless hats off.

I confess to a certain nostalgia when I hear Ehrhart's voice, and it goes back to a time, not so much of the war itself, but those days in the 1960s, hanging out at St. Mark's Poetry Project, Paul Blackburn ran the Monday Night Reading Series, and I can picture Ehrhart coming in the door with these poems—not that he did, mind you—but that I can imagine it. It is a tone, a temperament, a stance, which reminds me of that time. Besides this nostalgia, I have some tougher feelings about his work. The war and politics are not his only domains. His *Selected Poems* really expresses a range of tones, various landscapes and objects that his voice inhabits.

Book to book Ehrhart seems to become a better poet, a finer craftsman, I mean, and so he is able to extend his range considerably each time. A new ripple in his voice has to do with love poems, idyllic poems of the sea and the land, a poem to a grandmother, addresses to a woman. Tenderness is more apparent, even in the early war poems, than toughness, though obviously Ehrhart is a combat-ready sort of guy. I get the feeling, reading his latest collection, that our lives often depend on voices like Ehrhart's.

> I used to fear death.
> Now I only fear
> a slow and violent death;
> and even that, I know,
> will be bearable.
>
> ("Rootless")

Rootless, I would add, like a ronin untethered.

Two notable poets, besides Ehrhart, who write of the Vietnam experience in their poetry are Bruce Weigl and John Balaban, a combat veteran and a conscientious objector, respectively. Balaban was a student at Harvard during the war, when he notified his draft board that he wished to change his deferred student status to that of a conscientious objector. The draft board advised him not to do this, because it might mean that he would end up in Vietnam. But Vietnam is where Balaban wanted to go, and so his draft board accommodated him. From Harvard he went to the Mekong Delta, where he worked as a linguist until the Tet Offensive in 1968. Thereafter he served as a field representative for the Committee of Responsibility, ministering to wounded children. John was wounded himself. His stay in Vietnam, given his status, was considerably longer than a soldier's. He returned to the country again in the 1970s, ostensibly to make a documentary and to collect Vietnamese oral folk poetry, which he published in his book of translations, *Ca Dao Vietnam*.

Balaban's poetry and translations are no less striking than the above thumbnail biography suggests. As a poet he is quite skillful, a Poundian sort of technician, so that his voice emerges layered, even tropical, and allusive. His method is not so much to pare down as to build up, the voice ranging from the vernacular to the classical. He is a synthesizer, not in the sense of an artificer patching together disparities but rather like that electronic musical instrument, he replicates several instruments at once, keyboard to drums, I mean. Where Ehrhart's voice is reedy and folksy, Balaban's voice speaks in tongues and is backed by a Moog. Consider this poem entitled "Gardenia" from a longer sequence in his book, *After Our War*:

> The scent of gardenia and campsmoke shifts
> across laundries, hammocks, and tents.
> With white, thick, waxy, double petals a jasmine
> gardenia reeks, a prostitute in a stripped garden.

Under a planked jetty, some soldiers and their little sons
skinny dip, foaming the silted river with suds.
Below a lotus blooming in the mucky shallows,
a crab sidles through a basket rotting in the mud.
In midstream, huge egrets lift off the bamboo marshes.
I hear my name called: "Mr. American!"
by a pajamaed young mother who grins and beckons,
slapping a broken slipper and waddling my way.
Closing to her thumb the fingers of a white hand,
in the bud-hole of those loose doubled petals
she pokes her other index, and smiles. Tilting her chin,
she pokes her finger again and again and smiles.

Lush, even tropical in abundance, Balaban's poems make one pause about whether the lushness came from his Vietnam experience or whether Balaban's lush moods were imported into the country upon his arrival. This richness and density of language is likewise evidenced in his first novel, *Going Down Slow*, which chronicles the Dantesque lives and days of several Western characters after Vietnam. Their ultimate slide into drugs and passionless sex bring them into the Golden Triangle, the opium epicenter of Southeast Asia.

His poetry and prose often beat a rhythm between the ornamental and the elemental. Meaning, some of Balaban's writings are quite simple and direct. Take, for instance, his Vietnamese translations, *ca dao*, oral folk poetry, often transmitted by one—verbal rich, nonreading—generation to another, on the tongue, on the hoof, like the troubadours, like the ancient mimes. It was his intention in the seventies to record as much of this poetry as he could before it disappeared into the cultural defoliation with the fall of the South Vietnamese government.

Having translated Korean poetry myself, I can say there are similarities with Vietnamese folk poetry, but that is not surprising, since both countries, however distant geographically, share borders with China whose poetry is a wellspring for all nations, East or West. A shared imagery emerges, too, from both countries' utilizing Chinese characters to some degree, although in *ca dao* this influence would be negligible because of the poetry's oralness. Where real similarities exist is in the agrarian worlds that Vietnam and Korea inhabited until this century, with Vietnam more or less keeping that simpler, nonindustrial culture, while Korea became heavily industrialized after its civil war. Finally, to an American, there is that false similarity, because both countries are joined to our history by wars of liberation, South Korea having fought to a draw, while South Vietnam collapsed.

> The Saigon River slides past the Old Market,
> its broad waters thick with silt. There,
> the rice shoots gather a fragrance,
> the fragrance of my country home,
> recalling my mother home, arousing deep love.

Robert Olen Butler, the novelist, himself a former translator in the army while stationed in Vietnam, has told me how Vietnamese is an intonational language, meaning it literally it is not only *what* you say, but *how* you say it. One sound can be intoned seven different ways, resulting in seven different meanings. This aspect in Vietnamese language, less evidenced in Korean and Chinese certainly, was concretized at a reading where I heard Balaban recite some of the *ca dao* from his book. He chanted, he sang, he gave voice to those images; he literally made others weep in the room; it was extraordinary, as performance, as poetry.

In his own poetry Balaban is more likely to seek out the ornate and elegant, but that simpler impulse which he incorporates in his Vietnamese translations is also evident in his own poems at times. One of the loveliest examples of this simpler voicing is found in a poem entitled "Letter from a Bargirl":

> my dearest darling
> hi/ how are you
> ihop eeveything is abight with you,iam fine
> im imi i miss you verym m uch
> doy yóurh/   you miss me/
> fuck you
> iwant to fuck youó
>
> i think about you all time
> you alays in mha heart
>
> make love na
>
>   make.love.not..war........
>
> fuck....you
>
> Monique

As Philip Beidler points out so well in his study of this literature, Balaban creates a character here "who manages, as most of us do at one time or another, to get it all right and all wrong all at once."

Then comes Bruce Weigl, probably the finest poet to articulate the war experience both at home and in-country. A hallmark of the Vietnam writers seems to be their network of communication between themselves, and a generosity toward other writers which I've found nowhere else in the community of American writing. I am not saying there are no rivalries or competitions, because that would be a naive and incorrect observation. But there is a camaraderie among many of these writers because of a shared geography, emotionally, imagistically, experientially, and imaginatively. I mention this because I first heard of Weigl from Larry Heinemann, who strongly recommended his poetry to me. That was followed by W. D. Ehrhart's also recommending Weigl's poems. The only other instance of this mutual aid in a literary community that I personally am aware of is with the poets from the late 1950s (the New York School, Black Mountain, the Beats, the San Francisco poets), but ultimately those groups fractured and splintered over time.

One has to go back to James Wright's poetry to recall when a writer used the fallen, industrial landscape of the Midwest as effectively as Bruce Weigl does, or go back to Robert Frost to remember when an American poet used narrative as the primary strategy in poetic construction. These qualities are evident in Weigl's first major collection of poetry, *A Romance*, and even more strongly crafted and assured in his second, *The Monkey Wars*. His second book of poetry easily stands up to any comparisons. When his miniature dramas are not revealing a mythical and violent Midwest, they unveil a disruptive, war-gutted Vietnamese landscape in a way I can recall no other writer doing. Sometimes both of these worlds collide, spiralling into poems like "The Snowy Egret" and "Song of Napalm."

Weigl writes about ordinary people who find themselves—as the result of irreversible choices—in extraordinary conditions. His medium of address is a hard-edged, pared-down lyricism, a passionate open-verse style. These values often make his poems read like short short fiction or miniature dramas, and the effect is quite startling. The "plots" often spin off from dramatic reversals, for instance, a moment in which a grandfather kills a chicken, cuts off its head, and makes a puppet out of it, pecking his grandson ("Killing Chickens"). The narrator says, "He did it so I would remember him."

This is not an isolated example of how Weigl transforms a moment. By a kind of purposeful utterance grown into a dramatic complication, his narratives lead to recognitions. "Noise" and "For the Wife Beater's Wife" arc out in similar fashion, and this quality is best demonstrated in a poem like "Hope," in which a factory worker named Joe "drinks too much and hates / Anybody who is not white." Part of the genius of these "stories" is how Weigl makes us sympathize with characters like Joe, even after he tries to save an injured dog, but finally kills it because "it didn't have no hope."

The dramatic characteristics of this writing are best demonstrated in Weigl's poems about Vietnam. Some of the poems are reversals, turning tragic settings into epiphanies ("Girl at the Chu Lai Laundry"). This particular poem is remarkable for how it counters stereotypical war poems which dwell only on violations. Here in the most unexpected landscape, a moment of beauty blossoms:

> My miserable platoon was moving out
> One day in the war and I had my clothes in the laundry.
> I ran the two dirt miles,
> Convoy already forming behind me. I hit
> The block of small hooches and saw her
> Twist out the black rope of her hair in the sun.
> She did not look up at me,
> Not even when I called to her for my clothes.
> She said I couldn't have them,
> They were wet . . .

Without the rhythm of experience informing Weigl's voice, it might only be two miles back to the hooches, but to a poet who knows, it is "two dirt miles," in a war zone, in a war-torn country, out in the boonies, like they say, and seeing her "twist out the black rope of her hair in the sun," you only hope her ville never winds up in a free-fire zone, that while the image of her private moment is immortalized in a poem, you also hope that she at least lives a natural life-span, can excite in her private moments in fact, how she turns us around, turns us on, and thrills us in this fiction found in the emotional machinery of a poem.

But this one beautiful instance in Weigl's poetry is not enough to displace the greater reality of war. Other poems literally render this fallen, battered world:

> Into that pit
>   I had to climb down
> With a rake and matches; eventually,
>   You had to do something
> Because it just kept piling up
>   And it wasn't our country, it wasn't
> Our air thick with the sick smoke
>   So another soldier and I
> Lifted the shelter off its blocks
>   To expose the home-made toilets:
> Fifty-five gallon drums cut in half
>   With crude wood seats that splintered.
>   ("Burning Shit at An Khe")

The best of these poems begin in nearly pastoral elegance, and work into concussive illuminations. "Temple near Quang Tri, Not on the Map" commences with "ivy thick with sparrows," a detail which literally allows us to date this poem because by the end of America's involvement few terrains had sparrows to speak of. The poem culminates with a squad of American soldiers coming upon an old man muttering to himself in a small jungle temple.

> His face becomes visible, his eyes
> Roll down to the charge
> Wired between his teeth and the floor.

The poem ends with an eerie implosion, reminding me of Asa Baber's remark that wars begin quietly. Weigl's poem ends on that kind of pastoral silence when "sparrows/Burst off the walls into the jungle." As is the case in all great dramas, nothing is quite the same.

Weigl's poetry even offers interpretive readings outside the dramatic arena and its attendant fictions. I mean, there are pyschological aspects which have more to do with facts, with cause and effect, let's say. Take the preceding poem, for instance, which shows a jungle ambush where American soldiers get blown away. What feeling arises, not for us, but for those grunts in the bush? I would say anger, no, I would say *rage*, the killer instinct, where the mind blanks, the body works on fatigued reflex, and you walk, one step at a time because of mines, with the safety off, ready to rock & roll. The cause is the old man with the charge wired to his body in the little jungle temple near Quang Tri. Its effect does not come out until a poem like "Surrounding Blues on the Way Down," which is a companion piece to the other poem in this factual world of cause and effect, however dreary the conditions of these two physical elements. The narrator says, "I was barely in country," which shows us that *he* is not yet a wheel in the machinery of war's cause and effect. He is the tragic observer, though.

> Brothers of the heart he said and smiled
> Until we came upon a mama san
> Bent over from her stuffed sack of flowers.
> We flew past her but he hit the brakes hard,
> He spun the tires backwards in the mud.
> He did not hate the war either,
> Other reasons made him cry out to her
> So she stopped,
> She smiled her beetle black teeth at us.

This is a three-stanza poem that could as easily be called a three-act play. There is the setup in the first stanza, the complication in the second, and the tragic resolution in the third. The tragic perception is offered by the narrator, but the actors are really the old woman (protagonist) and the soldier driving the jeep (antagonist). Like characters in a play, they have objectives, and obstacles in the way of those objectives; they are motivated, they have emotional states which propel them into action. This is not Shakespearean so much or Chekhovian so much as it is Brechtian. *The Good Woman of Setzuan* and *Mother Courage* come to mind. It has none of the ha-ha perception of war that Sergeant Bilko provided our youth or the entertainment Alan Alda provided us in M*A*S*H, that most popular of Korean War diversions on television. The images are as assaultive as on-the-scene Electronic News Gathering (ENG), only the voice is not Walter Cronkite's, it is Bruce Weigl, a poet who plunges speech into the blackest depths of his soul to make a revelation.

> I have no excuse for myself.
> I sat in that man's jeep in the rain
> And watched him slam her to her knees,
> The plastic butt of his M-16
> Crashing down on her.

These violent moments are not gratuitous in the compact machinery of Weigl's poetry. Instead they are used to unmask, to reveal, to illuminate, and to articulate our deeper, more troubled emotions. That he accomplishes these resolutions of action in poem after poem is remarkable. A poem like "The Last Lie" is equally taut with fact bled into fiction, this time the victim not a mama san—though it could be suggested that the young soldier in the previous poem is the worst victim of all—but rather the children:

> Some guy in the miserable convoy
> Raised up in the back of our open truck
> And threw a can of c-rations at a child
> Who called into the rumble for food.
> He didn't toss the can, he wound up and hung it
> On the child's forehead and she was stunned
> Backwards into the dust of our trucks.

Weigl's midwestern poems are equally powerful, evoking lonely mill-town bars, violent husbands, crazed workers, young boys who kill egrets or blow off their fingers with fire-crackers, and these dramatic miniatures of our heartland merge with those historical instances of our war in Vietnam. I would venture to say that some of Weigl's war poems match any in the language in any period, including the poets from World War I whom Paul Fussell so brilliantly analysed in *The Great War and Modern Memory*. The totality of Weigl's achievment is quite extraordinary.

One way of explaining the deluge of Vietnam War writings in the last couple of years has to do with this need to break the silence, to merge image with voice, to let speech *see*. I am talking about a *necessity* to say, a kind of dramatic release from a sight caught in the throat like a fishbone. There was the experience to write about combined with this need to say it. Gradually, from the time the war was raging until the present, many of these ronins found their voices.

While nearly all the books share a landscape in common, the voices which sight the landscape vary. At their weakest, the voices are to a man first-person narrations, neither epical or dramaturgical, they are chronologies which begin on the first day of a tour and end 365 days later. Friends "buy the farm," i.e., they get killed. There is that eternal treeline. A monotony of bush. The berm. The rice paddy. Incoming. Take some. Give some. Hooches get burned to the ground. Dinks get it in turn. An eye for an eye. Someone souvenirs an ear. Old Farmer Bo's water buffalo gets killed for sport. The door gunner on the helicopter is a maniac. No matter where he comes from he has a Southern accent. Everyone speaks in witty scatological ways. They are deadpan humorous as a nightclub comedian, Lenny Bruce in camouflage fatigues. A white soldier becomes friends with a black soldier. They save each other's life. There is a lot of dope. There is some warm beer. The lieutenant is an asshole. The colonel is an even bigger asshole. This dasiy chain of assholes goes right up to the top to the Green Man. The grunt is a kind of king, mythic, scared but courageous. Early on he is a kind of young John Wayne. Later he will become a ronin, a walking ghost of a man, disembodied, disenchanted, broken and homesick.

Like all grunts, though, he is a believer. "You better believe it," he tells others. Or he says, as characters so often say in John Del Vecchio's epic-attempting novel, *The 13th Valley*, "It don't mean nothing," that double negative as obvious as, what? Probably Flannery O'Connor's pig on the sofa. In the end a boy becomes a man. A Man, I mean. A MAN, I mean. He gets laid by a whore, spouting unrepeatable slurs about her cleanliness and her race. He loses "his cherry," as they say, in two ways: 1) he christens his sexual organ; 2) he learns that his weapon is an instrument to kill others with. It finally is like the sunset in a Western, one fade replaced by another; one dissolve blurring into a million other dissolves. One treeline looks like all the other treelines.

But don't get me wrong; something fascinates me personally in even the drabbest of these Vietnam voices. They are adventures, vicarious, obscene, revealing, and telling, even when least expected. They tell us about being Americans, even the poorliest written of them. I would be lying if I said they did not fascinate me.

What I wish to address is a second form of reading which arises out of a different type of voice, a singular one, book to book. This second voice may "fascinate," but it also moves and instructs us, and finally it changes us—it turns the head around, it unravels us. On this second level one must read these voices carefully, even at times with a care like one brings to a good poem. As I said, the landscape is the same in each type of Vietnam War book: the jungle, units, incoming, dustoffs. There is a treeline. Hostile fire. A ville, Indian country. Boredom. The boonies. But in these latter works— surprisingly about 20 percent of the nearly two hundred novels which John Clark Pratt lists in his bibliography—something different happens.

In these latter instances Vietnam is conjured out of the American idiom, and the voice which evokes the landscape is a rich one, even a seductive one, full of coloring, sights, and the deepest feelings about our human condition. Even when the surface is tricked out with bravado, often the subtext bursts with the deepest emotions. Much about these voices has made an indelible trace across the rhythms of an entire generation's experiences, whether they are veterans or not. I know that as a writer I often feel envy for the symbolic action, the rhythm of that experience, in the fabric of this prose. I find myself, reading Stephen Wright or Kenn Miller or Joe Haldeman or nonfiction writers like Robert Mason and Philip Caputo—I find myself saying, I wish I had written that!

There are other times, even in the best of these works, where I cannot take it. The women who inhabit these landscapes so often are drab and one-dimensional, and observations about an entire people are focused into their whores. (Imagine a Vietnamese making conclusions about American women based on his experiences with disease-ridden, drug-infested, hot-pants and halter-top prostitutes working the Lincoln Tunnel area on Manhattan's West Side.) It amounts to macho at its worst, a condition with which I am familiar, if not through military experience, then from having grown up in a household of ten children, most of them male. When you come upon a novel that works against such female stereotyping, it is a marvel—it is simply marvelous, because a kind of habitual portrait of Vietnamese women has dulled your senses.

I can think of three notable exceptions to this tendency to caricature the voice of experience. The first is Robert Olen Butler's *Alleys of Eden*, which does not so much portray a relationship with a Vietnamese prostitute as it evokes a Vietnamese woman who happens to earn her living as a prostitute. That is a subtle, yet measurable, difference. Claymore Face, a prostitute in Larry Heinemann's *Close Quarters*, although described as being gruesomely ugly, somehow is real, a human figure, and a sympathetic one, absolutely due to the fact of how carefully the author evokes her with his seeing voice. Ugly or not, Claymore Face is quite lovable. Perhaps the most untrammeled of these Vietnamese women is a character in James Park Sloan's *War Games*. She is not a prostitute at all; in fact, she is beautiful, seems educated, and she is articulate, even in the borrowed idiom of American speech. Her job is to work as a clerk in the American PX. There are other exceptions besides these, but these come most readily to mind. Otherwise, in this male-centered world, the voices turn one prostitute into another, long black hair and *ao-dai* falling to the ground, revealing a kind of faceless creature with small breasts, honey-brown skin, a kind of ronin's succubus, a paper ghost. The male-centered voice provokes a landscape of whores and *mamasans* (old ladies).

That last female, the *mamasan*, brings me to my next observation about the voice in this landscape. So much of the vocabulary about Vietnam is a verbal garbage recycled from our other wars. *Mamasan*, a term as comprehensible to a peasant woman in the countryside of Vietnam as meatballs and spaghetti, is from World War II, a Japanese honorific for an older woman. *San* is the equivalent of "Mr." or "Mrs." *Gook* is probably one of the more degraded bastardizations, a Chinese word, it comes from the Korean War. It is Chinese in origin, but its sound is quite Korean, and in both Korea and China it means "country." Since it is one of the most commonly used derogatory terms for the Vietnamese, it is worth seeing its real pictorial meaning. It consists of

冂	enclosure or boundary
戈	"spear" for ruling
或	border
國	country

It is worth noting that a country, in its oriental sense, even today, also means the land and the people, very similar to the Greek's notion of *polis*, the "city-state," which is really a people in their national boundary and geography. Speaking to a Vietnamese woman I know, I said that I thought Vietnam was a beautiful-looking country, its trees, its vegetation, its colors. Her response was to bow her head and say, "Thank you." It was as though I had complimented her on her dress or new hairdo. Similar experiences have happened to me, time and again, in Korea, and also speaking with Japanese about their country or Tokyo. Perhaps maybe only our most flag-waving type of American has this sense of people and country, self and nation, so intimately connected, or even inseparable.

I know that even for American patriots this is a difficult concept to fathom; it certainly is one with which I am familiar only through travel in the Orient, not by personal temperament or inclination. It obviously is a quality, a state of mind, really, which few Americans, writers and nonwriters alike, understood about the Vietnamese. And yet it is a wonderful irony to think that in our American vocabulary created from the Vietnam War, one of our most derogatory terms for a Vietnamese was to call him a "country" in Chinese. The only fiction writer to note this is Kenn Miller in *Tiger the Lurp Dog,* in which Marvel Kim, a Korean-American LURP from Hawaii, observes this bastardization of his own beloved word "gook." Korea, in fact, is called *Han-Guk,* or "the land of the people," while the United States is called *Mi-Guk,* "the beautiful land."

Other bastardized words found in the landscape of Vietnam fiction are those left over by the last conquerors, the French. *Boo-coo* is Americanized French for "beaucoup," or "plenty of." *Ville* is the most obvious. *Hooch,* on the other hand, is surefire down-home corn mash liquor American, although it becomes a house instead of a whiskey in Vietnam. The richest of these words in the American voice are products of pure invention and even genius: point, incoming, dustoff, boonies, in-country, out-of-the-world. They are the products of the seeing American voice in Asia.

These are some of the conditions of voice in the fiction about the Vietnam War. When most sonorous, it is decidedly rebellious; at its most rebellious peak, it touches upon the revolutionary in our society. The rhythm of its experience is often tragic and comic, by turns, though in its former state it needs to be defined better by myself and others, so that its tragic condition doesn't become bastardized, as it has in the media. There is another term which Professor Pratt is fond of, and which I think appropriate to an investigation of this voice; it is often *fragmentary*. But I think this last condition bespeaks a broader context, which is our time itself, both in its Vietnam era and after the war. Writers like Donald Barthelme write in fragments; so do a lot of contemporary, non-Vietnam veteran writers. That is a condition of our time which Vietnam reflects; the other conditions are those of the war itself, reflected in our society.

Like "illumination," both a revelation and the artificial light for nocturnal combat assaults and interdictions, the word "fragment" is a loaded one in the literature of Vietnam. In addition to its traditional meaning of something being "broken off or detached," something "incomplete," it is also the hot explosive metal in a combat wound. It is something, a fragment, if not totally removed surgically, which constantly works its way to the surface of one's skin. A literary fragment, on the other hand, can be an incompletion, at its worst, and a dramatic leaving out, a suggesting, at best. Larry Heinemann has told me that he prefers the term "episodic" to "fragmentary," because the so-called fragment is often "the product of some writers' diminished ambition as well as diminished capacity, despite their supposedly elegant style." An excellent example of the fragment's dramatic values—as opposed to its diminished capacity—is Jack Fuller's novel *Fragments*, where a totality of experience emerges from the fragmentation of the narrative world.

At the outset I said that the warrior is a figure best suited for the epic, whereas I think the ronin is more a figure from drama. That said, it becomes an issue of in what kind of drama the ronin, especially the American ronin, locates his voice. In a classical time the choices were either in the empty space of tragedy or that of comedy. Today the instances of drama are everywhere in our lives, not only on the stage; as Raymond Williams writes, drama has changed from an occasional event into an everyday occurrence.

On television alone it is normal for viewers—the substantial majority of the population—to see anything up to three hours of drama, of course drama of several different kinds, a day. And not just one day; almost every day. This is part of what I mean by a dramatized society. In earlier periods drama was important at a festival, in a season, or as a conscious journey to a theatre; from honouring Dionysus or Christ to taking in a show. What we now have is drama as habitual experience: more in a week, in many cases, than most human beings would previously have seen in a lifetime.

(*Writing in Society*)

In this dramatized society, the ronin's experience is given a different rhythm. For him it is a question of 365 days or thereabouts. But shaped into the voice of our technology, the rhythm of his experience is something like two to six minutes of prime-time news, edited video tape, the smells gone, and even the seeing voice flattened into a pancakelike image without any depth illusion. No wonder the ronin is traumatized. All he has, like the figure in Frank Miller's cartoon, is his projected self as a warrior, a feeling mind, but his limbs sawed off. Is he a comic figure in this drama? Sometimes, yes. Or a tragic figure? Yes, he can be that as well.

Perhaps the best news to come out of the Vietnam War is this potential for it to become tragedy. I say this at the risk of sounding insane, heartless, and ridiculous. But I think it true. The reason for this estimate is that deluge of writings which followed the historical event, and how some of the voices in the deluge approach a condition which a generation has never experienced. It was not these soldiers who lost the war, but America did lose a war. Of that there is no question. But in that loss for a generation of Americans raised on a Vince Lombardi—winning isn't everything; it's the only thing—mentality, defeat is both sobering and potentially mind-expanding. As nations go we are as vincible as the next. That fifty-eight thousand or so Americans died in Vietnam is not tragic; it is horrible and disgusting, senseless and heartbreaking, it is a hollowed-out ronin-spirited misery. But it is not tragic. That is because the end of tragedy's arc is something like the pot of gold at the end of a rainbow. It is that perception, an enlightenment, an illumination—all of it by the seeing voice in this landscape. There is a W. B. Yeats poem entitled "Lapis Lazuli," which explains this condition better than any treatise on tragedy. Speaking of Hamlet and Lear, he writes that they

> Do not break up their lines to weep.
> They know that Hamlet and Lear are gay;
> Gaiety transfiguring all that dread.
> All men have aimed at, found and lost;
> Black out; Heaven blazing into the head:
> Tragedy wrought to its uttermost.

These are the tragic conditions for the American ronin, I think, and it is cause for celebration. His voice cleanses our souls; he brings his broken spirit into our spiritless land. But there is one more observation I wish to make before letting the ronins speak for themselves. Sometimes the spirit of the ronin is found in a character; sometimes it is found in both author and character. Combat veterans who write tend to be ronins by their deeds and how those deeds affect their conscious lives. These ronins tend to make other ronins in their prose, projecting their seeing voices onto the page. In terms of conjurings, their magic would appear to be the strongest.

Fragment One: The First Ronin Speaks. Here is the ronin in the bush, in the night, surrounded by death, masterless, full of his frenzies. He is evoked in this deadly night by Larry Heinemann in his novel, *Close Quarters*: "I let the bayonet slip from my hand and come down with all my weight on his chest, my hands around his neck. I squeeze his Adam's apple with both thumbs. I lift his head and push it back into the turf with a muted splash. My fingernails work into the back of his neck. The little man grabs both my wrists. He gurgles and works his jaw. His mouth stretches open and he wags his tongue. Lift. Push. Squeeze. Like working a tool smooth. His head splashes harder. His nails gouge my wrists. Lift. Push. Squeeze. Something cracks and my thumbs work easier, deeper. His mouth, his tongue, make thick wet murmurs. Lift. Push. Squeeze. His body shakes as though someone is trying to yank it out from under me. His face and lips and jaw go slack. His head and hands go limp."

I am not romanticizing the ronin figure when I say that his life is rootless and untethered. As we see in the fragment above, his mission is to kill men with his bare hands, and when we enter the rhythm of his experience, it is a terrifying voice we confront. That is one aspect of the tragic voice, though. His violent gestures, sculpted by words, is supposed to cleanse us. What is maybe even more terrifying is that John Pratt idea of mixing fact and fiction. Many American ronins, without the power of words to transform their deeds into tragedy, simply killed with their hands, pulled triggers, pushed buttons, cranked up the old war machine, and let it rip.

Already another ronin waits in the wings, ready to spring onto the stage like a berserking ninja. Here is how he speaks in the landscape of *Meditations in Green* by Stephen Wright, arguably, with Larry Heinemann, one of the best writers to come out of this experience: "The man blubbered with horror at his left leg which rested now incongruously beside his head, upsidedown and unattached. 'Well, shit,' muttered Kraft and kicked the useless leg off into the underbrush. The wounded man's white face looked as though someone had flicked a full fountain pen across it, a spattering of black marks like powder burns or bits of dirt driven by explosive force into the skin. At his other end black blood drained into the ground. Kneeling at his side, Doc quickly tied off the stump, stuck a needle in his arm. Then he cut open the shirt. 'Jesus Christ,' said someone softly in anger and disbelief. The chest resembled a plowed field. The man looked up at Doc, a child's look, as one hand reached tentatively for his groin, asking in a dry voice, 'My balls, are my balls okay?' and Doc nodded, patting his forehead, and the man died."

What the ronin speaks about is war, and being in a world of uncertainty, his voice sees uncertain things. He speaks out of his own nightmares, which are a combination of fact and fiction, the real and the unreal, the unreal given a reality in the cadence of his voice. The above words by ronin Stephen Wright are delivered from a trance, and when read carefully it is apparent that there is a rhythm in its prose measure as strict as any poem's. Masterless, stoned out, the ronin is still a disciplined figure, and his mission, after combat, is to deliver these messages back to the living, edifying but not distorting the details, he speaks from a trance in which the rhythm of the experience intoxicates him. Again, I think what he does approaches tragedy, and falling short of that claim, it is a drama, in the purest sense of that word.

In other instances the ronin invades the mind of a writer who is nowhere near the arena of Vietnam, but his rhythm infects a writer back in the world, perhaps even one who never laid eyes on Vietnam, and never will. Most often it is a case of an American writer thinking that he is possessed of the ronin, when in fact it is a lesser demon tormenting him. But when the real figure of the ronin invades a writer, even one sitting in his room on the Lower East Side, the rhythm of his experience, the sight he gives the writer's voice, these things are unmistakeable in their intensity.

This third projection of the ronin comes from Chuck Wachtel's *Joe the Engineer*. The protagonist Joe is a former combat veteran now reading water meters in Brooklyn and Queens. In a retrospective moment Joe thinks: *Imagine the thrill of hitting a target the size of a trash can from eleven miles away!* Figures like Cuchulain come to my mind. That is, a hero who is capable, in tranquility, of great poetry; but in a frenzy, working himself into warp spasms, his powers for destruction are immense. When Cuchulain has his tempers, he mows down thousands, even tens of thousands of men. Later, remorseless, he contemplates, dreaming of a breath and syllable to dance on the tongue. In a kind of postronin afterfrenzy Joe calms himself with these suasions:

What Joe hadn't realized at the time is that you cannot see for eleven miles, and if you can't see what you're hitting and if there's actually no one specific trash-can sized object you can draw a bead on, a *thrill* is not what you get. A thrill is what you imagine you get if you're sixteen and standing in a post office on Jamaica Avenue in Queens. What you do is fire, eject, reload and fire again and try to think of anything but what might be going on eleven miles away. Joe'd often think of the things he'd do with his whore back in Da Nang, things he'd never done before, things he could think about to keep himself from imagining a six-foot-wide scar in a patch of dried-brick pavement, where, perhaps sixty seconds before, an object the size of a trash can stopped to look up. After that Joe cannot look at something as complex and seemingly indestructible as Manhattan without calculating, at least for a moment, its total annihilation.

Back in the world, back in the U.S.A., the American ronin does not shed Vietnam like a snake sheds its skin. He does not shed it like another dirty garment. It is an experience that lingers, that ferments, that may even grow in size as time elapses, and goes by. Part of it may be the corruption that silence wields, whether self-imposed or imposed by a society. This silence works like rust on steel. Part of it may be the corrosion of guilt, as mentioned earlier, rotting, stinking, being the least illuminating of emotional conditions. Drugs, alcohol, these don't seem to dull it, but only heighten the experience. Yet the facts demand to be untrapped. That is when the imagination offers assistance. I am reminded again of that remark in Philip Beidler's study of the literature, that "one truly did not have to go to Vietnam to bring the experience home in literature."

Here is another ronin-type to consider; he is another type of dispirited, unfranchised, antiestablishment patriot. His name is Robert Dubois. We meet him in Russell Banks' novel, *Continental Drift*. Although Bob is not portrayed to us as a Vietnam veteran, let's say he comes across like one, I mean, we feel as though we have met him after the war in nearly every street of America, or more precisely, sitting at the end of the bar.

Until this night, except for the four years he served in the air force, Bob has lived all his life in Catamount (N.H.) and since high school has worked for the same company, Abenaki Oil Company on North

Main Street, at the same trade, repairing oil burners. He is thirty
years old, "happily married," with two children, daughters, aged
six and four. Both his parents are dead, and his older brother, Eddie, owns a liquor store in Oleander Park, Florida. His wife Elaine
loves and admires him, his daughters Ruthie and Emma practically
worship him, his boss, Fred Turner, says he needs him, and his
friends think he has a good sense of humor. He is a frugal man. He
owns a run-down seventy-five-year-old duplex in a working-class
neighborhood on the north end of Butterick Street, lives with his
family in the front half and rents out the back to four young people
he calls hippies. He owns a boat, a thirteen-foot Boston whaler he
built from a kit, with a sixteen-horsepower Mercury outboard motor; the boat he keeps shrouded in clear plastic in his side yard from
November until the ice in the lakes breaks up; the motor's in the
basement. He owns a battered green 1974 Chevrolet station wagon
with a tricky transmission. He owes the Catamount Savings and
Loan Company—for the house, boat and car—a little over
$22,000. He pays cash for everything else. He votes Democratic, as
his father did, goes occasionally to mass with his wife and children
and believes in God the way he believes in politicians—he knows
He exists but doesn't depend on Him for anything. He loves his
wife and children. He has a girlfriend. He hates his life.

Other than a reference, in passing, of Bob's four years in
the air force, there is no mention in this novel about the descent of a good man into an American inferno, from New
Hampshire to Florida, from a life of the typical working stiff
to that of a smuggler of Haitians to the mainland—there is no
mention that Bob Dubois is a Vietnam veteran. Yet he exem-
plifies a mood and spirit of Vietnam veterans after the war,
their rootlessness, their troubles, that untethered state filled
with tragic possibility. But let me offer that the ronin, masterless and footloose, is a raging, dangerous man if no vents are
given to his emotional life. Here is Bob Dubois, just before
Christmas, after leaving his mistress, after trying to buy

presents for his children. He stands in front of his 1974 Chevrolet station wagon. Bob's fist is raised. Then:

He brings it heel-first swiftly down, smashing it against the windshield on the passenger's side. The blow shatters the outer layer of glass and sends silvery cobwebs across the windshield, the force of the blow spraying the snow in fantails, clearing the windshield instantly. Again, he brings the heel of his fist down, and again, until he has filled the windshield entirely with spiderwebs of broken glass. Then he attacks the side windows, and the snow shudders and falls like a heavy curtain to the street. First he hits the front window on the passenger's side, then the back, then the rear window, until he has worked his way around to the other side of the station wagon, where he makes his way forward to the driver's window, pounding as he goes, as if trying to free a child trapped inside.

This chapter is entitled "Pissed," in that sense of anger, not drunkenness, as Bob himself explains. "No, I'm okay. I'm not drunk," he says. "Just pissed." He repeats that word: "*Pissed!*" Perhaps I have overintellectualized the ronin's condition, calling him untethered, disenfranchised, antiestablishment. How is this patriot feeling after that awful war? Probably exactly like Robert Dubois, full of rage, a little high, frustrated, unable to keep the silence any longer, he breaks. He raises his fist against an inanimate object for which he owes the bank money, even though the transmission does not work well. Read this to any Vietnam veteran, and ask if he has not felt this breaking point like Robert Dubois', this nearly quintessential ronin figure in our American landscape?

Ask the ronin what he feels?

Ask him to speak about it.

Invariably, he will say what Robert Dubois says.

"No, I'm okay. I'm not drunk," he says. "Just pissed."
And like Bob, he will repeat it:
"*Pissed!*"

Which brings me to that other aspect of the ronin, his facts told in fictional modes. Of this quality, the best examples are Michael Herr's *Dispatches,* Philip Caputo's *A Rumor of War,* Robert Mason's *Chickenhawk.* Because fiction is voice-centered, writers who operate through a medium of the voice can be clustered with the fiction writers. But it is important to keep in mind some advice which Philip Caputo offers in his own instance of the ronin; it is not good to have an imagination in a combat zone. You need to read a treeline as a piece of hostile landscape, a kind of jigsaw puzzle that is filled with poisonous vents waiting to annihilate you. The treeline is never, to borrow a phrase from Guy Davenport, "a geography of the imagination." It is not a landscape to become dreamy and poetic about; it is not something you look at as though it might be painted in the various shades of green like a contemporary Cézanne. William Carlos Williams, as mentioned previously, wrote that there is no news in poetry, but that men die every day for a lack of what can be found there. Michael Herr wrote back that there is no news found in the news, and that men die every day even if there is poetry. His prose, ronin-inspired, is infected by his sightings, by his confrontations with the masterless samurai, by an almost anti-zen of his observation (I'm a dead man, so now let me write). Robert Mason, a former helicopter pilot, wrote *Chickenhawk* in the ronin manner of facts in the rhythmical utterance of fiction, of facts so directly treated that his prose is at times like poetry; charged by human utterance, lyricized by emotion, made dramatic by precise tensions. Not only is John Wayne nowhere to be found in *Chickenhawk,* Mason is so thoroughly meticulous about his details that no romantic warrior can inhabit his terrain. All he presents is the ronin, tough but so terribly mortal:

"We waited for thirty seconds while Farris made sure everybody had unloaded. Machine guns opened up from three points. They had us pinned with fire from the front, the left flank, and the rear. I could see the muzzle flashes in the tree line fifty yards away, which blocked our take-off path. I pushed pedals furiously and wiggled the ship as we hovered, waiting for Farris. The only gun position I could watch was the one up front, and he was raking us at will. Our door guns couldn't swing that far forward, so the gunners concentrated on the flank attacks. As I oscillated left and right, I heard one *tick,* then Farris took off just to the right of the forward VC gun with the rest of us hot on his tail rotor. As we crossed the trees, another VC gun opened up, showering tracers through our flight. I pulled up higher than the rest of the flight and made small, quick turns left and right. As we climbed out, all the guns below us converged on our eight ships. I just kept floundering around, believing firmly that Leese was right: Anything you can do to make yourself a bad target is to your benefit. Moments later we were out of range. Six of the eight helicopters were damaged, and two gunners had been killed. Our ship had taken the one round that had hit us on the ground."

The distinction between fact and fiction is almost irrelevant in Mason's voice register, because his use of sight and rhythm—how his voice possesses an experience!—are hallmarks of good fiction, but certainly not restricted to fiction alone. By shaping and patterning the disorder of combat experience, especially in the precarious domain of a helicopter pilot, Mason produces drama, plain and simple. At the other pole of this fusion of fact and fiction turning into dramatic event would be the fiction which details itself with facts. Probably the best-known example of such a strategy in fiction is John Del Vecchio's *13th Valley,* a novel not so much concerned with voice as it is with an accretion of details. If Robert Mason seems to possess an innate sense of drama in his prose, Del Vecchio's impulse is toward epic, that most samurailike literary form, where types more than individuals inhabit the mythological plain. The danger, of course, is to distribute white hats and black hats, to draw an imaginary line and say, This is the fort and out there is Indian country. The danger is to re-create John Wayne, to rewrite *A Walk in the Sun,* and to bring in all the wooden Indians, urban cowboys, and cigar-store extras from Central Casting. An epic written in a nonepical historical period runs the risk of turning type into stereotype, of making voice a wooden vehicle, hollow and unresonating. Drama suffers as a result. But is John Del Vecchio guilty of such oversights by divining an epical approach to record the Vietnam experience in our writing?

There is something anachronistic about seeing the cowboy-warrior in the jungles of Vietnam, as though the samurai descended from a space ship or a time capsule. It is as though the samurai stepped onto the wrong movie set. Del Vecchio does write out of an epical impulse, and his strategy is to render fiction, not by voice, but by factual accretions joined to types and stereotypes in archetypical combat situations. His novel chronicles, for instance, a classic military confrontation between NVA regulars and U.S. regulars (Screaming Eagles), not Americans against Vietcong. In many respects this is a World War II novel transplanted to Vietnam, and it can be asked: So what is wrong with that? Like Stephen King, Del Vecchio heaps on details, turning his novel into a mountain of information, about how to eat in the jungle, about the rituals of stand-down, about supplies, gear, combat assaults, areas of operations, etc., etc. Read as a catalogue of information, *The 13th Valley* is a wellspring of myths and rituals of Vietnam for infantrymen in American units. Read as fiction, the novel is something else.

Del Vecchio's details, in and of themselves, isolated from the superstructure of his novel, are quite admirable. His scholarship is impeccable, his research is gargantuan, his instinct to write BIG is grand and even marvelous. He wants to write in a heroic mode even though he does not live in a heroic age. But he is more historian than poet, and by that I mean he is able to cull information and detail to create a pyramid of historical enormity, and yet his jettisoning of a voice, of a voice that sees and speaks, that seizes the rhythm of experience, allows some of this enormous potential in the material to slip away. What the narrator sees he won't say; like a pedagogue, he wants to tell us about it, rather than being like a dramatist—showing us. For Del Vecchio's narrative instinct is one which seems to make voice and sight separate entities in fiction, even disparities, not commingling energies.

Still, isolated moments in this novel are so good that one needs to reflect on Del Vecchio's attempt at panoramic fiction. Two examples come immediately to mind. The first is walking point, and how the author evokes this experience so precisely. The other is the section about the tunnel rats, which manages to be both factual and fictional, revealingly authentic and horribly nightmarish, real and yet sort of unreal. I think in these two instances Del Vecchio is in possession of a seeing voice that captures the rhythm of experience in Vietnam. Here is walking point:

"Very slowly he moved. One pace every five or six seconds, ten paces a minute, less than 300 meters in an hour. Whiteboy picked his way downward, generally westward, turning up here, down there, as obstacles in the trail dictated. He stayed below the ridge keeping the crest always uphill to his left. He did not cut trail. He did not use a machete to straighten the path. He simply moved toward his objective along the path of least resistance as imperceptibly as possible."

Two chapters later these nearly absolute rhythms of action and of experience rule the narrative voice with incredible authority:

"Step. Step. Climbing now. Climbing slowly. Climbing through the thick brush. The men in front waiting for the men with more difficult climbs. Staying in line. No sign of the enemy. Waiting for the first shot. Not even feeling their thighs twitching from the weight and the exertion of the climb. Not seeing, feeling the black before them. The sky became lighter, the floor remained dark. Not thinking. Like men with brains removed. No judgment. Just up. Step. Step. In line. Weapons on full automatic, aimed forward. Step. Not stopping. Step. Cherry could feel his biceps quivering. His back aching. Step. Step. Coming out of his rucksack and bending forward over his shoulder was his radio's antenna looking like a thin bamboo shoot. It caught in the vegetation. His ruck was caught by a vine. He frantically worked to extricate himself as the line advanced without him. Step. Step. Light now penetrated through the jungle ceiling down to them. Up. Step. Step. Toward the hilltop the canopy became thinner. Step. Step. The slope became more gentle. They surrounded the eastern side of the peak. Up, onto, over the top. Nothing. No one."

If you consider John Del Vecchio—these two quite well written fictional passages aside—as an historian, his novel *The 13th Valley is* a major achievement. But against the criteria of a seeing voice, of dramatic values like concision, of poetic values like the rhythm of experience, the novel is weak. Beyond its historical information—a veritable jungleful on every page—it is a serious entertainment, even a moving one at times. But I am thinking of a remark by Bertolt Brecht about how a drama should entertain and move before it can change our lives. Instead, it probably verifies lives that need verification—I am referring to veterans who experienced such combat actions—or enhances a political mood, given its epical inclinations, its tendency to mythologize, to aggrandize, to turn this historical action in the biography of samurai, the testament of the cowboy-warrior, that is, a cultural ghost, resurrected in our time for propaganda, personal aggrandizement, to give shape and pattern to a moment that finally remains amorphous, disconnected, and untethered.

Writers like Russell Banks and Larry Heinemann, whose prose is so muscled and taut, so elegant yet morally charged, remind us of a tradition going back to Herman Melville's master prose works. Neither fatted nor swollen with commercial ideals toward bestsellerdom, nonetheless they are popular fictions. By comparison Del Vecchio seems like a son of Dreiser, and the writer he most resembles, because of his historic and epical concerns as a witness of the actual, is Alexandr I. Solzhenitsyn, including that author's plodding and prolixity, but not excluding the seething vision. At times Del Vecchio's novel does possess a pitch similar, if not always consistently there, to writers like Banks and Heinemann. Take the tunnel rats:

"Whiteboy was alone on the CP when he heard digging. He had concealed himself beneath a bush on a small rise, south, above the exhausted column on the trail. The sound was faint. It stopped. He looked forward. The digging began again. Whiteboy poked his head out. The sound persisted. The usual jungle sounds of helicopters and artillery masked the faint scraping. He was not certain he heard digging noises at all yet he was sure someone was digging very near him. He felt it. He looked forward. It began once more. He looked down, between his legs, under his ass. It felt as if someone were digging beneath him. He turned again, he massaged the warm metal of Lit'le Boy's trigger mechanism. The sound stopped. He did not have the faintest idea what he was hearing. He relaxed. The sound became louder, nearer."

This sort of tension, set up in the opening paragraph, continues for at least thirty pages more into the next chapter. Here is how Egan, a quintessential boonierat, descends into a tunnel:

"His feet were above his head and he could feel blood pulsating at the back of his neck. He slid downward, inching forward under control, holding himself back, feeling if he let himself go he would fall tumble down to . . . to where? His shoulders were fatigued from holding himself back. It was like doing push-ups with feet elevated. He went deeper, pushed forward by curiosity and by his desire to find and destroy the enemy and by his need to show the boonierats how it was done. He could hear his own breathing into the mask. The mask smelled like rubber. At various levels the tunnel widened to perhaps two and a half feet, at other spots it narrowed to a tight squeeze through. Egan slipped deeper. He checked the sides carefully for closed or covered connecting tunnels. He found none. He jerked the rope once and edged down. The walls were the hard clay and shale stone mixture of deep foxholes and bunkers. They appeared to have been scraped with pointed sticks for the upper side of the tube was raked with inch-wide scratch marks. The bottom was smooth from having been crawled on. The entire radial surface was fresh. As Egan snaked down checking for booby trap wires he could not help but admire the work the little people had done."

Del Vecchio's novel *The 13th Valley* may betray voice for epical detail, but occasions like the tunnel rat's world above and his descriptive evoking of that experience of walking point, of breaking bush, are miniature refinements which bespeak an instinct for human-centered drama. Nowhere is that grand strategy for epic more undermined than in the bulk of this antiheroic fiction, though. And this tendency to underscore the heroic, the epical, and the grand reaches an apogee in Gustav Hasford's *Short-Timers,* a comic masterpiece. Hasford's way to deal with the samurai turned into a ronin is to laugh, because his own masters include men like Jonathan Swift and Rabelais, and in the recent past, writers like William Burroughs and Allen Ginsberg and Michael Herr. This is jukebox prose at its finest, blaring, raunchy, hip-shaking, pelvic-rocking, beer-drunk and pill-high. This is music from Aristophanes himself. It is where war is a game like Tom and Jerry, Wiley Coyote and the Roadrunner, Elmer Fudd and Bugs Bunny. Instead of the *zanno's* slapstick, the ronin uses an automatic weapon, and get this, folks, it's made of plastic, just like when you were a kid. Ha-Ha. Here the ronin's speech is clipped, staccato, precise, exact, nearly even a shorthand. He speaks in the present tense; it is cinematic. He knows about the dramatized society.

Crazy Earl is carrying an M-16 Colt automatic rifle slung on his shoulder, but in his hands is a Red Ryder BB gun. He's as skinny as a death-camp survivor, and his face consists of a long, pointed nose with a hollow cheek on each side. His eyes are magnified by thick lenses and one arm of his gray Marine-issue eyeglasses has been wired back on with too much wire. He says, "Saddle up," and the grunts start picking up their gear, their M-16's and M-79 grenade launchers and captured AK-47 assault rifles, their ruck-sacks, flak jackets, and helmets. Animal Mother picks up an M-60 machine gun and sets the butt into his hip so that the black barrel slants up at a forty-five degree angle. Animal Mother grunts. Crazy Earl turns to Cowboy and says, "We better be moving, bro. Mr. Shortround will punch our hearts out if we're late."

Hasford's ronin speaks as though from a cartoon; everything is unreal, absurd, and ridiculous, which finally is another way of looking at his tragic condition. The rhythm of experience is a spoken condition, a war story, another kind of tall tale. It is not didactic like the other ronins' voices. This ronin teaches by his worst examples. A moral tale, as they say, full of edifying detail, this is something Hasford's ronin can do without. His ronin tells us nothing; his condition is to show by isolating particulars, enlarging them, making them bigger than life. It is an amoral voice; it has none of those moral swells found in a writer like James Webb. Unlike John Del Vecchio's voice, this ronin could care less about epic, good guys and bad guys. It is as though Hasford's ronin were not only untethered, but that he floated in the big blue void like a giant balloon, ready to be burst at any moment by a simple pinprick. It is a voice filled with irony as well as wit, and it makes poetry out of its own cacophony; it is a kind of measured antimusic. W. C. Fields hated dogs and children; Hasford's ronin is related by blood to that kind of idea. But everything is inverted, so that the ronin's misanthropic details are ultimately what reveal his humanity.

In a chapter entitled "Body Count" the grunts are attacked by a swarm of rats in their dug-out hooch. They break up cookies and place them at the hole where most of them enter. This draws the rats out. Then Mr. Payback douses them with lighter fluid. Then the unit goes into a combat assault on the rat population. Daytona Dave "charges around and around with fixed bayonet, zeroing in on a burning rat like a fighter pilot in a dogfight. Daytona follows the rat's crazed, erratic course around and around, over all obstacles, gaining on him with every step. He butt-strokes the rat and then bayonets him, again and again and again. 'That's one confirmed!'" This ronin's voice is showing me a lot. First, he captures the overall lunacy of combat. Second, though, he reveals a fact which a combat veteran might tell you privately, but few writing-ronins reveal in their writing. Like tragedy, the energy of combat has a rhythm which also includes joy.

A friend of mine who spent his year in the Central Highlands said what I am trying to explain here: "Vietnam, it was one big party!"

A similar kind of rhythm of tragedy turning into comedy is Robert Auletta's play, *Rundown*. When another character sticks a fork into Pay's hand, asking, "could you loan me eight dollars and seventy-five cents?" we understand that the conditions in which this veteran operates is disenfranchised and rootless. It is there from Pay's first utterance: "What? Who's there? (Pause) Do you want me?" The paranoia is as thick as sludge. It reveals something that all good dramatists know about dramaturgical conditions; characters reveal themselves from first utterance. What they say resonates throughout the arc of the drama. It is the ronin's first choice, and those simple questions reverberate throughout the bending arc of Auletta's play.

It is not realism; it is not naturalism. The ronin's state is dreamlike; he is as nearly empty as the empty space in which he operates. Characters from the past slide in and out of the stage light like flashbacks in the ronin's mind. That, perhaps, is Robert Auletta's finest achievement in this work, how he captures the disordered inner workings of the posttraumatic syndrome through visible actions on the stage. It is as though the narrative were built from a series of hallucinations, and in fact they are. This is how that condition is reflected when Pay delivers a monologue directly to the audience:

I'm sorry. I've been a downer. I know I can get kind of depressing at times. I've got to learn to deal with certain kinds of shit. Some people can. I was over at OTB the other day, and ran into my friend Wendell. He was fucked up pretty bad in World War Two, lost his leg and other important parts of his personal physical environment. But does he let it get him down? No sir. Whenever the blues start to do a number inside his head he wraps his hand around a fifth of blackberry-flavored brandy and goes to work. I mean, he knows how to attack the root of his sorrow: (Slight laugh) the brain. (Pause) For a while there I used to go and see this guy who was specially trained, you know, hand-picked, polished specially to deal with . . . guys like myself . . . and their individual . . . problems. See, the two of us would sit down—a bunch of times we did this— and let me tell you what happened, what I realized: he was mind-fucking me! No kidding. I'd go home with the feeling that my mind had been violated, right down to the last inch. I had to douche the damn thing out with acid, and it still felt crawly, creepy. Sorry, I'm being kind of disgusting. (Pause) What I realized is, that nobody can help you: you've got to help yourself—and that's exactly what I did with this cute little secretary I met on the unemployment line, helped myself to . . . (Stops, looks around) I was trying to get to my mother's, but somehow I found myself down by the river.

Pay need say no more. He does not have to tell us anything, because he shows his condition, wearing it as though on his sleeve. Everything is made of fragments. It is one of the strongest ways to illustrate a war story. Start to tell about a cute little secretary you met on the unemployment line, lose the thought in the fractures of the mind, and dovetail this with the narrative line of the play. "I was trying to get to my mother's." This is something all the ronins can learn from a writer like Robert Auletta. Drama's only way to reveal ideas is through actions. The voice sees by doing, and by doing, a dramatic action unfolds. Here, the ronin is one of the walking wounded. He is back in the world. His girl friend teases him, telling him about her hot thighs. His old buddy Spear torments him down by the river. This notion of fragments, instead of being a narrative strategy, is part of a human condition. It is perhaps one of the strongest examples I can offer of the fragment operating in the voice of a ronin.

In America, the ronin begins quietly, but then his angry voice emerges. He explodes himself onto the frontier; or he negotiates himself by insinuations and dangerously antisocial behavior onto our stage. He might whisper sweetly, full of cadences and song, as he does in the work of W. D. Ehrhart, or overpower with lush details as he does in the poetry of John Balaban, or overwhelm us with narrative moments, of miniature dramas, as Bruce Weigl does. Sometimes his voice manifests itself in a more traditional narration, as in books by Winston Groom, Smith Hempstone, Robin Moore, Jonathan Rubin, Tom Suddick, Robert Roth, and Bo Hathaway. At other times he uses traditional fiction as a cover to subvert by an incandescent language. My copy of William Pelfrey's *Big V* is so dogeared from thumbing through it, rereading it, and bending back pages to mark certain sections that I've replaced it several times already—and what I wouldn't do to get a hardcover of that novel. "Fuck you" is such a worn expression that its abundance in this literature is numbing; but Pelfrey's grunts curse like no one this good since Mark Twain, and invariably the expletive is: *Fuck me!*

As in:

He took the machete and started chopping with short angled strokes, but soon stopped, running his fingers along the blade.
"Where'd you get this machete?"

"Why?" asked Fi Bait. He walked over to us.

"It don't look like regular issue."

"It's NVA. Welch got it at Dak To."

"NVA?" He examined it carefully. "Did you fill out a tag on it?"

"You gotta be shittin me, Kell. Tag, shit!"

"This never even was turned in, was it? You know it should have been turned in for G-2."

"Fuck me, Kell. It's only a goddamned machete."

Pelfrey's *Big V* is allseeing voice, and its scatty, scatological dialogue has a verbal magnificence to it. Nearly every page is filled with snippets of verbal banter that exude humor, authenticity, drama, and revelation. Another voice-centered novel is *No Bugles, No Drums* by Charles Durden, which like Pelfrey's novel, is finger-snapping prose, full of bebop rhythms, and verbal riffs.

Tryin' to describe the country we moved through is like what old what's his name musta felt tryin' to describe the circles of Hell. Foliage thick as hair on a sow's ass. Lots of time you couldn't see ten feet to either side of the track, or twenty feet straight up. Two 'n' three layers of green growth, vines the size of soda bottles, some the size of whisky jars, sixty to seventy feet long running' down the trees 'n' across the ground. You'd bust your ass at least once or twice a day. Thorns like twenty-penny nails. Rip you to shreds, rake your glasses off, hang you up 'r tear your weapon right outa your hand.

Durden's narrative descriptions blend with his dialogue, all of a kind of Southern wash, the poetry of natural speech, that old Southern gift of tongues. Pelfrey's is via Kentucky transplanted to Detroit.

That is only part of it, though.

There is Josiah Bunting's *Lionheads*, John Cassidy's *A Station in the Delta*, William Eastlake's *Bamboo Bed*, Joe Haldeman's *War Year,* Norman Mailer's *Why Are We in Vietnam?,* Robert Stone's *Dog Soldiers,* David Winn's *Gangland.*

Some of these I have not dealt with, because—like David Rabe's *Streamers* and his other Vietnam War plays—other writers have addressed their work quite well. I strongly recommend, for instance, Philip Beidler's study, especially for his analysis of Rabe and for his incisive analysis of the early writings when the literature was as quiet as the origin of this war. As popular as some of this literature may appear presently, I still perceive of it as a fugitive art form, meaning, I don't think it can ever be totally popular, because it remains subcultural, even if it occasionally captures wide audiences.

In many respects the ronin is our perfect follow-up to John Wayne, because there is something about antiheroes that Americans love, from Huckleberry Finn to Yosarian. It goes back to our constitutional beginnings as a people; we are a nation of individuals, not a well-knit fabric speaking in one voice. The ronin, as I said, can even speak with several voices at once, as though he were a ventriloquist. From an untitled work in progress, in another visitation from the American ronin after Vietnam, Joseph Ferrandino places his ronin in Valley Forge Hospital, a psychiatric military installation in Pennsylvania. Ferrandino's ronin sums up, for the moment, at least, the condition of the masterless samurai. After a tour of duty in Vietnam the narrator is trying to convince the captain-doctor that he is crazy. He hears voices. But there is a twist, because even though he fakes being crazy, perhaps the narrator really is crazy.

"He asks me do I hear voices. *Do I hear voices?* I know what he is up to. I say *yes* and the doctor writes it down."

The ronin hears voices; not only does he hear voices, but he *sees* voices, and over and over again, he repeats the rhythm of his experience, to himself, to others, showing us, not telling us. Yes, he is untethered, because he began franchised and established, but by breath and syllable, in the strict joy of tragic rhythms, often laughing all the way, he finds himself, and us, disenfranchised, antiestablishment. And yet like the samurai from the epics, the ronin in his drama remains a patriot, he wants to believe, and, finally, if nothing else, he believes in his disbelief and disillusionment. That is his way. Or he will say, "That is the way." Then he walks, not into the sunset, which cowboys and samurai do, no, no, he limps, he hobbles, while in the darkness of night, he finds illumination in the rounds lighting up the warrior sky. And, as John Clark Pratt says, there is nothing more beautiful than someone else's firefight.

8

Korea: Theresa Hak Kyung Cha

Notes from an Abandoned Work

It is nearly a year since I first read Theresa Cha's *Dictee,* and I have not made any revisions on the essay I wrote, nor have I managed to expand it as I intended. Right now [summer 1984] I am in the Sorak Mountains, an isolated mid-coastal region on the Korean peninsula. Up early, from my hotel window, I see the great mountain range in front of me, the jagged peaks shrouded in low clouds. It is raining, but the summer air is wonderful, the humidity is not as cloying as it has been in Seoul, 120 miles, and seven hours away, descending the snakelike roadways out of these mountains, and then through lesser ranges, rice paddies, and rivers to cross. The phantomlike mountains look exactly like those folk paintings. Korea is a rocky, mountainous country, and as my mother-in-law said, it is the rocks in the folk paintings which distinguish Korean art from either Chinese or Japanese paintings. It is nearly impossible, even outside Sorak San, to not see a mountain or river, and this is true in Seoul as well. I often think that I experience Korea not with my eyes or ears but through my legs, my thighs, and calves, ascending and descending hills and mountainsides.

Back in Seoul a few days earlier I would rise at dawn and take a long walk up one of the northern mountains with my brother-in-law, who is married to my wife's sister and in whose house we are staying. If I did not get up and go out this early in the morning, walking as far as the crumbling wall of the ancient city, where a soldier is posted, because the top of the mountain is restricted to military personnel only—if I did not get up early—the sun baked the streets and mountains, making it impossible to go out until nightfall. The peninsula is a wintery cold place mostly, but in July and August it becomes nearly tropical, the monsoon rains come daily, and the heat goes into the nineties and sometimes over one hundred degrees, and the humidity makes it awfully uncomfortable.

The Sorak Mountains are cool, though, and the mountain air is even better than coffee and a cigarette to wake up. I am thinking about a lot of things, watching a group of older people, workers, lugging heavy bundles down a mountain path, fording a stream, and going off to market. Later I discover that they have been gathering roots. This is an industrious land, only a few steps behind Japan in industrial production. Seoul is big and polluted, a city of ten million hardworking people. Out in the countryside the farmers still backbreakingly plant rice plants, one by one, and the farm life is arduous and difficult. I seem to be the only person in the country not working. But I am thinking, standing on this tiny balcony, watching several of the hundred waterfalls breaking from the mountain rocks, their loud music filling my ears.

It is all about numbers, and I am looking at a book of Chinese characters used in the Korean language. The character which interests me most in this early morning hour in the mountains is that for "novel." *So Seol.* Small talk/ small story. The second sound is made up, on its left side, with a classifier for speech or words. Its right top contains the number eight, which means "breaking up." The bottom part is a character I know quite well by now, and that is "older brother," the mouth with legs. The walking mouth. The big mouth. The loud voice. Somehow it comes down to this: to explain by talking. It is a "story" but it has come to mean "novel."

Numbers are important in Theresa Cha's book, *Dictee,* a work whose essence is really a talking story like the Korean definition for a novel. There are the nine muses which inspire the nine chapters of her book. There are the faces of nine women on the back of the paperback edition. There are eights, too, the number which means "breaking up," and there is ten, as she wrote, "a circle within a circle, a series of concentric circles." But I am thinking of the number four, because I am on the fifth floor of this hotel, but I am only four stories off the ground. That is because there usually is no fourth floor in Korean buildings. Four is bad luck, like our own number thirteen. Four also means death. *Sa.* Each time I have returned to my essay about Theresa Cha's writing that number four has haunted me, and each time I walked away from finishing the essay, because I knew that the best I could do was to abandon this work in despair. That is because Theresa Cha's *Dictee* was published in 1982, and shortly after it was released—she was murdered.

It happened in New York City, where I mostly live, and which is ten thousand miles away from where I am now. This is the country where Theresa Cha was born and which she left as an adolescent, going from there to Hawaii, and finally San Francisco. She attended Berkeley, and she also studied in France. Her interests were writing, for which task she was eminently qualified, both as fiction writer and scholar. She also was involved in video. Her husband, Richard Barnes, a photographer, had moved with Theresa, one and a half years before her death, from Berkeley to New York. They had known each other for six years, but had only been married six months at the time of her murder. They lived downtown, in an old Italian neighborhood east of SoHo. They were newlyweds. As Richard told me when I met him the day after Thanksgiving in 1983 down at the Caffe Dante in the Village, "We were only married a short time."

He paused there, looking blank and lonely, then he continued.

"We were still getting to know each other in this new relationship."

This meeting came about because I had ordered her book from a small-press catalogue. I have lived in Korea, am married to a Korean, and I try to read any books in English either written by Koreans or about the country. There still are not many Koreans writing in English. Of an older generation I think of Richard Kim and Young-Ik Kim, the translator Peter Lee, and a handful of other poets, scholars, and fiction writers. I honestly did not expect to find very much by ordering this work, but her name sounded Korean, and I decided to read her book. I thought Theresa Cha an extraordinary writer, and I still think *Dictee* an important, singular work. Some of it has to do with its Koreanness, but it also has to do with her influences, like Samuel Beckett, her own intelligence, and how she fuses these things with a nearly meditational force. I could not stop singing her praises, to my wife, to our Korean friends. Finally I decided to see if she lived in New York, she was listed in the telephone book on Elizabeth Street, and I called. It was Richard Barnes who told me that she had been murdered.

I think at first he did not know what to think; I was calling him nearly a year after her book was published and she had been murdered. Obviously, it was still an impossible experience for him to sort out and put together. Shortly after that I wrote what amounts to the second part of this essay, hoping to revise it and expand it, as I said, but I have not. When I went back to Korea in the summer of 1984, I brought along one of my two copies of *Dictee,* the hardcover which Richard had given me, and I hoped that given some time, while relaxing with family and friends, I'd reread the novel, make new notes, and write the essay I wanted to write about Theresa and *Dictee.* That morning on the balcony of the hotel in Sorak San I held the hardcover in my hand, rereading passages, trying to write down some notes. But I was not getting anywhere, and decided to take a walk to the seventh-century Silla dynasty Buddhist temple up the road.

It was that old thing about experiencing Korea through your thighs and calves, and I thought maybe this walk would clear my head about *Dictee.* Understand, this is a beautifully difficult work of fiction, and I have no problem articulating my admiration for its listening ear and its seeing voice. Theresa Cha was perhaps more voice-centered than any of the writers I have studied in this work. Her writing is not the problem; it is her death which troubles me. It has to do with the fact that we get to know writers in their work, and I feel, without ever having met her, that I know Theresa Cha, and I also have this certainty, from meeting her husband, Richard, several times now, that she would have been one of my good friends, I mean, I am certain that we would have gotten along very well. Theresa Cha is a kindred spirit to me. But it is the idea, so painful, that a voice so rich and talented, a voice so useful to the landscape of fiction, would be silenced so early on in her career. That is what drives me to inaction;

that is what troubles me, even in this idyllic mountain setting, walking in the heady air, of Sorak San.

But it is this landscape of mountains and rivers without end, which has to be evoked to understand the roots of Theresa Cha's voice. Her voice contains the mountain spirits, I mean, the mountain god, and its simple, jagged pattern, the short sentences, the steady accumulations of words and details and emotions, it is like the Diamond Mountains themselves, Kum-Gang, only a few miles north of here, alas, in North Korea, over a treacherous DMZ. The Communists got Kum-Gang and Kaesong. The latter was legendary for its beautiful women and its entertainers, its woman poets like Hwang Jini and Myung-Ok. The former was known for its roaming tigers. It is probably a good idea to keep in mind the roaming tiger and the beautiful poets of Kaesong when thinking about Theresa Cha's voice. I think qualities of both are trapped there.

As I walk toward the ancient temple I realize that Korea's mountains have drunk so much blood, that on the bus to Sorak San the guide tells us about different battles, of nearly two thousand wars in as many years, and I recall with a good deal of sadness how so many Korean writers died young. When I spoke earlier about tragedy regarding the Vietnam War, this condition is perhaps even more eminent in the Korean landscape, and once breath is given to circumstance, it becomes a question of which tragedy to pick. This is a beautiful country, and it can be unremittingly sad as well. What makes Theresa Cha's story the saddest for me is the fact that she was a writer and a contemporary and a burgeoning talent, that her life was snuffed out by some dirty-handed psychopath loser in the basement of a New York building with nothing to offer the world but his disgusting violence and a rat-minded dream.

Beauty and sadness, they seesaw in my mind, placing one foot on one stone, the other foot on the next stone, feeling Korea, as I say, in my legs, ascending this mountain path. Stillness. Inwardness. Language. I keep thinking of those qualities in *Dictee*. I say to myself, the world turns. You must go on. My legs move as though in a cadence with a sentence from Samuel Beckett, "it can't speak, it can't cease." Or in the rain splattering the big-leafed paulownia tree, I hear another Beckett cadence, "nothing ever but nothing and never, nothing ever but lifeless words." And I go on, my copy of *Dictee* inside my Gore-Tex raincoat so that it won't get wet. I am thinking about something one of my brothers-in-law said, which was that Korea was a great country—if you are a man. That is because it is still a most Confucian country, and nearly all privilege is male-oriented. Marriages are arranged by families; women become mothers and raise families, they take care of the household. In this light it is especially interesting to read a Korean woman's voice so charged by intelligence and life, so ascendant and liberating in its range, so honest and wise, and even after it is Americanized, so unwilling to give up the spirit of this rocky place. Korea is a nation of music lovers, and Theresa Cha's prose is as musical as a talking song. She might baffle these Korean men around me, in their slickers and carrying umbrellas, cameras slung across their chests like eternal tourists. But I think, let them be baffled.

They would be baffled by Yu Guan Soon or Joan of Arc or St. Theresa, the women evoked in Cha's fiction. They might be baffled by her mother, whose story *Dictee* is. Or they might not be. These are earthy, real people, and their native spirit is innately artistic, which explains why China and Japan and Russia, the surrounding countries, always tried to conquer the peninsula. Part of it is the sheer beauty of the landscape, these mountains, I mean, but the greater part, I think, is professional jealousy. It was difficult for these larger countries to tolerate the creative mind which Koreans bring to their lives. A lot of it has to do with that native instinct for song. People are always singing in Korea, children do it, adults do it, and as I leave this Silla dynasty temple, I hear an old man in front of me, his throaty old voice belting out a song, no doubt, to the local mountain god.

Dictee is like that, too. It is a recitative, and perhaps it is best understood, not as fiction, not as philosophy, not as religious meditation—all of which it is to various degrees—but as song. Its sound is that of a Korean woman speaking in her invented English. It is how I hear English all over the peninsula, jagged and broken like the mountains, and always resonating. But it has been nearly a year since I wrote anything about this gifted writer. Perhaps, I think, this will be the day of a breakthrough; I will walk up this mountain trail, stone to stone, for a few miles, always going upward, and I will breathe this mountain air, and I will locate syllables. I will finish my essay about Theresa Cha.

In a mountain stream there is a white crane, standing near the water. Since leaving Seoul a few days ago, coming these 120 miles through mountains and over rivers, alongside of rivers and over mountains, I have seen many white cranes, usually in pairs, meditating, as it were, in the center of rice paddies. They remind me of some notes Richard Barnes provided about Or-Da-To who watched an ape and a white crane fight in the mountains. From the ape's footwork and the crane's wing beats he created eight fist forms, eight footwork forms, eight finger techniques, eight kicking techniques, eight slapping techniques, and eight grasping techniques. That covers eight, I think, watching the white crane, so majestic, so calm in these mountains, but what about nine?

My mother had an impossible number of children; a sister once told me there were seventeen pregnancies. But there are nine children living. I know about the number nine. If I did not have the hardcover of *Dictee* with me and I looked at the paperback, I would see those nine Korean women on the back, and I would understand what it is like to have your photograph taken with eight other people. It was the standard operating procedure of my childhood. But my own family is a broken, fractured entity. Here in Korea the family is everything, a curse and a blessing, the overriding principle of an entire society. Children are adored, in and outside the home, by relatives, by strangers, by policemen on corners. As a member of my wife's family I enjoy an incredible privilege among the men, and I am given even too much respect and deference. But my father-in-law is the patriarch, and there are little things which must be followed. No grown man as long as he is of a younger generation than the head of household would dare smoke a cigarette in front of the patriarch. Last night was typical of this, and at the end of dinner my father-in-law rises, even if he is enjoying conversation, and leaves the dining room in order that the men at the table can smoke.

That tight family is evident in Theresa Cha's writing, not only in the tale itself, the daughter taking dictation for her mother, but in other documents I have seen about her, a white memorial book which Richard Barnes gave me, its covers filled with pages of homage, a love letter from her mother, a poem from her father. I call it Korean magic, that togetherness, that tightness, and when it works, it is beautiful and terribly powerful, and when it intrudes, it is probably worse than having ten wives fighting for your affection at once. Inside my copy of *Dictee* I have a letter from Theresa's mother, thanking me for what amounts to the second part of this abandoned work. It is written in elegant script, using *hangul,* Korea's phonetic language, and since my Korean is poor (I speak a little/I can't read at all), my wife had to translate it. I thought I had misplaced the letter, but I am surprised to see it inside the book, and that it traveled ten thousand miles with me, that I have it in my hand in Sorak San. I owe this essay to Mrs. Cha and I owe it to Richard Barnes and I owe it to myself and to the memory of Theresa Cha. I know all that, and my sore legs know it, as again I hear a rhythm as though from Beckett.

"I can't go on, I must go on . . ."

It is easy to understand geomancy and shamans and animism in these mountains. Of course there is a mountain god, and of course there are spirits in the air and spirits in the earth. Of course Tangun was a bear and the founder of this peninsula. When I think about Theresa Cha, whom I know by her writing and nothing else, and a few photographs I saw in the white memorial book, I tell myself that her spirit is everlasting, she wrote a great book. But maybe even in my own lifetime this idea of a book will be obsolete. The rhythm of experience will be trapped elswhere, or maybe first a nation and then a world will forget entirely about the seeing voice, about breath and syllable, and everything that I think is good in a life and in the life of our fiction.

I go beyond a stone patio and some girls hawking soft drinks and beer and I find myself alone in this elevated place, the sun blocked out by the tall pines, the rocks full of water running down them. It is slippery and precipitous, and I move carefully through this part of the trail. I am walking to a place called Bi-Son (Place of Flying Angels), and I am going to sit and listen to white water, breathe mountain air, and find syllables. I wish my wife were here, but she is further back on the trail with our daughter. I wish Richard Barnes were here. And I only wish I knew his wife, and maybe all of us would discuss movies and Beckett and language and fiction and . . . But that is only a saddening wish, a frustrating one, even a ridiculous thought. I keep moving up the trail, my clothing soaked, not by rain, but by perspiration. My heart is pounding; this is excercise.

Dictee is like this climbing; the rhythm of the experience is Korean, but the words are in English. That involution of thought. The tongue going inward, scraping the walls of memory. Like tomb rubbings at King Onjo's burial mound, gargoyles appearing on the waxy paper. I sit down. I must rest. I hear the white water running, the granite mountains, rising, rising, forever upward. I am near the place of angels. I sit on a granite slab of rock and I crack open the book, and I read, "From all deaths. To the one death. One and only remaining. From which takes place annunciation. A second coming." I close the book. I stare off into the water, listening, listening. The rain has stopped, the sky lightens, but there is no sunlight. Some dog-weary mountain climbers, not hikers, come down the trail, probably having gone miles and miles into Sorak San. They look like grunts from photographs of the Vietnam War. They are tough and lean and kind of hippyish, a fashion not often encountered in this martial land. There are three men and a woman, and they appear to be college students. Their thighs are bulging with muscles. They wear headbands like Willie Nelson, backpacks harnessed behind them, one carries a carved stick. They smile at me.

"It's a nice day," he says, his English too careful and slow and finally too perfect.

"Yes, it is," I say.

"Hello," another says.

The woman lowers her eyes, that shy gesture you see a million times by women in Korea. She giggles.

"So long," another says.

I wave goodby.

When they leave, I return to my thoughts of that white memorial book which Richard Barnes gave me, and I am thinking about a long letter her mother wrote and a sad poem by her father and how he has not even seen Theresa in his dreams, and I think of a Myung-Ok poem which begins, "It is said that a lover seen in dreams/will prove to be an unfaithful love," but that it is only in dreams that she sees her love, and she ends by saying, let me see you in my dreams always. When I first met Theresa's husband, he had just returned for *jae-sa,* a memorial service for her in California. This made me think of that ceremony, which is not morbid, at least the one I saw in Seoul was not, and how human and touching it is. There are objects which the deceased was associated with, some food or drink they liked, personal effects, that sort of thing. It made me think what someone might have for me, a can of Budweiser, a shot of Bushmills, Selby's novel, a poem by Robert Creeley, my cigarettes, maybe a paddle-ball racquet, a beat-up boxing glove, *sushi* (probably *neggi toro* handroll). Some music. What would it be? Thelonious Monk, I would imagine. Someone might read a Yeats poem. Someone would read a passage from my work.

I recall a letter from one of Theresa's friends in the memorial book and a letter she wrote back, which I find quite touching. "I have a soft constitution. And a strong one, at times, or at least at the center, nothing seems to deter it, to dislocate it, it is there, I am certain of it, whatever it is . . . but there is a constant light still, inside us, in me, that lives, that moves." And there is a poem by one of her siblings.

> Watch me. Captive of linen.
> I am a butterfly.
> My winged heart flutters, trembles, quivers.

But I must move on, I realize. And I stand up and move up the mountain trail, wondering how much farther it is to the Place of Flying Angels, to Bi-Son. Then the sky lightens, I see the sunlight, and ahead of me I come upon a bridge, and there it is—the Place of Flying Angels. It is as though I walked into the landscape of a great folk painting and find myself a character in a many-paneled screen, an unending series of nines. It is nearly too marvelous to believe, and so I go inside a pavillion and order myself a bottle of OB beer and I take a long drink from the glass bottle, then I sit in the shade at a table, the white water now deafening.

Finally, I suppose this is addressed to Theresa Cha as much as to myself or to her family and friends. I am afraid that I can only offer these notes, which I abandoned in the Place of Flying Angels, realizing that I had something to say, but I do not have the emotional content with which to say it. This is an abandoned lecture, even an abandoned homage, but I think Theresa Cha would understand the reference. She understood her Beckett. What follows then are the notes I wrote upon first reading *Dictee* [in New York City, 1983], and which I have not been able to amplify. I drink some more beer and now light a cigarette; I raise my glass in a toast, even though I am sitting alone.

"Here is to study (*hak*) and respect (*kyung*). Here is to you, Theresa."

Dictee

Dictee is a fiction, a prose, a daring and poetic work, brilliantly original, full of charged idiomatic utterance, as well as being vanguard, even deeply philosophical, in its thought. It is the synthesis of a life, which is formed from the disparities of our age. First, it is the utterance, the speech, the language, of a young Korean exile. (More often it appears to be Ms. Cha's mother or herself personified by her mother.) It is mystical, nondenominationally catholic, though also quite Catholic, too, and chilling in how it penetrates memory and experience with its detail and observation. Parts are written in an idiomatic Korean-English rhythm; other parts use French. The thought I take to be quintessentially Korean intellectual, but it is filtered through several strata of ethnicity and culture.

All of this is said with a kind of hollowness in me. When I read this book, I immediately found a kindred spirit in terms of experimentation and experience in Ms. Cha's writing. There were murmurs of Beckett, of language philosophy, of Korea's two great twentieth-century poets, Kim Sowol (1903–34) and Yi Sang (1910–37). Kim was Korean's great lyric poet; Yi Sang was its darker conscience, a drug addicted, tubercular *poete maudit*. The assumption that one would like to make about Korean writers is that they might flourish beyond their short years. Too many of them die young, and tragically, and for all the life in Cha's *Dictee,* unfortunately, she likewise is part of a Korean literary pattern to be exquisitely brilliant and poetic, and to die young. But these are afterthoughts, because I read this book ignorant of these biographical details.

Dictee itself is discontinuous in its structure, which consists of nine parts, each section given two titles, one classical, one generic, for instance, "Clio"/"History." This includes Calliope, Urania, Melpomene, Erato, Elitere, Thalia, Terpsichore, and Polymnia, as well as Epic Poetry, Astronomy, Tragedy, Love Poetry, Lyric Poetry, Comedy, Choral Dance, and Sacred Poetry. Koreans are shamanistic first, and the number nine has mystical associations going back to an ancient text entitled *Nine Cloud Dream.*

The book begins with a prose poem, written first in French and then in English. "Open paragraph It was the first day period She had come from a far period tonight at dinner comma the families would ask comma open quotation marks How was the first day interrogation mark" The next short introductory section is titled "Diseuse," setting the tone for the entire work. "She mimicks the speaking. That might resemble speech. (Anything at all.) Bared noise, groan, bits torn from words. Since she hesitates to measure the accuracy, she resorts to mimicking gestures with the mouth."

Self-conscious, reflexive, language-centered, and charged with the music of spokenness, Cha invokes Sappho as her muse, and proceeds into the voice of her book. Immediately following these invocative passages there is a French excercise. "Ecrivez en francais: 1. If you like this better, tell me so at once. 2. The general remained only a little while in this place. 3. If you did not speak so quickly, they would understand you better." The purpose of this "excercise" is to create the context of emotional biography in the exiled voice of Korea. These seemingly innocuous language excercises actually mask a deeper utterance, for each one of these commonly phrased sentences has a haunting resonance throughout *Dictee*. Rote gradually gives way to a deeper significance; mimicry is replaced by the exhilaration of discovery and invention. The transitional passage in this journey occurs in the next apologia, a catechism as it were of Cha's spiritual life.

"Black ash from the Palm Hosannah. Ash. Kneel down on the marble the cold beneath rising through the bent knees. Close eyes and as the lids flutter, push out the tongue.

"The Host Wafer (His body. His Blood) His. Dissolving in the mouth to the liquid tongue saliva (Wine to Blood. Bread to Flesh.) His. Open the eyes to the women kneeling on the left side. The right side. Only visible on their bleached countenances are the unevenly lit circles of rouge and their elongated tongues. In waiting. To receive. Him."

Speech as mystical utterance. It is a chant, an ancient belief in the word being holy. In this section another language lesson appears. "Translate into French," followed by a series of numbered sentences, prayers, journal entries, poetry. Here, for example, is sentence 7, full of Korean speech in English yet also echoing Samuel Beckett's *Comment c'est*: "Forget and would be forgotten close eyes and would be forgotten not say and they are forgotten not admit and they are forgotten like sins say them they are forgiven forgotten and they are forgotten."

The first formal section of *Dictee* is "Clio"/"History," being a poetic biography of Yu Guan Soon, the great revolutionary and patriot, a woman, from the early part of this century. I am reminded here of Williams' *Paterson* and Olson's *Maximus Poems,* even though this is prose, because Cha seamlessly mixes her own words and utterances with historical materials, juxtaposing, hammering out her earthy rhythms, experimental yet deeply Korean traditional. As Cha points out, Yu Guan Soon is a Korean Joan of Arc, even a kind of Wonder Woman in terms of myth, legend, and ritual. It is the image of feminine transcendance in the minds of every Korean schoolgirl. Yu is what every Korean becomes were she able to transcend custom and manners, fly off from the hearth, and be as courageous as any warrior. Maxine Hong Kingston's *Woman Warrior* is written out of a similar legend, though it should be stressed that Yu literally was real and did the things historically as well as mythically ascribed to her.

What needs pointing out here, because it is typified in the strategy of this first major section of *Dictee* and is repeated in subsequent sections is that Cha manages to transcend autobiography by creating personae for herself, going inside history, assuming the countenances of others, a Yeatsian thing, that is. "Calliope"/"Epic Poetry" continues this historical personification in the guise of biography. This section is based on the journals of Hyung Soon Huo, whose mother is the first generation of Korean exiles born in Manchuria, the result of a diaspora created by the Japanese annexation of Korea earlier in this century. Again, the voice of the exile is articulated, historical materials are worked from the inside out, and an emotional pitch, a personal voice, is given to the generalizations of history.

"Mother, you are a child still. At eighteen. More of a child since you are always ill. They have sheltered you from life. Still, you speak the tongue the mandatory language like the others. It is not your own. Even if it is not you know you must. You are Bilingual. You are Tri-lingual. The tongue that is forbidden is your own mother tongue. You speak in the dark. In the secret. The one that is yours. Your own. You speak very softly, you speak in a whisper. In the dark, in secret. Mother tongue is your refuge. It is being home. Being who you are."

Cha flavors this document with her own rhythms, her emotional sounds, her exile's voice. What she is documenting here is a brutal campaign by the Japanese to force all Koreans to abandon their own language and assume the language of the conqueror. During the time chronicled in this journal it was against the law to speak Korean. Parts of this journal read like Cha's translation; other parts show her own blend of highly charged rhythms, and an enviable way the writer works from these specifics into philosophical abstractions. Some of her own more idiosyncratic passages race with the speed and accuracy of the mind itself in action, breathless, discrete, haunting.

"You are going somewhere. You are somewhere. This stillness. You cannot imagine how. Still. So still all around. Such stillness. It is endless. Spacious without the need for verification of space. Nothing moves. So still. There is no struggle. Its own all its own. No where other. No time other conceivable. Total duration without need for verification of time."

Again, there is the theology of this moment as well, and Cha ends this passage on epic poetry with a blending of Christianity (the rhythms of the Bible) and what appears to be an early dynastic form of Buddhist transcendance from late Silla or early Koryo dynasties from about a thousand years ago. The certainty of the spoken is what allows Theresa Cha to synthesize these disparities into a homogeneous fabric of writing.

Korean is a phonetic language, and it was invented by King Sejong about five hundred years ago. Its sound values are earthier than Japanese, and capable of greater abstraction than Chinese. (There are begrudging aspects of Japanese language superimposed on modern Korean language, albeit minimally so; and the Chinese language was that of Korea's several dynasties until the present moment.) In spite of Korea's geographical wedge between China and Japan, linguistically it is related to Altaic languages, running up through Mongolia and either with a terminus or origin in Hungary. It is a language, used by a rigorous Korean scholar, eminently suited to conceptual thinking, and this quality is evidenced throughout the history of Korean literature. As one who has attempted the translation of Korean poetry I can say that this abstract quality in the language is virtually untranslatable in English. In a verse section entitled "Urania"/"Astronomy" Cha captures many qualities, in English, of this Korean penchant for conceptualizing. How she does this, I cannot say, except to testify it is done. More remarkably, this is an *en face* text, one side of which is French, the other English.

> There. Years after
> no more possible to distinguish the rain.
> No more. Which was heard.
> Swans. Speech. Memory. Already said.
> Will just say. Having just said.
> Remembered not quite heard. Not certain.
> Heard, not at all.

"Melpomene"/"Tragedy" fuses qualities which Cha wove into earlier sections: theology, history, emotional and autobiographical images, and the unwavering rhythmical integrity of her prose. Tragedy is a Western song of passion/purpose/ perception; it is a construct which demands language to propel it, yet so often it grows organically from everyday occurence and from the momentum of historical events. Korea's collective tragedy is partly its geographical location, the locus of superpower unrestraint. Wars have been fought on Korea's land since its historical beginning. If it was not China, it was Japan; if it was not the Mongolians, it was the Manchurians (once Koreans themselves). Or it was the Russians and the United States. A personal moment in that tragedy were the student riots of April 19, 1962, an important moment in postwar Korea.

"Coming home from school there are cries in all the streets. The mounting of shouts from every direction from the crowds arm in arm. The students. I saw them, older than us, men and women held to each other. They walk into the *others* who wait in *their* uniforms. Their shouts reach a crescendo as they approach nearer to the *other side*. Cries resisting cries to move forward. Orders, permission to use force against the students, have been dispatched. To be caught and beaten with sticks, and for others, shot, remassed, and carted off. They fall they bleed they die. They are thrown into gas into the crowd to be squelched."

All of these experiences are recounted in a letter to Cha's mother, her eleven-year-old's memories triggered by a visit to Korea eighteen years later, her first time back since leaving. "We left here in this memory still fresh, still new. I speak another tongue, a second tongue. This is how distant I am. From then. From that time."

"Erato"/"Love Poetry" is written, in part, like a movie treatment: "She enters the screen from the left, before the titles fading in and fading out. The white subtitles on the black background continue across the bottom of the screen. The titles and names in black appear from the upper right hand corner, each letter moving downwards on to the whiteness of the screen. She is drawn to the white, then the black. In the whiteness the shadows move across, dark shapes and dark light."

Love in this section is first glimpsed seductively by the medium of film. It is also about spiritual love as portrayed by St. Theresa's marriage to the Holy Face. It is also about the love between a husband and a wife.

"He is the husband, and she is the wife. He is the man. She is the wife. It is a given. He does as he is the man. She does as she is the woman, and the wife. Stands the distance between the husband and wife the distance of heaven and hell. The husband is seen. Entering the house shouting her name, calling her name. You find her for the first time as he enters the room calling her. You only hear him taunting and humiliating her. She kneels beside him, putting on his clothes for him. She takes her place. It is given. It is the night of her father's wake, she is in mourning."

Cha's love is transcendant, yet not sentimental. Her images cut deeper than romance. It is etched in the real, the harsher side of relationships. And because of her gift of personification, the passage is Cha and is not Cha. Partly it is a movie of her life; partly it appears to be another life, or her life through her mother. The simultaneous push and pull of distancing and the whispers of sensual intimacy make this the tensest, and therefore most dramatic passage in *Dictee*. With her resource for abstraction and intellectual grace, Cha seems to suggest that she likewise is a writer rooted to the earth, and that memory and experience are palpable, real, and painful.

"She is married to her husband who is unfaithful to her. No reason is given. No reason is necessary except that he is a man. It is a given." "Her marriage to him, her husband. Her love for him, her husband, her duty to him, her husband." At the moment when Cha's persona appears to beg the reader's sympathy, there is a Brechtian kind of distancing which occurs. See, it seems to say, this is only a movie. "He leaves the room. She falls to the floor, your eyes move to the garden where water is dripping into the stone well from the bark of a tree. And you need not see her cry." The overlap of the real and illusory weaves further when the voice of the narration turns from marital love to mother love. "Mother you who take the child from your back to your breast you who unbare your breast to the child her hunger is your own the child takes away your pain with her nourishment/Mother you you who take the husband from your back to your breast you who unbare your breast to the husband his hunger your own the husband takes away your pain with his nourishment." The last quotation suggests that Cha's greatest strength, beyond her intellectual and conceptual abilities, beyond her images, beyond the historical and cross-cultural allusions, is her lyrical force, a voice charged with energy and emotion.

"Elitere"/"Lyric Poetry": *Dictee* in its final arc, devolving
upon these latter sections to summarize what has been articulated throughout. By this point in the overall text it is clear
that the nine central elements of Cha's voice have been filtered through each section as well as being highlighted in
their specific contexts. By this I mean that a quality like
"erato" is nearly a given by this point in her inner narrative
as is the "lyrical" of this section. Thought and memory
haunt this author, and she never evades their greater implica-
tions. "Let her break open the spell cast upon time upon time
again and again. With her voice, penetrate earth's floor, the
walls of Tartaurus to circle and scratch the bowl's surface.
Let the sound enter from without, the bowl's hollow its sleep.
Until." Here the need to break lines, to draw in breath is apparent as it was in "Urania"/"Astronomy." Speech is broken
into breath and syllable, Charles Olson's measures, even Cicero's measures, though the latter included "tongue" as well,
a most appropriate ingredient in a recipe to understand *Dictee*. Cha is a better prose writer than she is a poet, but once
her poetry is understood within the lyrical and intellectual
traditions of Korean literature, even the poems have their
grandeur.

> Make numb some vision some word some part
> resembling part something else
> pretend
> not to see pretend not having seen the part.

The poetry is followed by Cha's most meditative passages,
reminiscent of Beckett's *Texts for Nothing*. "Retour" takes the
object of a room partition, and renders the metaphor into a
geopolitical realm of Korea's partition. "Fine grain sanded
velvet wood . . . pale sheet of paper " becomes the human
partition, the act of separation, of division. "If words are to

be uttered, they would be from behind the partition." This seemingly harmless phrase has a signification in Korean, which has to do with powerful women, who in a Confucian world cannot rule overtly, but rather from "behind a screen" or partition. This section ends with what amounts to a recapitulation of the chapter as well as the entire book to this moment—as well as a summary of the book's future, the remaining three chapters.

> Dead words. Dead tongue. From disuse. Buried in Time's memory. Unemployed. Unspoken. History. Past. Let the one who is diseuse, one who is mother who waits nine days and nine nights be found. Restore memory. Let the one who is diseuse, one who is daughter restore spring with her each appearance from beneath the earth.
> The ink spills thickest before it runs dry before it stops writing at all.

"Thalia"/"Comedy": This is the humor of the unsmiling, silent comedian, a Buster Keaton. The voice does not waiver from its initial pulse. Again, Cha is probing self—her mother's and her self. Why? "To keep the pain from translating itself into memory." I cannot remember how I first read this passage, but there is now a hollowness when I read, "She says to herself that death would never come, could not possibly. She knowing too that there was no displacing death, there was no overcoming without the actual dying."

But this is a writer dictating the words upon the page, and a writer's life is in her words. *"She says to herself if she were able to write she could continue to live."* Two "memories" follow, and these are followed by "Memory." In the first memory the act of writing, fired by the coals of memory, is evoked as a kind of ultimate sensual act. "The forefinger touches the lip skin, as

her eyes now close she might have sighed she might have
moaned she takes the forefinger on her hand and barely
reaches over to the shoulder the jacket where the pen is
placed inside the pocket." The second memory is an epitha-
lamium, a marriage poem. It is sensual, but again it is not
sentimental, not nostalgic in any sense. Cha dices her experience, splitting it by the centimeters of language. "It would
not be unforgettable. It would be most memorable." How
nuanced, exact, and subtle the juxtaposition of those two sentences! Separated, they are innocuous; braided into this narrative, they resonate with authenticity.

The final two-and-one-half pages of this section are subti-
tled "Memory." Like a theme and variation upon the "Erato"/"Love Poetry" section the narrator enters a theater.
There is the interplay of light and shadows on a screen. "Second day in the theatre. Second time. She is sitting in the same
place as the day before. As the first day. Turning left to see
her, she is alone, immobile in her body. Her hands are folded
on her lap with her other belongings. She hovers in a silent
suspension of the simulated night as a flame that gives itself
stillness and equally to wind as it rises. Her eyes open to distance as if to linger inside that which has passed in shadow
and darkness." "She remains for the effect induced in her,
fulfilled in the losing of herself repeatedly to memory and simultaneously its opposition, the arrestation of memory in
oblivion. (regardless. Over and over. Again. For the time.
For the time being.)" The meditation is that of a silent woman
in a darkened room, with only one other person there, a
stranger. The dramaturgy of this moment is the narrator lost
in thought, and that thought-provoking memory—the curse
and blessing. It spirals into a religious moment. "She says to
herself she would return time to itself. To time itself. To time
before time. To the very first death. From all deaths. To the

one death. One and only remaining. From which takes place annunciation. A second coming."

> Before Heaven. Before birth and before that.
> Heaven which in its ultimate unity includes earth
> within itself. Heaven in its ultimate generosity
> includes within itself, Earth. Heaven which is
> not Heaven without Earth (inside itself).

The section ends with the writer coming back to her dictation from angels: "She returns to word, its silence."

"Terpsichore"/"Choral Dance": One of the more deeply abstract passages, it reads, at least, initially like a birth cycle. I say "initially" because much of *Dictee* is sculptural, presenting one set of values in a reading, then unveiling another set upon second reading, and so on. The surface of Cha's style—the first take as it were about her voice—is that of a notational writer. There is a kind of emotional shorthand working. Below this idiomatic surface the text is charged by its lyrical impulses, the repitions more musical in their values than philosophical, though this last quality is present.

"You remain dismembered with the belief that magnolia blooms white even on seemingly dead branches and you wait. You remain apart from the congregation."

In its fetal interplay of darkness and light, stillness and silence, I am reminded of the Japanese writer Tanizaki's architectural treatise *In Praise of Shadows*. "In making for ourselves a place to live, we first spread a parasol to throw a shadow on the earth, and in the pale light of the shadow we put together a house."

Theresa Cha's house is of words, but her words seem to be written in the shadow of that parasol which Tanizaki writes of. It is not a question of utter darkness or of incredible light, but the median of these extremes out of which this text arises. Yet from a Korean point of view there is something almost odious to compare their writing style with a Japanese analogy. In their arts the Japanese are obsessed by the delicate. Koreans are more metaphysical, rendering the spiritual through the aspect of earth. Their songs are hollow-throated, comparable to the West's flamenco in Europe and the blues in the United States. Or take Korean pottery, which goes a long way toward understanding the artistic impulse of *Dictee*'s prose style.

Silla vases are literally earth-colored, dark and still, even silent in their unadorned shapes. Their only designs are seemingly prehistoric comb-markings. A few hundred years later in the Koryo dynasty's vase work, celadon dominates, a greenish blue which eerily approximates the sky behind the yellow-brown granite mountains of the countryside. Like a newborn child's white around the retina of the eyes, Yi dynasty white porcelain is almost blue-white. In things which are bright there is always the shades of darkness. In objects of sky colors there is always the reflection of mountain darkness. With some Korean folk paintings, even discounting their faded colors because of antiquity, the parchment and the pigments thereon are so earthy dark they only can be viewed from a few feet away. It is this latter earthiness of color which I find imbuing so much of this writing. Or put in a comparative way: other language-centered texts are singularly devoid of a "feeling" informing them, whereas Cha's lyricism nearly always is rooted—to the earth, to life, to human feelings. "Muted colors appear from the transparency of the white and wash the stone's periphery, staining the hue-less stone."

"Polymnia"/"Sacred Poetry": this is the most literal of all *Dictee*'s sections. There is a well, a woman at the well, and a child come there. "The wooden bucket hitting the sides echoes inside the well before it falls into the water. Earth is hollow. Beneath." The *ajima* (a housekeeper) seems to represent some otherness, though. It is almost as if she were a *moodong* (a shaman). Sacred poetry is not only myth; there is the ritual as well, and this last section is rounded out by such ritual. "She took off the kerchief that she wore and placed it on her lap. She took the bowl and said she must serve the medicines inside the bowl. After she had completed her instructions, she was to keep the tenth pocket and the bowl for herself as a gift from her. She placed the white bowl in the center of the white cloth. The light renders each whiteness irridescent, encircling the bowl a purple hue. She laid all the pockets inside the bowl, then, taking the two diagonal corners of the cloth, tied two knots at the center and made a small bundle." It is with this bundle that the narrator/persona moves out of the formal structure of the book and enters "Tenth, a circle within a circle, a series of concentric circles."

The envoi is a paragraph about a small girl being lifted to a window, a most appropriate image, because of its outwardness, coming out of the self, the house of the inner life, and looking out to the world, which I take to mean the act of writing this book.

9

Stephen Dixon

A PARADOX ABOUT Stephen Dixon's voice is apparent, and so needs mentioning immediately. His characters nearly always run on, say too much, don't seem to know when to stop. The author does know, i.e., he never says more than he has to. It is perhaps the first noticeable tension in how Dixon's voice sees the landscape of his characters. Then there is a secondary quality which needs mentioning, too. There are all kinds of New York writers, and the kind of New York writer he is needs to be sketched. He is not that kind of New Yorker who comes from Chicago, moves to Manhattan, and becomes the essence of a New Yorker. Dixon's voice is that of the native New Yorker. Its nervous surface, its jitteriness, is not merely urban; it is New York cadenced, even more regional than that, in fact. It is the voice of a Manhattanite (the native sort), though it could be mistaken for a voice from Brooklyn or the Bronx. Yet Dixon's voice centers itself in specific areas of Manhattan, mostly on the Upper West Side, not those chic warrens; his Upper West Siders are working people, middle class, a high school substitute teacher, say, or a paste-up graphic artist. The secondary location of Dixon's voice would be the Lower East Side of the sixties and the early seventies, not hippy, yet hip, more easily found in a bar than a drug den. Again, it is bohemian, but of a working, responsible sort.

Ethnically, Dixon's voice could be called Jewish, only in the sense of that Lenny Bruce line, "In New York, everyone is Jewish—until proven otherwise." How many times, outside of the New York area, someone or another decided I was Jewish, too! It's that voice, its conflicts, and, of course, much of the cadence from New York speech derives from the rhythms of Jewish immigrants on the Lower East Side. But a careful ear will detect Irish and Italian rhythms as well. And, today, the Hispanic, "Yo, my man," which originates with blacks hearing Hispanics begin sentences, "Yo quiero," "Yo soy," "Yo tango." To speak of Dixon's voice being ethnic, which it is, is to suggest that his ethnic background is New York itself. He is a New Yorker.

Again, it is important to be specific in what I mean by New Yorker. For instance, John O'Hara wrote a kind of New Yorker prose; so did John Cheever. Donald Barthelme has his own brand of Texas-bred New Yorker style. (I do not mean here the *New Yorker* magazine voice, even though all the writers mentioned wrote for that publication; I mean writers whose voices are influenced by the geography of this city.) Dixon's New Yorker voice is at times subterranean, but never fugitive. It is a voice that can be strung out by the times but never seems to succumb to the tremors of a particular place. There are problems in abundance which this voice addresses, but it rarely skirts those problems facilely. There is something intelligent in that voice, struggling yet willing to make the struggle. It is a voice with both ideals and objectives.

A casual reading of one Dixon story reveals a nervous surface to that voice; the appearance of the "I" in the narrative, certainly deceptive. Dixon writes the most characterized—and changing story to story—first-person narrative I've ever come across. By that I mean, it is especially unwise to substitute Dixon as the "I," although the author slyly welcomes the misconception, even encourages it, in order to work a greater irony out of a voice which appears to have little or no irony at that first, casual reading. His first-person narrators, in that first misreading, come off autobiographically, and yet a more careful reading shows them to be as fictional in their range as any conventional, third-person narration. In fact, I recall, first reading Dixon's stories, not in book form, but in little magazines, thinking his tone was unironical, too flat, and that he was writing the fiction really out of nonfictional compulsions. Of course, I was wrong about this, as the stories, collected in book form, more than prove. I go; I walk; I sit; I read; I drink; I sleep; I talk. Dixon knows how to place his first-person narrator into a different context and set of circumstances story to story, thus making that "I" different each time. The geography of the fiction is what makes the rhythm of the experience so different in each narration, though to quote these sentences out of context, i.e., without their geographical emphasis, is to create the illusion that each cadence, story to story, is the same. That is a mouthful, but let me explain by example.

Here is the opening of "Mac in Love" from Dixon's first short-story collection, *No Relief:*

"She said 'You're crazy, Mac,' and shut the door. I knocked. She said 'Leave me be?' I rang the bell."

In *14 Stories,* the story "Signatures" begins:

"I'm walking along the streets, on my way from this place to not particularly that, when a man stops me. 'You in show business?' "

"The Barbecue," a story in *Movies,* starts:

"I'm at this apartment with several people who came over for a backyard barbecue at nine o'clock but hadn't known because the hosts couldn't get ahold of everyone that the barbecue had been postponed, when someone says 'I've got to tell this story. All of you—no, everybody, you've got to listen to one of the wildest stories I've ever heard and which is all true. Every last word.' "

The opening story of Dixon's most recent collection of stories, entitled *Time to Go,* commences: "Each year when spring comes I do a lot of handyman work for the row houses that line Wilmin Park Drive on the 2900 to 3300 blocks" ("The Bench").

Out of context, and without the emphasis of a geography—which is what makes Dixon's voice dramaturgical—the "I's" of his fiction seem interchangeable, of one note, i.e., all the same "I." But that observation has more to do with the weakness of literary analysis than it has to do with Dixon's prose. For instance, it has been pointed out many times that William Carlos Williams' poetry does not really change tonally from beginning to end. Yet the objects which that voice sees do change, both in Williams and in Dixon. Put another way, Dixon has found a voice which operates rhythmically the same through all experiences, but the particulars that voice dwells on do change, and that is where the shadings and variations occur.

If there is a dramatic arc to follow in Dixon's ongoing dramaturgy, it is a progression from bachelorhood (the avuncular voice of the early stories), into relationships (commitments), to marriage (the deepest commitment), and recently into fatherhood (the greatest responsibility). In other words, nothing changes in that voice from book to book, and yet everything has changed, completely and totally. That is part of the irony in Dixon's voice, that it appears to be the same but is different each time. Even a casual perusal of a Dixon story isolated in a little magazine reveals measurable qualities about his style. He writes everything, not only his dialogue, with an ear to the spoken. Part of his grammar is undiagrammatic, yet consistent. His sentences don't parse, they sing the American idiom. Toward the end of "Layaways" that everchanging "I" (this an old man) says:

"I return for the funeral and because I don't like the South much with all that sun and beach and older people having nothing to do but wait for death and me with them, I move back for good and open another store, but a much smaller one for candies and greeting cards and things like that in a much safer neighborhood."

And things like that in a much safer neighborhood is not linear; it is presentational. It is how a voice operates in the kingdom of fiction. It is how prose becomes not only fiction but a kind of poetry, because it captures the rhythms of common speech and idealizes it in the dimensions of a sentence.

Let me return to something which was said at the outset and needs elaboration now. Dixon's characters always say too much at the same time that the author is not saying too much. In the title story of *Movies,* Joan has this to say to Bud, her husband, after he left a movie theater after the first showing and she stayed to watch the movie a second time. Joan mentions a separation. "Because of one movie?" Bud asks. "It's a long continuation of things," she says. The dialogue is short, terse, full of its tensions. Then Joan talks, though monologizes would be more accurate: "All right. As I said, it didn't change my life as much as open new things up. Its ideas on women and men and relationships and sex. On the sometimes absurdity of living together as couples and the possibility of undiscovered courage and different lifestyles. It almost documented, as if it knew us, what's been wrong with our personalities together and relationship since its inception, things I've thought about but which that movie made much clearer to me and confirmed. Of the voices we hear. Not so much that. The movie said to me that if your present life is too confining and frustrating and unsatisfactory for reasons you've so far unsuccessfully tried to bring to light, then go out and discover life, that's what. Don't wait for the answers to come from the people and sources that have been most faithful and helpful to you till now, that too. In other words, what it said with that image of the woman feverishly digging around with her hands in the desert and the numerals falling off her watch and then out of her eyes was don't keep looking for water where you've already found there's a ninety-six percent chance there's nothing there but dry sand." And Joan goes on like this for another page. Joan finishes by saying: "And after speaking to Holly—well it's obvious she's gained from her sixteen to seventeen viewings of it as many insights and insights in insights about her life and outsights she also says, that her whole life has changed."

A few sentences later, "She shuts the light. He begins crying."

Locutions are where Dixon characters short-circuit themselves, turning their feelings into an undigested babble. The context is what evokes them and makes them real, even when their verbal ramblings approach the surreal. But like a soliloquy in a play, his characters have a purpose, even when they go on too much. In the end, for all her words about art and life, Joan has one simple purpose. She wants a separation from Bud. Bud's purpose is clear, too. He wants to stay with Joan. Because Joan herself is the obstacle to Bud's objective

(Joan)—Bud cries. The rest is what might be called the stage "business" of Dixon's fiction. Joan's going on, well, it is sad but more importantly it is comic. Her ramblings are a kind of schtick; she speaks where a comedian would do bits. But speech, when Dixon's characters stretch it out, becomes its own kind of bit, i.e., stage business. Lucky in *Waiting for Godot* is also this kind of comedian. So is Molloy in Beckett's novel of the same name. And Dixon himself frequently shows his love and understanding of Beckett's voice by often paying homage to him in the course of the prose.

Something about Dixon's narrators reminds me of Buster Keaton. They are isolated, yet they seek company; in a group, they prefer to go it alone. Their philosophy is common sense—they are as literal as Christ, Buddha, Francis of Assisi, or Gandhi—the very thing which usually gets them and Keaton's characters into complications. These are characters too lovable to get into real trouble, but their souls are those of complicators, like the *zanni* of the *commedia dell'arte*. They would be Kafkaesque except they seem to love life too much to become grim about it. They are gracious plodders, journeymen, workers. Their only revelations seem to be those they strive for, not are given. They do not have revelations like Zen monks. There is even something trampish, in a preppie sort of way. They are not befuddled like Woody Allen characters; they are befuddlers, though. I could see them as friends or colleagues or both of Allen's creations, but not those gentlemen themselves. Mostly they are believers, but even his disbelievers possess a nutty kind of hope about them.

I imagine his characters in Oxford blue shirts, khaki pants, sneakers or boat shoes (really old ones), and if they wear ties, they are out of fashion, and the top button on the shirt is undone. Nowhere does Dixon say this; I am talking about what *I* imagine *his* "I's" to be dressed like. Disheveled, they are still clean-cut, not threatening. It's that lovableness I mentioned about them. Women who do love these characters would call them teddy bears, hopelessly abject, that is, and cuddly.

They are characters who read books and go to movies often. They use the telephone, have arguments (so often) in front of their brownstones or apartments. They seem to go to bars, not obsessively like the Irish drunks of our literature, but as a matter of course. They drink beers in the afternoon, and yet don't misbehave because of that. They are not elitist, yet they are not bleeding hearts. They have compassion, but it is distilled through their own problems. His artists seem so real, not just the writer-types, even when he doesn't give them that occupation. (Usually his writer-types are schoolteachers.) But his dancers, painters, actors—they appear so real. Not one of them is able to live off of his art; rather, they live by it. They must work in restaurants or schools or wherever. They are not famous, though often I think they deserve such a status. They are feeling humans, vulnerable yet not sentimental. They are not *tough*. I cannot imagine Dixon's characters getting into heavy physical violence with each other, even though their verbal assaults are frequent in moments of crisis.

Stephen Dixon's seeing voice works out of two other aspects of his style. Flatness creates dimensions and shape. And this in turn creates coloring. That flatness and coloring in his voice remind me of the American painter Milton Avery's work, how authenticity is achieved by keeping the canvas a surface. It is simplicity worked in such a way that it becomes profound. It is colors bled thin until everything primary is a pastel. There is a painting by Edward Hopper on Dixon's book, *Movies,* but I do not see the bleak isolation of a Hopper in these tales. Dixon's own drawing for the cover of *14 Stories* graphically indicates the urban nature of his work, but also bespeaks that simplicity of line which is his trademark. There is a lyricism in this flatness, just as there is in Milton Avery's paintings, just as William Carlos Williams' poetry sings with a simple lyricism that has a spirit akin to Avery's or Dixon's. Again, this flatness is illusory, because there is just as much depth to it as a perspective canvas. Part of the illusion of Dixon's flatness in prose has to do with his simple, declarative sentence, a chain of subject-verb-object sentences, successively rendered:

"So I've an hour to kill. I walk along 34th, cross over to Paddy's Clam House when I see it. My father took all of us kids to it once on my birthday. Big round tables and large crowds and sawdust on the floor I seem to remember and the place doesn't seem significantly changed, except it's empty. A man kisses his fingertips at me through the window and points inside. I lift one of my shoulder straps and point to my shorts. Don't be silly, he says and holds open the price list of the menu. I shake my head and continue east and go into Macy's to get out of the sun and heat" ("Bars" in *No Relief*).

This early instance suggests how Dixon employs seeming flatness in his prose. In an early example like the one above, this aspect is nearly a quirk, but from one collection to the next over the next decade, the flatness actually creates its own density on the page, and it becomes a major significance in how Dixon's voice operates. It could be suggested that this quirk in his style has become one of its operational virtues, both a signature and the landmark by which we know his fictional landscape. What may have begun as an eccentricity has evolved into a major characteristic of his fiction. It is what allows us to identify his voice in the sea of other voices which our little magazines publish. It is a seductive and attractive quality, one which I imagine a lot of young writers will copy and emulate because it does appeal. At least at its surface it is a style that hints at being easily duplicated, but I would suggest that it is harder to imitate than those first appearances suggest. Why? The flatness is able to be xeroxed onto another voice pattern, but the coloring is too much Dixon's own for another writer to tamper with it.

By his most recent collection of stories, *Time to Go,* the declarative sentence has been worked into a fine-tuned machine-like vehicle for transporting the voice of Dixon's fiction, effortlessly yet complexly. Let me quote from the opening beat of "The Package Store" as an example:

Larry said "Rose, listen, I've decided, something very important—we have to get out of the store. We can't take it anymore. For once we have to do something like this for ourselves."

Rose said "Go back to sleep. It's too early. It's still dark. The birds aren't even chirping. I'm not kidding, Larry. I'm too tired to talk."

"Okay, but tomorrow we'll have to talk about it. Today—later this morning I mean. We have to get out of that store. Sell it for what we can get. Hopefully we can sell it for something high. The price. I'm also confused now because I'm sleepy, but you know what I mean."

"I know what you mean. But you can't be sleepier than I. You woke me up. Worse, you're keeping me up. Sell it for high, sell it for low—right now I don't care but I'm sure tomorrow I will. But that's it for now—no poking me awake again—all right?"

"For now, maybe, but not later today. I've been lying here thinking about it for hours."

'I'm sleeping, Larry. I'm fast asleep, or would be."

Later that morning when they were dressing, Larry said "Remember what I spoke to you about the store and our lives earlier before?"

"No, reacquaint me."

The above example not only illustrates the latter mentioned qualities in Dixon's voice but also highlights some pictorial concerns of the author. As in the drama, often how we know Dixon's characters is by what they say and what they do. If there is introspection, it is vocally trumpeted, not inwardly scraped from the walls of a mind. It also introduces—though it has been latently there from the beginning—a character type which Dixon has articulated lately, that of an older, frightened, working couple in the city. Both "Layaways" and "Darling" from his second-to-last collection portray older types, though the former story also includes the working couple who own a shop and who are conncerned for themselves over urban violence. The recent work has less of his bachelor-type characters, too. They seem to have gotten older, married, drifted off, and the pickup bar seems to have vanished from Dixon's landscape.

Dixon uses dialogue in the way that dramatists do, not like other fiction writers. He can create whole characterizations by its force alone, as in the previously mentioned story, "Darling," which pits the voices of a young man (inwardly spoken) against a moribund old woman (outwardly verbalized) whom he is charged with taking care of in her bedridden state. But like a good playwright, his dialogue, while it reveals, likewise withholds information, creates tensions. "Darling" is more inner and outer monologues contrapuntally arranged than a story using dialogue per se. Yet the receiver of this story's information, the reader, is given something that resembles dialogue, because her outwardly spoken dialogue is juxtaposed by the attendant's inner vocabulary. (Pinter employs a similar device in his chamber works, *Landscape* and *Silence,* although in play form, the system is reversed, where the inner world is verbally externalized, the outer world becomes meditative.)

"Darling?"
I go to her room, turn on the light, stand by her bed.
"Could you turn me over please?"
I turn her over on her back.
"And get my pills?"

The old woman receives a silent, obedient medical attendant, an orderly, a domestic helpmate of extraordinary cour-
tesy and efficiency. The reader, though, is presented with a
jabbering, dislocated, edgy and inefficient male, his monologue unceasing through the duration of this story. Outwardly,
as much is not said as gets said. Inwardly, the narrative voice
wags on and on. Dixon leaves out; his character grows prolix.
This sweep of worlds, simultaneously presented, of silence
and incessant babble, is expertly rendered in "Darling," setting up some exquisite tensions, structurally and dramatically.
What is said or not said is arranged with what is done. He
will leave, but he does not leave. He thinks he will stay, but he
leaves. The outcome is both theatrically comic and dramatically tragic-comic.

When I think of the *mise en scene* of Dixon's stories, I imagine a production of graceful movements. (What I am saying
here is that I often imagine his stories as plays, and I try to
imagine how I would direct them.) Both his male and female
characters range from being educated to being smart, with
his female characters earning the latter appellation more often than the males. His women are anything but sex objects,
because so often they are the ones controlling the interpersonal
situation. One character's attraction for another is declared.
They make love in the afternoon, but their lovemaking is not
graphically analyzed. The women are interesting more often
for their verbal wit, their professions, their aspirations—than
desires. I would note all this in any dramatic production of

his work; I would cast the characters according to these types. Also, I would want naturalness, even a kind of grace, in the actors. What is the quality of light in these stories? It gets back to that Hopper painting on the cover of *Movies;* I would not light a dramatization of Dixon's work with Hopper lighting. I'd go for those pastel colors—really primary colors bled thin by turpentine—of Milton Avery. The only exceptions would be those scenes in bars and movie theaters. Mostly, though, his characters move in the light of day, and if not in an apartment, there is that argument outside of it, on the street. That street scene is quite Plautian, even a hallmark of New Comedy in the Roman era. I would note that historical parallel in designing the street scene, which would include a row of brownstones on the Upper West Side.

Finally, in terms of directing, I would employ the old adage that 90 percent of directing is in how you cast. There would be nothing as clunky as a narrator—shades of *Our Town* rearing its head—but I would keep in mind that Dixon's narrators nearly always are also characters in the drama. Let the story happen from their point of view, but don't let them stop the action to comment. Then, again, they never do in the stories, either, because what often appears as commentary is really another fictional vehicle which Dixon employs to reveal character and to move the action forward. Opinions decidedly rest within characters, not the author. In that sense, as a director of one of these tales I would try to let the actors discover the story for themselves. I would not intrude on their discovery but might occasionally offer—perhaps like Dixon himself does as the author—some helpful advice, "Move a little closer to her when you say that. Good."

If this seems beside the point of a fiction writer's creations, it is not. Dixon writes as though he were a benign director. He only becomes an actor in so much as it might help his characters come alive. He seems willing to step back, and let them flourish, prevail, or even perish on their own terms, not his. Of course, this type of supportive director is secretly a dramaturge as well. But I cannot help but listen to Dixon's voice in the stories as though he were an old-time playwright/director, I mean, the kind of writer, before this century, who also directed his own work, Molière, Shakespeare, on back to the Greeks. The voice of Dixon's prose is not intruding, never judgmental, often even supportive of his characters. He more often suggests them instead of commanding them. He never traps them in a space and abandons them. But he allows them to make their own choices, and therefore discoveries.

Often his dialogue echoes a writer like Beckett (the fiction and the plays), but the overall invention of the prose is uniquely Stephen Dixon's. Partly this is because Dixon writes out of the rhythm of his own experience, urban, American, New York. Partly this is because the different set of experiences has put Dixon in a different place than Beckett. His voice does not waiver, yet the circumstances have changed. The voice of early Dixon stories often is as scattered as his characters' voices. The later voice enjoys an observer status in the chaos, not omniscient, just calmer than previously. It becomes, I think, a matter of the author becoming a finer craftsman. It is as though the early voice had to go where it wanted, whereas the present voice goes where it wishes to go through a more conscious exertion of will. It is as though in the recent work the author is confident enough to allow the prose to take off, and he gives it his blessings. That is a sure indication of a writer's voice confidentally working the landscape of fiction.

The voice of Stephen Dixon comes directly out of his experiences. Because that is so, you notice a progression from a

younger man to an older man in his work. I would imagine
that more of his older couples will emerge in future writings.
Likewise, I see children appearing more often in the stories.
Work—even the work ethic—pervades his writing voice from
the beginning. It would be hard to imagine a Dixon character
without a job. The early occupations were often those of a
high school substitute teacher or a graphic artist. The most
recent occupation for his characters has been that of a university professor. That is the occupation of Will Taub, his most
recent characterization in *Time to Go*. Within the progression
of experience—the gathering of particulars in a life occurs.
But in the rhythm of experience Dixon employs the same
steady beat.

At times that rhythm appears formless and experimental,
but really it is calculated. It is worth harkening back to the
stage for an apt analogy. When young actors engage in improvisation, it is often a series of unremitting chaoses. The
practiced actor takes improvisation to mean a worked-out set
of patterns of action in advance, so that at any given moment
in a performance, the actor can draw from these patterns to
advance either character or plot. Stephen Dixon's prose is
improvisational in that sense. It has the appearance of being
spontaneous and intuitive, but in reality it is worked out
carefully behind the scenes. His prose, like the live performance, relies on creating that *illusion of the first time*.

I do not wish to suggest that this calculation resembles
plotting (or even plodding). He is not a chess master, even
though his voice operates within the traditions of the short
story, which is our most mathematical literary form, even
more so than the sonnet, for instance. Dixon inhabits a
checkered landscape in his fiction, and so it is full of quick
successions of forward and diagonal moves, jumps, and
crownings, and then backward across the board in pursuit.
From the body of work already published, several short-story

collections and a few novels, his métier would appear to be the short form. Framed by the short story's rigors, his jittery voice is more explosive. Untrapped, and let to wander in the landscape of the novel, it loses some of its explosiveness, i.e., the flatness literally becomes flat. Which is not to say that Dixon can't write novels, but only to suggest that so far his short fiction is stronger than the novels. *Too Late* and *Work* still read like his short fiction, but they suffer as a result of that comparison. The short fiction has the simple virtue that it leaves out as much or more than it puts in. The novels seem to put in all that the short fiction has left out. Although I have not dealt with it here, *Quite Contrary*—being a collection of interconnected stories—is characterized by the virtues of Dixon's short fiction, while creating a novelistic effect.

When I first read Stephen Dixon's prose, I thought his roving, singular narrative voices were the offspring of an only child. I mean, its yattery, chatty style suggested the indulgence of a man singularly raised, even a spoiled quality to it. I should have known better. It is really a voice trying to speak in the multitude and from it. That is, there is a quality in the voice which comes from someone in a big family, not an only child's voice. I think it an important distinction. People in big families eat fast, drink fast—and talk fast, because it is the only way to get a word in edgewise, quench a thirst, or fill a stomach. Being a New Yorker is part of it, too, growing up in that other kind of multitude, but there is something unique which happens to a voice in a large family. Ask García-Márquez. Or James Joyce. Or Stephen Dixon. In fact, it is worth asking what these three writers might have in common with their voices as a result of that trait in their backgrounds. One thing that immediately comes to mind is that all of them *people* their writing, often taking themselves away from the central point of view. Where—in *One Hundred Years of Solitude*—is there a character similar autobiographically to the author himself? In time, I venture to say that some lesser character—in the same way that Shakespeare played important characters to the plot who were not central to dramatic action—will reveal himself to be García-Márquez. Joyce showed this positioning of himself away from the center in *Dubliners, Ulysses* (Bloom is more central than Dedalus, Joyce's alter ego), and *Finnegans Wake.* Some of Stephen Dixon's first-person narrators may in fact be autobiographical, but most of them are not.

Part of my own impulse to write comes from a need to speak, but because of a large family hierarchy I was assigned the role of the silent brother and son. Even to this day it is quite impossible for me to assume a talking role within my family, though with friends there is no problem. Stephen Dixon's voice does not strike me as the silent kind within a family. There is a writer at ease with speech, operating in this landscape. There is even something of an actor in the voice, i.e., the presentational voice suggests gestural qualities, too. Also, in an American age, what with cultural stresses on the young; what with the proliferation of writing programs at universities—there is a marked rise in the number of really young writers who emerge into print while still in their twenties. Richard Price was just out of graduate school when *The Wanderers* appeared. I sold my first novel when I was twenty-one years old, and published my second when I was twenty-six years old. That is not unusual today. Dixon's own ascent was slower, even more classical, when you consider that the average age of a first novelist in America is around thirty-seven to thirty-nine years old. He had published stories, I believe, since his mid-twenties, but he was closer to forty when those stories started to be collected in books. His first collection, *No*

Relief, came out in his fortieth year, and there has been a fairly steady succession of publications since then.

There are real advantages to his accumulation of books later in his life. First, it has allowed him to sharpen his skills over a longer period, perfecting that voice. But, more importantly, Dixon has a body of experiences from which to draw. Some of the younger fiction writers do not have these experiences. Take an author like Richard Price. His first novel is tight, rhythmical, concretely realized through felt experiences, i.e., I doubt whether Price himself was a member of a Bronx youth gang. But each successive novel he's published appears more bloated, stuffed, and filled out. The prose is padded to make a "fat" book. And, mutual to this tendency for "padding" the voice, Price's most recent novel is a university memoir, something I never imagined a writer like him doing. Part of it is perhaps writing too many books in too short a time. But the greater part has to do with not having enough experiences to write about. This has not been a problem with Stephen Dixon, nor could I imagine it ever becoming a problem, because he still has not written outright autobiographically, and so has that direct experience to draw on yet.

A major problem with fiction, poetry, and playwriting today is the fact that so often the author puts himself or herself at the center of the experience. This is especially true in early novels set in foreign, often exotic lands in which the narrator or the protagonist inhabits the landscape imperially. In reality the natives could care less about this character's importance to their lives. But in the fiction all eyes in Jakarta, all ears in Katmandu turn toward this egotist's center. A dramatic writer, though, tends to shape each character as though he inhabits the center, not the author's alter ego. This is true in Ibsen, Strindberg, Brecht, Checkhov, Beckett—all the great modernist playwrights. Even in an American masterpiece, Eugene O'Neill's *Long Day's Journey into Night,* Jamie Tyrone, though important to the drama, is not its central character, because he is subordinated to his mother and father and brother, and that larger structure—the Tyrone family itself. Very often Stephen Dixon's first-person narrator is not central, though remaining crucial and important, to the dramatic arc. I believe this to be an aspect of coming from a large family and growing up in a city in which it is hard to imagine anyone central to its overall energy. This is a major quality in my mind, because it suggests a writer who is both mature and responsive and who has learned, through experience, that our lives are incidental to the Grand Machinery of our human universe.

None of these assumptions surprise me very much, because I do think Dixon's voice is mature and responsive, even from his early work outward. It is a voice that is of the tradition, yet it consistently breaks new ground for the world of fiction. But I have said enough. I have extolled and picked and verified and tried to calibrate this voice. Finally, it possesses qualities which I have yet to fathom, but which I find interesting to my ear, and moving emotionally; moving, interesting, and real. How do you know a Dixon character from other characters? By how they speak. And how do they speak? Rather than elucidate further, I simply wish to end by letting one of them show us how he speaks. This "I" appears in a story called "Names" in *14 Stories:*

"Finally I become depressed by her. I walk around the room. I lie in bed. I try and read. I try to sleep. I look in the refrigerator. I open the bread box. I drink. I go outside. I walk the streets. I look in the apartment windows. I look at the store windows. I go to a movie. I leave the movie halfway through. Maybe quarter way through. I go to a bar. I sit and order a drink. I stand and set my beer down and go to the washroom though I don't have to. I go because I want to walk through the crowded bar."

That is an essence of the rhythm of experience as it works the landscape of the seeing voice. That is Stephen Dixon's voice.

10

Harold Pinter

THE HEALTH OF THE American theater owes its vitality in no small measure to the genius of Harold Pinter, an Englishman. By that I mean to say is that he acts as a model and ideal for many younger writers, myself included. This reputation is based on such major plays as *The Homecoming,* the film version of *Betrayal,* and chamber masterworks like *Landscape* and *Silence.* Pinter makes few bad choices in his writing. He may be difficult to fathom on the page, but this is resolved in the rehearsal hall. Sometimes I think I was blessed, at the age of fifteen, seeing *The Caretaker* and *The Dumb Waiter* at the Provincetown Theatre on MacDougal Street. It is not that the event transformed me into a playwright; I was not. But to this day I think of those plays as dramatic foundations, mysteries, initiations into the theater, experiences I am not easily able to articulate.

They provide an essence, these Pinter works, of what the dramatic experience is all about, not meanings but states of being. I cannot tell you what Davies means by his monologue on boots, but I can say there was a rhythm of experience, a concision, a direct treatment of object, no ideas but in things, a right-word kind of feeling, i.e., poetry, in his utterance.

Can't wear shoes that don't fit. Nothing worse. I said to this monk, here, I said, look here, mister, he opened the door, big door, he opened it, look here, mister, I said, I come all the way down here, look, I said, I showed him these, I said, you haven't got a pair of shoes, have you, a pair of shoes, I said, enough to keep me on my way. Look at these, they're nearly out, I said, they're no good to me. I heard you got a stock of shoes here. Piss off, he said to me. Now look here, I said, I'm an old man, you can't talk to me like that, I don't care who you are. If you don't piss off, he says, I'll kick you all the way to the gate. Now look here, I said, now wait a min-ute, all I'm asking for is a pair of shoes, you don't want to start tak-ing liberties with me, it's taken me three days to get out here, I said to him, three days without a bite, I'm worth a bite to eat, en I?

Recently, I saw a dramatization of James Joyce's short story "A Mother" at the West Bank Cafe's Downstairs Theatre Bar, where Mrs. Kearney's husband is represented onstage by a boot. Why not? He is a bootmaker on Ormond Quay. But what was so extraordinary in this ensemble was that the actress playing Mrs. Kearney made us feel as though Mr. Kearney was present onstage with her. Likewise, that first time I saw Harold Pinter's work I was transformed not by the meaning of Davies' monologue—I still don't know what it "means"—but I felt Davies' emotional state, his objective to get new boots, and his willingness to walk three days to attain that objective, and the obstacle in his way, that churlish monk who tells him "to piss off." There is even a resolution to this drama within the overall drama of *The Caretaker*.

Aston offers Davies a pair of shoes. The stage direction— and a director and the actor better pay good attention, be-cause Pinter so rarely employs them—reads: "Davies takes the shoes, takes off his sandals and tries them on." I saw Donald Pleasance follow those directions when I was fifteen, and he took such care to render that detail into illuminating stage business. It was as though those shoes were his greatest love; as though his entire life waited for this moment. It was a ritual, and because it was a ritual, the audience was filled with ritual expectation. Davies says, "Not a bad pair of shoes." He is all understatement. "He trudges round the room," the directions say, but imagine a walking dance, Fred Astaire, Gene Kelly, Jimmy Cagney, but Pleasance is *just* walking around:

"They're strong, all right. Yes. Not a bad shape of shoe. This leather's hardy, en't? Very hardy. Some bloke tried to flog me some suede the other day. I wouldn't wear them. Can't beat leather, for wear. Suede goes off, it creases, it stains for life in five minutes. You can't beat leather. Yes. Good shoes this."

Shoes are important to Beckett's Didi and Gogo, too. They are important to us because they are objects which reveal emotional states in characters and situations. Mrs. Kearney caresses her boot, scolds it, flings it across the stage. A buffalo-head nickel becomes similarly endowed in a David Mamet play. A harvest of fruits and vegetables becomes this in one of Sam Shepard's plays. A glass of water has this effect in a later Pinter play. A glass of water! Imagine that. In my own play, *Our Father,* which Bill Foeller directed at the West Bank Cafe, a dead father becomes that emotional object. Not written in my text, but realized by the actors through their gestural lives onstage, John Gould Rubin's Mumbles affects a swizzle stick in his mouth whenever he speaks, thus epitomizing his character's name. Peter Crombie's Beaky affects a "literary" air about him; Randy Foerster's Psycho crawls across the bar— *stands on the bar*—a real psycho move in bar etiquette and physical grammar. Knowing that his brothers have heard his tales a million times, Ken Ryan's Bones goes into the audience, sits at a table, chats with the people there; he charms them. "He said this; I said that." That's how the characters in my play speak. It goes back to Davies, but it goes back to him for several reasons.

First, Pinter is an education for any younger playwright, no matter what his peers or that generation between his and mine thinks of his pauses and silences and minimal wordings. This is the real thing, the source, a wellspring. But it goes back to Davies because Harold Pinter understands how we speak, and his play traps the rhythm of speech into the dramatic voice. The playwright makes us see through his characters' utterances. What might be opaque on the page becomes crystallike on the human tongue. It is that simple. Pinter captures the poetry of human speech, focuses it, and turns it into a dramatic situation.

I have read of Pinter's infatuation with T. S. Eliot's writings, and often his characters can fit into that universe nicely. Yet Pinter's spareness, the tunneled effect of his realism, is a product of the post–World War II world; he is a writer whose work comes after modernism. The writer from whom Pinter draws most of his inspiration is Samuel Beckett. Interestingly, though, Pinter seems the better dramaturge, because his sense of drama comes from the inside out, whereas Beckett's dramaturgical instincts come from without the theater, even against drama's grain. Let me suggest that Beckett is a far greater novelist and fiction writer (my unproved opinion) than he is a playwright, even though he primarily is known as a world dramatist. There is nearly a lack of sympathy for actors in Beckett's texts, as though he did not trust their instincts, whereas Pinter learned how to write plays from the actor's point of view. His introduction to the theater was with a touring Shakespearian company in Ireland. In his prose eulogy to Anew McMaster, the last of the great actor-managers, as Pinter says, he writes of this commencement.

I toured Ireland with Mac for about two years in the early 1950s. He advertised in "The Stage" for actors for a Shakespearian tour of the country. I sent him a photograph and went to see him in a flat near Willesden Junction. At the time Willesden Junction seemed to me as likely a place as any to meet a manager from whom you might get work. But after I knew Mac our first meeting place became more difficult to accept or understand. I still wonder what he was doing interviewing actors at Willesden Junction. But I never asked him. He offered me six pounds a week, said I could get digs for twenty-five shillings at the most, told me how cheap cigarettes were and that I could play Horatio, Bassanio and Cassio. It was my first job proper on the stage.

("Mac")

The Dresser not only seems Pinter-inspired, but it seems to draw much of its portraiture from this Pinter essay on McMaster; the harumphing Sir character played by Albert Finney in the movie, and the efficient, obsequious dresser played by Tom Courtney, they seem almost like McMaster and Pinter, right down to the Lear scene when Sir demands more thunder. Pinter writes: "He did Lear eventually. First performance somewhere in County Clare, Ennis, I think. Knew most of the lines. *Was* the old man, tetchy, appalled, feverish. Wanted the storm louder. All of us banged the thundersheets. No, they can still hear me. Hit it, hit it. He got above the noise." I point this out by way of illustrating the depth of Pinter's theatrical experience from the inside out. I mention *The Dresser* because that Finney/Courtney film version is a kind of epitome of the rehearsal play, or the play about the play, and therefore of the world of theater, from which Pinter's playwriting ability evolves.

That Pinter trusts actors is implicit in how he writes plays. These are people who are not only his friends but a class of theater person—its hottest center—from whom Pinter emerged into his writing career. There are little stage directions in Pinter, because I suspect that the writer in him implicitly trusts the instincts of actors, something that cannot be taken for granted with other playwrights and writers. It is as though Pinter is saying, A text is one thing, but the drama depends mostly upon a subtext, which I can suggest, but which the acter must realize. He is also saying that an actor's discovery will be greater than a writer's directions, and I think that Pinter is not only theatrically correct in this thought but also right. A pattern of discovery within a production is sacrificed when director and actors follow too carefully the writer's directions.

Even in a legal sense regarding copywright and fair use and union laws, it is only the writer's dialogue which cannot be tampered with, not his stage directions. In contrast to Pinter, Beckett's own stage directions by comparison almost appear wordy, although diehard Beckettians might throw the property shop hobo shoes from *Waiting for Godot* at me for making such blasphemy. Before the actors sound one beat of dialogue in *Endgame* there is a fairly rigid set of stage instructions and business to be adhered to. Or consider a recent American Repertory Theatre production in Cambridge, where Joanne Akalaitis' setting of the play in a subway station almost brought down the house, because Beckett found this freeing up of directions to be an infringement of his intended purposes. It would be hard to imagine Pinter finding himself in a similar legal imbroglio.

Beckett is a dramatic writer who uses the theater as a kind of vehicle for his utterances, while Pinter is a dramatist, and it is hard to imagine him operating outside the empty space of a theater or a movie set. The latter writer provides blueprints for theater and movie people to realize an edifice of sound and gesture. The former writer gives the actors and director an already built house which they must inhabit according to his instructions. Conversely, there is literally no way to compare the body of Beckett's prose and poetry with that of Pinter, whose depths ring superficially in these other mediums. Beckett is one of the greatest prose writers in the English language; Pinter is a passably good prose writer. Beckett is a poet's poet, while Pinter is a playwright who has written some passably good, some lovely, and a few elegant poems. That said, let me contradict myself by quoting, not from Beckett's poetry, but Pinter's.

> The sound of light
> Has left my nose.

When I speak of a seeing voice, of a dramaturgy of style, I think I also mean that "sound of light." But let me return to these two masters.

Another dramaturgical distinction between the two writers is the range of characterization and the scope of stage business which each writer uses. Beckett's characters are mostly male, older, even decrepid. A young boy speaks a few lines in *Godot;* a woman soliloquizes in *Happy Days* and most recently in *Rockaby.* But the general tenor of Beckett's world is male-dominated. Pinter's world also has its share of male-centeredness as witness *The Homecoming.* Yet Pinter has the good dramaturgical sense to make Ruth central to that male universe which until her arrival is untempered by women. The men are violent and impotent; Ruth may make them more violent, but she arouses them as well. She is not merely a catalyst; she is both catalyst and a central figure in this drama. She lives and breathes; she is the play's centerpiece.

After Lenny finishes two long monologues to Ruth, one about punching out a prostitute with pocks who had the hots for him, the other about brutalizing an old lady, he attempts to remove Ruth's glass. Ruth says: "If you take the glass . . . I'll take you." *She picks up the glass and lifts it towards him.* Again, if Pinter wrote that direction, it has to be significant, and it is. Ruth says: "Sit on my lap. Take a long cool sip." Ruth completely disarms the violent Lenny with her glass. She *seduces* him with it. She teases him, she taunts him, she undresses Lenny with that glass, she exposes him for what he is—she *reveals* him. She ends by saying, "Oh, I was thirsty."

Beth, in *Landscape,* is an equally lush and complicated woman character, whose interior monologue, given an exterior voice, works in counterpoint to Duff's gravelly male utterances. His speech is about men drinking pints, about gruffnesses, whereas Beth's is a sensual catalogue, a love scene given shape by a human sounds.

I drew a face in the sand, then a body. The body of a woman. Then the body of a man, close to her, not touching. But they didn't look like anything. They didn't look like human figures. The sand kept on slipping, mixing the contours. I crept close to him and put my head on his arm, and closed my eyes. All those darting red and black flecks, under my eyelid. I moved my cheek on his skin. And all those darting red and black flecks, moving about under my eyelid. I buried my face in his side and shut the light out.

Duff terminates his monologue by talking about having her in front of the dog, banging a gong, and if the gong isn't loud enough, banging her against the gong. It is animallike, primitive. He says, "You'll plead with me like a woman." Behind his words I hear that zipperlike sound of electronic backup in certain rap music recordings. For Beth, I hear wind chimes.

He lay above me and looked down at me. He supported my shoulder.

Pause

So tender his touch on my neck. So softly his kiss on my cheek.

Pause

My hand on his rib.

Pause

So sweetly the sand over me. Tiny the sand on my skin.

Pause

So silent the sky in my eyes. Gently the sound of the tide.

Pause

Oh my true love I said.

Lacking the counterpoint of Duff's gruffness, this would be sentimental mush. But in that push and pull, of the violent male, of the grittiness, this tender moment becomes a fully realized occasion in the drama. This is likewise true in *Silence*, but instead of only a male and female to bounce their sounds off of each other, there is a woman sandwiched between two men. Ellen shares a quality of speech with Beth: "He sat me on his knee, by the window, and asked if he could kiss my right cheek. I nodded he could. He did. Then he asked, if, having kissed my right, he could do the same with my left. I said yes. He did." But in addition to speaking at odds with one another, the characters in *Silence* intersperse their outward ruminations with snippets of dialogue.

RUMSEY

Find a young man.

ELLEN

There aren't any.

RUMSEY

Don't be stupid.

ELLEN

I don't like them.

RUMSEY

You're stupid.

ELLEN

I hate them.
Pause

RUMSEY

Find one.
Silence.

Beckett's characters are involved in a dance of death turned comedic at the last moment, while Pinter makes a dance—and, as the last examples show, a musical score—of life and death. Pinter's stage business includes young and violent characters like Mick in *The Caretaker* and Lenny in *The Homecoming,* and Beckettian hobos like Davies. There are the old people of *The Birthday Party,* and the youthfully middle-aged of *Betrayal;* there are the downtrodden of his early plays, the advantaged of *Betrayal,* and the two meeting in the same room as they do in *No Man's Land,* whose stark title is only surpassed by the following setting:

Summer.

Night.

Hirst and Spooner may or may not be university classmates. One is affluent; the other is destitute. Both are joined by drink. Not the simple taking of *a* drink. They are alcoholics; they have met at a pub. Hirst brings home his new friend. Drunk already, consider how much more alcohol they consume in that book-lined room. With deepest, drunken modesty, the shabby Spooner, himself in visual contrast to the austere setting and the dapper Hirst, declares: "I was about to say, you see, that there are some people who appear to be strong, whose idea of what strength consists of is persuasive, but who inhabit the idea and not the fact. What they possess is not strength but expertise. They have nurtured and maintain what is in fact a calculated posture. Half the time it works. It takes a man of intelligence and perception to stick a needle through that posture and discern the essential flabbiness of the stance." Spooner concludes: "I am such a man." What appears to be late-night rationality and civility actually is as bonkers as Lucky's soliloquy in *Godot*. It is a gibberish of *Dottore* and Pantalone in the *commedia;* it is Moliere's bourgois gentleman. These are characters from Old Comedy, going back to Greece, back to Sicily, back to the animal mimes. Like Beckett's creations, they suggest that less is more, but somehow Pinter cuts an even thinner slice of pie to make this detail happen. His pauses and silences are downright musical notations, and there literally is as much in those hollow voiceless moments as in any part of his plays. Some of Pinter's synaptic notations resemble Far Eastern drama's business, for instance, the elongated dramatizations of the Japanese Noh theater. (The one Noh drama I saw was three pages long and lasted well over three hours in its abbreviated form.) Some Buddhist dance-dramas I saw in Korea several years ago likewise stretched the time sequence into this slow-motion dreamlike cadence. In this sense Pinter has as much connection with W. B. Yeats' poetry and drama as he does with Beckett, though admittedly his connection with Beckett is quite linear and direct. Pinter shows early versions of his plays, I am told, to Beckett before revising them.

Both Beckett and Pinter have asserted considerable influence on how playwrights write plays all over the world, but the strongest influence from these writers, besides the immediate influence on their native places, is found in America with a generation of writers who matured in the mid-to-late sixties and into the seventies. Two of the strongest examples of this influence is that of Sam Shepard, America's dramatist of the countryside, and David Mamet, our country's city-slicker poet of the stage.

Some historical information is necessary to disspell any notion that America is still begging for its culture from abroad. Both Shepard and Mamet are distinctly American playwrights, maybe even moreso than Eugene O'Neill, Arthur Miller, though not Tennessee Williams, who is pure native genius. The dramaturgical tradition in America, by comparison to other nations, is a relatively new one. O'Neill's star is comparable to Aeschylus' in terms of origins of a national drama. And it is not until O'Neill that America can speak of a national drama, since everything prior to that consisted of imports from abroad, mostly from London. (This condition still exists on Broadway, to a lesser extent off-Broadway, and not at all off-off-Broadway and in our regional theaters.) But not many playgoers or playreaders, even ones enamored of O'Neill's romantic and dissolute biography, are aware of his debts—sometimes amounting to outright thefts—to August Strindberg. Writers like Shepard and Mamet still are pioneers of the American drama, and it is not until Shepard came along that anything resembling native intuition in our drama existed, with the one exception being Tennessee Williams.

By comparison England enjoys the longest unbroken tradition of drama of any country in the world, starting with liturgical tropes in the tenth century and building to the great religious, and later secular, cycle dramas outside of London. London's own tradition predates Shakespeare by many years, tracing its origins to university dramatic societies and—imagine this happening in America—law schools. Shakespeare did not so much create Elizabethan drama as he walked into it and elaborated upon it. The Bard was an actor, too, like Harold Pinter was, and like Sam Shepard.

This English tradition had only one brief hiatus, during Cromwell's rule, from the 1640s to the 1660s, when no legitimate theaters were open in London, but the Restoration more than made up for these twenty years of darkness on the boards. When one considers Harold Pinter, he descends from a long line of playwrights; he writes out of a tradition. His play *No Man's Land* even uses stock characters—Pantalone and the Professor, if you will—but evoked through the tunneled realism which is Pinter's trademark.

Sam Shepard did not appear always to be learning from Pinter. His early plays are sui generis, dramatically speaking, but I think they do have strong influences from the climate of American poetry at that time, especially as it was written by the nonacademic New York/Lower East Side "St. Mark's-in-the-Bouwerie" crowd, Blackburn, Oppenheimer, et al. Shepard's poetry comes out of the American idiom, a rhythm which Shepard mines so well. It is not until he spends some time in London that he comes to write his first really major pieces, though, and these larger works carry the stamp of Pinter's influence, especially his Pulitzer Prize-winning drama, *Buried Child,* which is the story of a homecoming, just as Pinter's play *The Homecoming* deals with that subject, and this theme can be traced back through all of Western drama to its source in the first play of Aeschylus' *Oresteia* trilogy, *Agamemnon.*

Not only does *Buried Child* have parallels and echoes from Pinter's play, its characterizations, its business, nearly everything about the play, are an Americanization of that British drama. (And Americans talk about the Japanese stealing ideas and refining them!) The odd thing about his, though, is that Shepard is not plagiarizing; he is working on one of the finest traditions in all the theater. That is, take what's already there (say, the story), and make it over into your own *voice,* and with that voice resee the dramatic potential. It is something which Pinter himself has done with Beckett. Brecht was the most famous of these dramatic pirates in our century; Shakespeare was the most famous pilferer in his time. The

Greeks did it, too. Like I said, it is part of the dramatic tradition.

Instead of Ruth and the seduction around the glass, there is Shelly and a hand shoved down her throat. Bradley's hand. The amputee. Vince's brother. Instead of Teddy bringing home Ruth for his homecoming, there is Vince with Shelly. Instead of Lenny, there is Bradley. Instead of a house in North London, there is a house in the American heartland. But as Brecht's *Threepenny Opera* is to John Gay's *Beggar's Opera,* Sam Shepard's play is to Harold Pinter's. Beat by beat, scene to scene, act to act, Pinter's superstructure is interpolated into Shepard's text. Sam in *The Homecoming* speaks at length about Max's wife Jessie. By the final moments of the play he blurts out, "MacGregor had Jessie in the back of my cab as I drove them along."

He croaks and collapses.
He lies still.
They look at him.

Dodge in *Buried Child* also spills the beans, as it were, giving him coronary arrest.

Halie had this kid. This baby boy. She had it. I let her have it on her own. All the other boys I had had the best doctors, best nurses, everything. This one I let her have by herself. This one hurt real bad. Almost killed her, but she had it anyway. It lived, see. It lived. It wanted to grow up in this family. It wanted to be just like us. It wanted to be a part of us. It wanted to pretend that I was its father. She wanted me to believe in it. Even when everyone around us knew. Everyone. All our boys knew. Tilden knew.

But Dodge—a character a bit wordier than Pinter's inventions—has a few more things to say, about killing a baby, about making his "last will and testament." It is this voice, this object-laden voice, by which Sam Shepard transforms himself from an epigone to his own kind of mastery. Shepard's voice works nicely in this vehicle of Dodge. Here is what he lets Dodge say as his final soliloquy in the play, as though Shepard were also saying, I am influenced by Harold Pinter, but I am my own man, my own sort of writer, my own kind of American playwright.

The house goes to my Grandson, Vincent. All the furnishings, accoutrements and paraphernalia therein. Everything tacked to the walls or otherwise resting under this roof. My tools—namely my band saw, my skill saw, my drill press, my chain saw, my lathe, my electric sander, all go to my eldest son, Tilden. That is, if he ever shows up again. My shed and gasoline powered equipment, namely my tractor, my dozer, my hand tiller plus all the attachments and riggings for the above mentioned machinery, namely my spring tooth harrow, my deep plows, my disk plows, my automatic fertilizing equipment, my reaper, my swathe, my seeder, my John Deere Harvester, my post hole digger, my jackhammer, my lathe—(to himself) Did I mention my lathe? I already mentioned my lathe— my Bennie Goodman records, my harnesses, my bits, my halters, my brace, my rough rasp, my forge, my welding equipment, my shoeing nails, my levels and bevels, my milking stool—no, not my milking stool—my hammers and chisels, my hinges, my cattle gates, my barbed wire, self-tapping augers, my horse hair ropes and all related materials are to be pushed into a gigantic heap and set ablaze in the very center of my fields. When the blaze is at its highest, preferably on a cold, windless night, my body is to be pitched into the middle of it and burned til nothing remains but ash.

Buried Child is the story of a homecoming, and that is saying a lot about Sam Shepard. The new word in that last sentence is "story," something which Shepard was not interested in in his earlier work. Voice. Image. Tensions. Suspensions. These seemed to be greater concerns than story. It is nearly impossible, given these conditions, to say what early Shepard plays are *about*. They are not about anything; they just hapen to be. I think these urges go back to Shepard's days on the Lower East Side, when the poetry scene dominated in the way that the off-off-Broadway scene was to dominate the mid-to-late sixties, and how the music scene took over, first with jazz and the Beats, now with rock and punk. At the same time the poetry workshops were going on at St. Mark's Church, Theatre Genesis began there as well. This was one of the early theaters in which Shepard's work was performed. I remember going to the Old Courthouse on Second Avenue and Second Street on the Lower East Side, the abandoned building where St. Mark's workshops were held—a place I lived in for more than a year—and I remember running into Shepard there frequently. He was teaching the playwriting workshop for awhile; his rock group used to rehearse downstairs. His plays were often put together in that space. His poetry appeared in the one-shot magazine, *The Genre of Silence*, which Joel Oppenheimer edited and named after the statement from Isaac Babel, the Russian's last speech before going off to Gulagland forever.

Later plays like *Tongues* and *Savage/Love*—maybe performance pieces better describes these works—reflect some of Shepard's earlier concerns with poetry. They were created in collaboration with the actor Joseph Chaikin. In a note to the former play Shepard writes: "We agreed on a piece to do with the voice. Voices. Voices travelling. Voices becoming other voices. Voices from the dead and living. Hypnotized voices. Sober voices. Working voices. Voices in anguish, etc." Where this poet's urge for a voice-centered text really blossoms is in *Savage/Love*, which reads more like a chapbook of poetry than as a play or performance piece. There are no directions, no cues, no directionals about the empty space. Instead, there are titles like "Savage," and this text:

YOU
Who makes me believe that we're lovers
YOU
Who lets me pretend
YOU
Who reminds me of myself
YOU
Who controls me
YOU
My accomplice
YOU
Who tells me to lie
YOU
Who is acting as though we're still in the first moment
YOU
Who leads me to believe we're forever in love
Forever in love

They are more lyrics than lyrical poetry, more pop song than poetry. Shepard, from the beginning, has been interested, as listener and as participant, in our popular music. It inspires so much of his writings, not just these later experiments. Like poetry—voice, rhythm, image are concerns, but lacking precision, bereft of *le mot juste,* they are finger-snappers, melodies that riff through the mind, then vanish. They are sentimental, but so are even some major works of this writer; he is not hard-edged by any means. There is a very conventional, even a deeply conservative, American heart beating underneath the surface of nearly all Shepard's writings. *Buried Child* and *Curse of the Starving Class* are conventionally structured and dramatically presented, using fourth wall techniques. *Tongues* and *Savage/Love* are sentimental, and therefore emotionally conventional, conveying as they do worn-out feelings. Compared to Pinter in these lights, Sam Shepard is a pale rider. But that is not the quality I wish to highlight here. Once you learn how to read Pinter on the page, reading him on the page is quite pleasurable. I don't think Sam Shepard lends himself to reading on the page, though. So often I have read his work on the page, finding it sloppy, inelegant, bastardized, clunky. Yet in performance something happens; his text comes to dramatic life. Shepard's best medium is the stage itself, the one exception being *True West*, whose blackout scenes I found turbid in performance but elegant upon the page.

While early Shepard is terse enough, often even too oblique, his later plays seem almost prosey, including *Buried Child, True West, Fool for Love, Curse of the Starving Class*. The seeing voice is replaced by this O'Neill-like urge to preach instead of sing; by a Neil Simonish urge to communicate to a "common" audience, to the average Joe and Mary. Shepard is a physical writer, though, and often his verbal inelegance is saved by the stage business which his sentimental words demand. His actions are not sentimental; they are brutally real. Shepard, like Pinter, not only respects actors but seems to depend on them to realize what he suggests in his writing. His women are often as interesting, or moreso, than his men. Finally, the way a writer renders characters of the opposite sex becomes a crucial way to distinguish the good from the great playwright. At least this is true of all our modern playwrights with the possible exception of Samuel Beckett. And no actress can complain, if she were playing Shelly, when a writer provides her with the following lines:

Don't come near me! Don't anyone come near me. I don't need any words from you. I'm not threatening anybody. I don't even know what I'm doing here. You all say you don't remember Vince, okay, maybe you don't. Maybe it's Vince that's crazy. Maybe he's made this whole family thing up. I don't even care any more. I was just coming along for the ride. I thought it'd be a nice gesture. Besides, I was curious. He made all of you sound familiar to me. Every one of you. For every name, I had an image. Every time he'd tell me a name, I'd see the person. In fact, each of you was so clear in my mind that I actually believed it was you. I really believed when I walked through that door that the people who lived here would turn out to be the same people in my imagination.

That is not stingy writing; it is a gift from a writer to his actor. It is nearly saying, I can only do so much, and I need you to carry this the rest of the way. I like that quality in Shepard. I admire it. I finally respect its dramatic instinct, too.

Ibsen, Strindberg, Chekhov, Brecht, they all understood that kind of largesse, a sort of gift which always brought back a multitude of returns in performance. Shakespeare could not claim it because women were sequestered from the Elizabethan stage, and so his feminine creations were thinly veiled boys or effeminate men. But Euripides understood it, and it was what got him into so much trouble with his elders. What I am saying is that Shepard's women—Halie, Shelly, Luna, Laureen, Paulettea, Mom, Ella, Emma, Becky Lou—if not always fully sketched, are not stick figures or solely male projections either. They breathe, they have syllables, they speak lines, they talk, speechify, they signify, they hurt and give hurt, they live.

If I were going to articulate a weakness in Shepard's dramaturgy, it would be with his rural concerns in an urban world. His pastoral nature, I mean, where the ideal is always found in nature, not in man or woman per se. A romantic thing. Or maybe even a Romantic thing. Even his characters in the city seem countrified. They get places in four-wheel drive, not by subway. They sleep in trailers. His urban cowboys were made for nonurban actors.

There are actually a good number of urban playwrights in America today. Robert Auletta comes to mind immediately, especially his Vietnam-inspired piece, *Rundown*. But perhaps the best known of these urban dramatists is David Mamet, who is something of a quintessential Chicago writer. Unlike Shepard who has been producing plays for close to twenty years Mamet's notoriety is more recent, starting with a string of successes several years back, including *American Buffalo, Sexual Perversity in Chicago,* and *Duck Variations.* Like Harold Pinter, Mamet has had successes in screenwriting, too, most notably with the *The Verdict,* in which Paul Newman delivered one of his better performances.

Mamet has learned about spareness and synapse from Harold Pinter, but a lot of these qualities are native-bred. Although from Chicago, Mamet has spent a lot of time in New England, and the voice in his dramas often bears an architectural resemblance to the spare, clean, direct, and functional majesty of white clapboard houses in Vermont and Massachusetts. His voice is not unlike William Carlos Williams' poetry in this sense. That is, Mamet may be influenced by Harold Pinter, and certainly Samuel Beckett as well, but his voice has as much to do with American poetry and painting as it does with these sources from abroad. His urban voice puts him squarely into the geography of the American landscape of the present moment; what his voice sees makes him one of the finest examples our drama has produced.

Like Shepard and Pinter, David Mamet writes plays like an insider, i.e., he has acting instincts in how he writes. What he sees are things which actors see, and how he says what he sees comes unquestionably from the spoken, not the written. If I were to articulate a dramaturgical weakness in Mamet's seeing voice it would be in his depictions—and often lack of depiction—of women. His most successful play, *American Buffalo,* is a retelling of Chaucer's three thieves' tale, which in turn goes back to Aesop. It is a play for men, not women; and so is his most recent triumph on Broadway, the Pulitzer Prize-winning *Glengarry Glen Ross,* which resembles Pinter's *Homecoming* minus Ruth. In a shorter play like *Reunion* the young girl is nearly a projection of a daughter by the father. She seems to lack human quirks and idiosyncracies. The girl-child in *Dark Pony* is merely the catalyst for the father to tell his story about the Indian Boy from the radio.

Dark Pony is not so nearly bereft of the feminine character-izations as Mamet's other work. In fact, its other qualities, which are so strong, make it one of my favorite shorter works of any writer, coming in a personal list right after Pinter's *Landscape* and *Silence,* the apogees of short plays which blend drama, fiction, and poetry. Like the Pinter shorts, Mamet's *Dark Pony* is a pardigm of what I mean by the dramaturgy of style in which the seeing voice fuses elements from drama, poetry, and fiction to create a living, breathing moment which must be spoken, because at the moment when the words enter human speech, they become music-mechanisms of powerful conjuring. I had the good fortune to be in New Haven during the time this short piece premiered at the Yale Repertory Theater, and it still remains an excellent instant of what Robert Brustein refers to as poetic realism and a *trans-forming* moment on the stage.

From beginning to end this is a lovely thing, in perfor-mance, and even on the page. I wish all poems and works of fiction were this spare and exact. Here is the front matter be-fore the text:

The Characters
The Father
The Daughter

The Scene
An automobile.

The Time
Night.

It begins with the father saying: "Once upon a time there was an Indian."

My own experience working with American actors has been that they get nervous about line breaks on a page, because that is poetry, and they do not like poetry in the theater. The same writing, unbroken, left-to-right, linear, like prose, is all right. Most contemporary playwrights, even when heightened in their utterance, when their seeing voice operates and evokes, tend to steer clear of line breaks, preferring prose to verse in order to appease the actors. But Mamet, I think, is quite daring in how he aligns his play on the page, using line breaks, and making it clear that this is a seeing voice inspired by American poetry, and at times even an instance of American verse, albeit in play form. (Anyone who has attempted to write a play knows that the form is perhaps even more demanding than, say, a sonnet or villanelle.) What Mamet is doing is some highly formal poetry writing here, using strophe and antistrophe, musical counterpoint, and variations on what a voice sees by contrasting it with what another voice sees, something like the children's chorus in Mozart's *Magic Flute*. Right from the beginning of the play these conditions are operating.

> DAUGHTER: When was this?
> FATHER: A long, long time ago.
>   (*Pause.*)
> DAUGHTER (*to self*):   Long ago.
> FATHER: He was a Brave, and very handsome.

Note that he "was a Brave, and very handsome," not that he "was brave and very handsome." Mamet always makes these kinds of distinctions in his characters' voices, splitting hairs, but also making poetry.

DAUGHTER: What's a Brave?

And here come the line breaks!

FATHER: A man who fights in war.
A young man.
And his body was like Iron.
and he could see like an Eagle.
And he could run like a Deer.
You ever see a deer run?

The first part of the father's voice reminds me of Gary Snyder's long poem *Myths & Texts,* but the last line is pure schtick, the playwright knowing from poets like Frank O'Hara that humor is a valid emotion. What the voice sees here is also a sight gag, Milton Berle more than John Milton.

What follows suggests that Mamet may be more of a father than a husband or lover, because the moment with the father and daughter, while not corny or one bit schmaltzy, is downright feeling and tender.

FATHER: And swim like a fish.
DAUGHTER: And he ran like a deer?
FATHER: Yes.

A lesser dramatist might have written:

FATHER (*incredulously*):   Yes.

But Mamet trusts an actor to understand the subtext there, and a good actor will.

DAUGHTER: Hopping?
FATHER: No. Not hopping. But as fast as deer run when they
    run.
DAUGHTER: And could he hop a fence?
FATHER: He could jump over it. Yes.
DAUGHTER (*to self*): Good.
FATHER: His name was . . .
FATHER AND DAUGHTER (simultaneously): Rain Boy.

Of course, anyone could have written that, if they had a
dramatic instinct, understood the music in words, were fiction writers, and had a poet's ear for dialogue. Of course, few
writers could. Mamet has the good sense to know that narrative stops action, that a description of a story is not a story on
the stage. This is a static play, as are Pinter's short pieces
mentioned earlier, but Mamet has only made it seven pages
long, and when I saw it it could not have played for more
than ten minutes, if even that. What makes it remotely dramatic is its poetic device, its seeing voice, its imagery, its
rhythms. This is really a poem in dialogue form. Here is the
last big chunk of the father's monologue before the play ends
with the daughter saying, "We are almost home."

FATHER: But he bore down upon them.
    (*Pause.*)
    And through their midst.
    (*Pause.*)
    Through the dying fire.
    The snow grew red with their blood.
    (*Pause.*)
    Then all became quiet.
    The wind blew.
    The snow drifted.
    He lay in silence.
    He had become cold.
    Dark Pony walked over to him, and he nudged him with
    his nose.

(*Pause.*)
And he neighed.
(*Pause.*)
And he licked his face.
(*Pause.*)
Slowly he opened his eyes.
(*Pause.*)
He looked up above him.
Dark Pony was standing there.
(*Pause.*)
"Oh, Dark Pony," he said . . .
(*Pause.*)
"I thought you had forgotten me."
(*Pause.*)

Harold Pinter has inspired both David Mamet and Sam Shepard, but both writers have found their own voices in the midst of that inspiration. How their voices see goes back to something I first noticed in the poetry of Frank O'Hara, early Gilbert Sorrentino, and LeRoi Jones. There is as much myth and ritual in a comic strip or a Grade B movie as there is in any so-called highbrow American cultural source. No, I take that back. There is more myth and ritual in comic books and Hollywood movies than anything else in the cultural landscape. Go to the Far East and people would much rather ask you about Elvis Presley or the latest rock star than what Arthur Miller is writing, if anything, lately.

Yet some of America's finest poetry is rendered in its small theaters, a fact which makes our dramatists in a kinship of neglect with our poets and fiction writers. All of these voices are endangered, though not yet extinct. Instead of telling our children to turn off the radio, stop reading a dumb comic book, or watching a stupid movie on television, maybe we should let them keep doing what they do best. If they have a voice which sees, these things will hone them for the future.

Some of our best writers were raised on such things. The bottom line of what I have been saying is not so much that our generation and the ones which follow should be weaned from bubble gum music and other pop phenomena, but rather that our writers should be unembarrassed by the riches which this culture has produced. Poets can and should learn from fiction writers and playwrights. Playwrights should learn from the poets and the fiction writers. Most importantly, our fiction writers need to be aware of poetry and of drama.

Part III

Envoi: The Act of Darkness

WRITERS RARELY MAKE a living from their writing. Instead they tend to acquire teaching positions in universities. The tendency magnifies in this decade with the proliferation of writing programs throughout the country. One of the only exceptions to this observation is Hubert Selby, Jr., who the last I heard had moved back to Los Angeles, where he formerly lived for many years, and was pumping gas. His old friend Gilbert Sorrentino, an editor and part-time teacher at the New School for many years, is now a full professor at Stanford University. For the past eight years I've taught a writing course at Columbia University; and for the past six was in the communications department at Fordham University. Nearly all writers today are educated people, i.e., they have some college experience, both as students and as teachers. A writer like Gore Vidal can fire up his romantic venom for such a phenomenon, but finally this is a trend both natural and good. Why? There are many reasons. When Black Mountain College went under, Charles Olson told his tribe that the future was in the big university centers.

He was right. And he shuffled off to Buffalo. So did Robert Creeley. So did a lot of other good writers.

But there is another reason as well why universities are good for writers. It is an arena in which inherent dramaturgical instincts can flourish. Teaching is more like performance—an outwardly public gesture—than like the act of writing, that most private, isolated act. This is more than merely the clownish side of a writer emerging into a public sphere. It is how workshops in this country operate, their emphasis on the voice, showing and not telling, evoking without commentary, making fiction interesting and moving and real. The test of student writing is usually in an out-loud presentation, so that this inherent aspect of all good writing, its voice, is brought to the fore. But this dramaturgical instinct comes from other sources as well.

Again, I use myself as the example here, but it is less egotistical than instructional, i.e., I'm typical of this development, not unique. I really did not begin to teach until after I was thirty years old, with one commercial fiction, one small-press fiction, and one small-press chapbook of poems published already. My degrees were awarded after I was thirty as well. Before joining the Writing Program faculty at Columbia I had taught a writing workshop at a state university outside of New York City, and within the City University sytem I had taught a compostion course for English-as-a-Second-Language students. In the two and one-half years of college I attended as a teenager at a state university I had been exposed to several writing workshops. (They were good experiences.) I also had attended the workshops at St. Mark's in the Bowery for many years. Again, good experiences. I was probably no better or no worse equipped than any other young writer except one maybe who had really strong pedagogical instincts. I did not. The playwriting workshops I attended at Yale Drama School in 1971 and 1972 were likewise good experiences. Dramatists absolutely need workshops to develop their scripts, whereas fiction and poetry workshops, even though I feel positive about them, are arguably beneficial. When I was hired by Columbia to teach an introductory writing course which included fiction, poetry, and playwriting, I may have perhaps anticipated another slightly negative experience for a writer, but I was wrong. It was J. R. Humphreys, the director of this program, who gave me the greatest advice about how a writer teaches and also laid bare what dramaturgical values teaching had for a writer's craft. His advice was simple.

He said, "Teach yourself."

The program and the course I was teaching were two of the oldest in the country. And Humphrey's said what I always believed anyway.

"Style is voice. If they can find their voice, they are half-way home."

He knew this as a teacher, but he also knew it because he was a practicing novelist. His first novel came out in the forties and his latest was about to be published. And he studied drama as an undergraduate at Michigan. The dramaturgy of style, you could say, was a second-nature thing to him. All he was saying was that the voice is something we are born with, and the idea of teaching was to use your own voice, as example, on the page, in the classroom, to get them to trust their instincts to release the voice. This is not mental. At one faculty meeting I remember a writer present saying—and she was right—"You need to be a little dumb to write good fiction." That is, dumb people *see* and *hear,* and can be concrete about these phenomena.

Fiction is as much a pictorial art as painting, film, or stage-craft is. One's expressive nature in language has to be combined with an ability to see things and to hear others speak. The human voice, as any singer will verify, is a sublime musical instrument, and a writer needs to learn all of its musical planes. A voice is sensuous, expressive, and musical. It is capable, word to word, of great rhythm, and, sentence to sentence, of even a melody. Its paragraphs can build harmonies, an expanding musical structure, just as its movement, chapter to chapter, and overall, end to end, creates incredible tone colors.

The voice of fiction has a rhythm, unique to each writer and each experience the writer has. But there is also a motion to the voice, a pattern. Designs are evoked; and these designs add to the greater sequence. This is a dramaturgical experience, the voice in the arc of its tensions, the old push and pull of the stage.

What I considered to be a good experience about that newest job teaching (and still do), was that Humphreys wanted us, in those introductory workshops, to stress interrelationships, not differences, among the writing forms which included fiction, poetry, and scriptwriting. It was as though fifty years earlier someone created a syllabus which was waiting for me to come along. A writer has a voice, yes. But that is not enough to make that voice happen, I mean, the simple act of being aware of it is not going to make it warble and trill. Don't start with language. That's too grand a construction. Start with a word. Pick a concrete image from the labyrinth of the mind. Let's call it CLOCK. Spell it large. Give it life. Picture it. Go through the senses. Locate some feelings about that "clock." From here the dramaturgy takes hold.

Through playwriting a fiction writer learns about dialogue, not only the veracity of things in a character's voice, but how the playwright manipulates the voice toward dramatic ends. A good contemporary example would be David

Mamet's *Glengarry Glen Ross,* act 1, scene 3. A real estate hustler named Roma is seated at a booth in a Chinese restaurant. In the two previous scenes we have met the other real estate operators, each vulgar, harsh, obscene, edgy con men—and *human.* Mamet's ear for human speech, its poetry of object, rhythm of experience, exact word, and energy is literally *fantastic.* He is a writer as sensitive to the waves and nuances of the American idiom as anyone around today, poet, fiction writer, or playwright. Yes, the ear is the first thing. But dramaturgy is a sense of character objective and obstacles in the way of that objective. It is purposeful speech.

Roma is talking with Lingk at the next table. Because two previous dramatic situations involve characters who know each other because they are in the same business, the dramatic assumption is that Roma and Lingk know each other, too. Because Mamet is a good dramaturge, he knows that we think we know this. He leaves out information. It is the mark of knowing how to shape experience into a dramaturgical moment. Mamet leaves out as much or more than he puts into his script. (Another thing which short fiction shares with drama and poetry.) This scene is less than five pages long, most of it Roma talking, with a few bits of dialogue from Lingk. Roma expounds upon his philosophy of life. It is sincere, even honest-sounding. The con man is casting his net. Not only has he trapped Mr. Lingk with his words, Roma seduces the entire audience as well. Here is Roma's voice:

"Stocks, bonds, objects of art, real estate. Now: what are they? (*Pause.*) An opportunity. To what? To make money? Perhaps. To *lose* money? Perhaps. To 'indulge' and to 'learn' about ourselves? Perhaps. *So fucking what?* What *isn't?* They're an *opportunity.* That's all. They're an *event.* A guy comes up to you, you make a call, you send in a brochure, it doesn't matter, "There're these *properties* I'd like for you to see." What does it mean? What you *want* it to mean. (*Pause.*) Money? (*Pause.*) If that's what it signifies to you. Security? (*Pause.*) Comfort? (*Pause.*) All it is is THINGS THAT HAPPEN TO YOU. (*Pause.*) That's all it is. How are they different? (*Pause.*) Some poor newly married guy gets run down by a cab. Some *busboy* wins the lottery. (*Pause.*) All it is, it's a carnival. What's special . . . what *draws* us? (*Pause.*) We're all different. (*Pause.*) We're not the same. (*Pause.*) We are not the same. (*Pause.*) Hmmm. (*Pause. Sighs.*) It's been a long day (*Pause.*) What are you drinking?"

This is what they call the payoff, because Mamet tricks us thoroughly. We have been *seduced* by Roma. It is not a question of what he is saying (meaning), but how he says it (voice). It is how a drama comes alive through its dramaturgy. The moment simply—*is.* It is part of drama's "illusion of the first time," but it is also how "the act of darkness" turns into an illumination. That act of darkness which Edgar mentions in the guise of Poor Tom about his mistress is as much, to quote from Creeley, about "my love's manners in bed" as it is about the dramaturgical moment itself. Are we seduced by Roma? Yes, we are, because we have suspended our disbelief, and because he is a con man—he strikes. Roma ends this phase of his hustle by saying: "Well, let's have a couple more. My name is Richard Roma, what's yours?"

Good dialogue is not only the rhythm of experience in the voice of a character. It is a vehicle which moves the drama forward, into its arc, across the landscape of its imagination into the full range of its possibility. An imaginary world comes to life. But I would say that David Mamet, in this instance, in this play, in this scene, knows as much about poetry and fiction as he does about playwriting. But what a fiction writer learns from Mamet's example is that a character reveals from first utterance outward. That the first impulse toward speech propels an action into the highest range of that voice's resonance. Words reverberate from first to last in a dramatic situation.

When Masha, a character in Chekhov's *Sea Gull,* is asked why she always wears black, her first impulse to speech is to define herself for the rest of the drama. She says, "I am in mourning for my life." Fiction writers learn from this, because they find out that a voice not only reveals itself by speaking but propels itself into an action. When Blanche DuBois says that she's always relied on the kindness of strangers, her voice reveals and propels simultaneously. Through the music of human speech, the voice of the character (through the voice of the writer) comes to life in the context of an imaginary space.

Yes, there are differences between the play and the poem, between the poem and fiction. But their interrelationships are more striking. Take the writing of poetry in a workshop setting. Young writers seem to bring the most ill conceived and stubborn notions about what a poem is more than they do about fiction and playwriting. They are most reluctant to give up clumsy theories learned from second-rate high school English teachers and third-rate professors in college. My own daughter, in second grade, came home in tears because her teacher (otherwise extremely competent) told her that what she wrote could not be a poem because "it did not rhyme." Another time her autobiography was rejected because instead of commenting she chose to evoke experience. She began the passage by describing her first remembered experience in this life, blowing a giant spit bubble from her mouth as she swung on a swing in a playground in New Haven. Of course, prior to submitting either of these assignments, she assayed my opinion, I being the resident writer in our apartment, and I told her this was sterling material.

What is a poem? You will be told that it is something that
rhymes. You will get terrible imitations of Shakespeare's son-
nets, usually not in American idiomatic English and usually
not in Elizabethan English either. The macho bandits in a
workshop will tell you that poems are feminine things. Mostly
the poems lack a voice, are pictureless, and do not approach
the experience which motivated the words in any direct fashion. I call it dancing around the object and the experience.
More than poems you get greeting card copy. Or you get imitations of other poets' voices. The majority of the people in
my class at Columbia want to write fiction and they will ask
aloud what writing a poem has to do with it. Occasionally
someone is interested in playwriting, and they likewise will
ask that question. You learn, first, how to channel a voice
into a construct of maximum energy, which ideally is something that can approach song. You learn about words, how
each one is important, article, preposition, noun, verb, ad-
verb, conjunction.

"*But* I did wash the car" is a different voice, rhythm, experience, and coloring, than to say, "I washed the car." The
first might be whiny, conditional, defensive, whereas the second is firmer, surer, more absolute. Not the noun, not the
verb, not the pronoun—it is the conjunction which reveals
the voice in this instance. Why do playwrights and fiction
writers learn from poetry? Stuff like this. But it is a two-way
exchange. I see a fiction writer and a poet learning from a
passage like David Mamet's quoted earlier. There is concision, energy, images, a field of composition. Even the syllables count in Roma's monologue. Even the pauses count.
What is *not* said counts, for instance, in the beginning, that
Roma wants to sell Lingk some bogus real estate. The language is visual. "Stocks, bonds, objects of art, real estate."
These are things, not abstractions. Busboys, carnivals, lot-

teries, drinks—these are things, too. It is concrete, pictorial, if you will. That is what poetry is.

Let me return to this teaching thing which writers get themselves into. Over the years I discovered that the more aware a playwright is of physical details the better the script. Writers think through their bodies. Their senses. William Carlos Williams' "no ideas but in things" is a good rule to follow. One semester at Columbia I taught a scriptwriting class instead of my usual introductory course. I discovered that some elementary acting excercises are useful to writers, *all* writers, not just playwrights. Yes, but especially playwrights. It is not a coincidence that Sophocles, Plautus, Moliere, Shakespeare, and Pinter are all playwrights who have acted.

The chairs and the table in the classroom were pushed to the side. A space was created. I was going to start simply. It was an excercise which an actor friend told me about, and I think he said he learned it from a class with the director Lee Breuer, but I can't verify this. The excercise is called walking through life. You start at your youngest memory and start walking up to the present moment. It is revealing for writers because so many images, feelings, and emotions can arise in that simple journey. Other excercises are equally rudimentary. Some stretches, working with a partner; becoming aware of vertebrae on the spine. Closing the eyes and touching a partner's face, then trying to find a partner in the room. Eyes closed, hands resting on a partners shoulder, you are led through the room in which, all your trust in a weld formed by your hand and the partner's back, you navigate around a room in which everyone else is hooting and hollering.

Writing is a product of the physical world, not a by-product of a mental process. It is creating objects, word sculpture, dimensional, plastic, and resonating. It consists of objects as palpable as ashtrays, beer cans, and roast beef. The writer starts with a voice negotiating an experience, working it through the medium of language. But, as I said, language is almost too grand a construct. It needs to be broken down into words, into a word, and from there to the syllable, to the breath—the way you breathe. Often the rhythm of the experience dictates the form, turning it toward the play, the poem, the fiction. Even with the interconnectness of forms, one form is more strongly felt to be right.

Finally, I conclude this part and its last passage by saying that I wanted to articulate some concerns about short fiction primarily, although I have used the drama and poetry to set down my own definition of it. When Aristotle wrote about poetry, he meant the cadenced, rhythmical language of the drama. Drama is poetry in action. Fiction is only different from the drama in its choice of a medium (prose), not in its method (the voice). By dramaturgy in the narrow context of my exploration I mean the poetry of the theater as it translates into the prose idiom, particularly that imaginary kingdom known as fiction. The origin of fiction, like that of the drama and poetry, is in entertainment. It is worth recalling Bertolt Brecht. First, it must entertain before it can move you; and it must move you before it can change your life. Early manifestations of fiction—works like Sterne's *Tristram Shandy*—are both entertainments and experiments. This has been true of the history of the drama as well.

And the dramaturgy of fiction bears many similarities to the theater's verbal art. Both use voice to see. Both are best when palpable. Both use a poetry that is looser than a poem on the page and whose ultimate measure is found in speech. Fiction used to have an edge on inwardness and stillness, but when you consider a playwright like Harold Pinter, his two short plays, *Landscape* and *Silence*, and one of his major achievements in a longer work, like *The Homecoming*, this is an edge which fiction does not own exclusively. One of Pinter's greatest contributions to drama, and to literature, in our time is how he is able to characterize inner feelings through the externalized medium of the stage. Some of Pinter's recent work is as meditative and still as any prose fiction by Beckett.

We must presume that the inside of the human skull is a dark place and how that locale gets illumination is through the landscapes of poetry, fiction, and the drama. Pinter is a good example of how light is shed in a drama. Inwardness, stillness, and meditation are not dynamics of daylight. They suggest the nocturnal, or at least the shadowy climate of candlelight. The light of poetry, as Aristotle saw it, came out of his recipe, starting with plot and character, working down to spectacle. At this point I think it is safe to say that our greatest insights about plot came from Chekhov, because he often was accused (wrongfully) of lacking a plot. This, in turn, becomes an important consideration about contemporary short fiction as well. Here is what drama teaches: if a character is different at the end of a dramatic action than he or she was at the beginning—then there is a plot. This notion of plot, ancient and still worrisome to some, is not incidental, not worthless, but somehow has been overcharged since Aristotle voiced it as a kind of primacy in his *Poetics*. But it should be understood that he was addressing a particular type of drama, one which was devoid of psychology as we know the term; the drama was emblematic, more of type than character. Costumes resembled football uniforms; voice was large, stilted, and inhuman.

Through these concerns, from Aristotle to the present, of the drama as well as poetry, I have attempted a study of short fiction. My concern was with the voice, as I said, the seeing voice. I do not wish to reduce the meaning or the moral/ethical considerations of fiction. Nothing I have said is a radical departure from anything that is already known, at least among creative writers, now, in the past, in antiquity. As I said, I wanted to create a context and an emphasis about the seeing voice. That is all. The emphasis was with the prose itself, not meanings, because I have found that the meaning of a play is useless to an actor creating a character through the medium of his voice. An actor looks for lines, objectives, and obstacles. That is what I planned for my emphasis in this work. I wished to create some "business" about short fiction, as they say in the world of theater. Business: schtick, bits, routines. I was not looking for meanings in a voice. We never do that in life, so why start in literature? But I was after the qualities of *purpose*. Like the actor, once purpose is found, objectives can be made visible. Then I asked, What are the obstacles? What things must the voice confront to arrive at its objective? Actors physicalize a script; that is how they know it.

This is not a matter of infinite space in which a voice operates. The universe of the stage is proscribed, finite, and blocked. So is short fiction's universe, meaning, some things work, and some do not. There is a context for the fictional voice. The context which I chose included fiction's older tropes as well as ones from drama and poetry. The context of short fiction, as I see it, is framed by these other literary media. There are interrelationships which I wished to explore. This context, this emphasis, is an act of darkness, sensuous, amorous, rhythmical—the guilty pleasure of a fiction writer, playwright, and poet, not in the voice of a critic. It is the voice of a practitioner. Like Mamet's character Richard Roma, I'm after drawing you into this real estate—buy a piece of short fiction for your retirement years!—the imaginary world of a voice, as much by how I say it as what I say. If you've gotten this far in my sell, I can ask what you are drinking? I can introduce myself. Here is my hand. Glad to meet you.

"My name is Richard Roma, what's yours?"

Index

Michael Stephens is the author of the novel *Season at Coole* as well as seven other small press books of fiction, poetry, and translation. Many of his plays have been produced off-Broadway, and *Our Father* enjoyed a year-long run on Theatre Row in New York as well as a European tour. He has degrees in writing from Yale University and the City College of New York and has taught in the Writing Program at Columbia University for many years.